Praise for
14 Days to Die
AN AMAZON BESTSELLING PSYCHOLOGICAL THRILLER

"This may be called 14 DAYS TO DIE but it only took me 1 and 1/2 days to read it. I was hooked from beginning to end... I have read lots of thrillers from each type from psychological to mystery, from the daft to the sublime, and this one is written in a fantastic way that keeps the pace up and keeps you alert at all times. I am going to say: This really needs picking up by some film company I would love to see this played out visually."
— *Sue and her Books*

"Whoa...I was not prepared for this. This is a gripping thriller full of twists and turns... We see all these pretty suburban homes and we don't really know what happens inside. Sarah and Mike seem to have a happy, stable life: The American suburban dream. Only, they don't."
— *Michelle Only Wants to Read*

"14 Days to Die is very entertaining, and I read in one sitting. I felt sorry for Sarah but also laughed at her. Her life is of a typical housewife struggling day to day to keep house, husband and children happy whilst also fighting against the ravages of age that time does to a woman."
— *Tracy Shephard*

"Talk about a fantastic plot and premise for a thriller! Not only was this one fast-paced, but it also had exceptional character development in a short book. I could feel my heart beating faster with each call she got reminding her of the impending doom hanging over her head... This book was thrilling with a side of romance that I could stomach. Overall a fantastic read that I highly recommend!"
— *Suspense is Thrilling Me*

"I'm pretty hard to please when it comes to psych thrillers (probably because I read so many of them), so I was pleasantly surprised by how much I liked this one."
— *Kelly and the Book Boar*

"...a debut psychological gripping thriller with many twists and turns that keeps you guessing until the very last page. And I never guessed the brilliant ending! I loved this book!...After reading this book, you will now look at your husband and other people in your life in a new light. What comes around goes around!"
— *Sue, NetGalley Reviewer*

"You will NEVER see the ending coming and if you are anything like me.....that ending will totally piss you off. AB Whelan.....that ending knocked me on my behind and left me speechless and ready to scream! BTW......I LOVED THIS ONE BIG TIME!!"
— *Jamie Submits to Books*

Praise for
As Sick as Our Secrets
AN AMAZON BESTSELLING PSYCHOLOGICAL THRILLER

"This is going to be one of those books that everyone talks about!! A Great read!"
—Steven deBruin, NetGalley

"A devious thriller that's as chilling as this never-ending winter... Whelan delivers a sexy mind-trip that had me both dazed and dazzled. There's a dangerous feel throughout this book, but it's one that creeps up on you slowly."
—*Suspense is Thrilling Me*

"As Sick as Our Secrets by A.B Whelan is going to be one of this year's best psychological thrillers! ... It is dark and real, with windows of light to make the book very close to perfect."
—*Cloud of Thoughts*

"As Sick as Our Secrets was a fast-paced psychological thriller that kept me gripped right up until a very satisfying ending." --Dee's Rad Reads and Reviews

"An enticing, thrilling mystery with fantastic heroines."
—Kate, *CreateSpace*

"This was a dangerously addictive thriller… ! It may not be everyone's cup of tea due to some scenes of sexual violence, but nothing was so graphic that it spoiled my enjoyment of the powerful narrative and immersive plotline, which I have to say reminded me of "Big Little Lies" at times. Well worth a look!"
—My Chestnut Reading Tree

"While I fell in love with each of these 3 strong, witty women, the mystery is what held me captive. So many layers, so many secrets, and so many lies. All leading up to a final confrontation and twisty ending that really worked for me. Highly recommend, as my review doesn't do it justice---you really need to experience this one!"
—*Goodreads* Review

"Another unique thriller by A. B. Whelan. Full of interesting characters and details, I was riveted the whole time!"
—*Goodreads* Review

"What a great fast-paced tale that delves into a dark subject matter that should not be read by the faint-hearted."
—*NetGalley* Review

"...a superb writer. You can feel every bit of emotions of the characters... A must-read book."
—*Goodreads* Review

14 DAYS TO DIE

A NOVEL

A. B. WHELAN

TITLES BY A. B. WHELAN

Young-adult fantasy series:

City of Shame

Valley of Darkness

Safe and Sound

Fields of Elysium

Stand-alone psychological thriller:

As Sick as Our Secrets

Summary:
To what extent would you go to avenge your husband's infidelity?

Stay-at-home mom Sarah Johnson has the perfect family—a handsome, hardworking husband and two healthy and beautiful children. At least, that's what she's been telling herself for years. After the tragedies in her youth, Sarah deemed living a lie easier than dwelling on the past and facing her everyday failures. To avoid any kind of confrontation at home, she doesn't read her husband's emails or spy on him like most jealous wives do. She wouldn't jeopardize her comfortable but dull life for anything.

But Sarah's world is about to crumble around her when she receives a phone call from a man with a heavy foreign accent telling her that her perfect husband has put a price on her head. She is offered two weeks to come up with a counteroffer or die. Why would her model husband Mike want her dead? Hasn't she been the perfect wife? Or has her karma finally caught up with her—making her pay for her former transgressions? The final countdown begins and now Sarah has to race against time to find out what went wrong in her marriage and find a way out of this nightmare.

So the game of life or death begins. Secrets are unveiled. Emotions are unleashed. Actions are taken.

Will there be a winner in this dangerous game when no one can escape the twist of fate?

Whelan, A. B., 1977-
14 Days to Die : a novel / A. B. Whelan—2nd edition
1. Psychological thriller   2. Suspense—fiction   3. California—fiction
4. Domestic—fiction

ISBN: 978-1523363360
(CreateSpace)

Cover image copyright: Valuavitaly

To my mother

<u>CONTENTS</u>

My mother used to tell me that being a mother is the most underappreciated job in the world. I never really understood what she meant until I gave birth to my first child.

It was a fine winter day that eighth of February when I decided to kill my husband. When I come to think of it, I mean really think of it, it wasn't the first time I had considered erasing him from the face of the Earth. But let's be honest here; what wife, after a day of emotional abuse, hasn't found solace in the thought of getting rid of her husband? Sometimes when Mike came to bed drunk, yelling at me and cussing me out, I imagined putting a pillow over his face and keeping it there until he stopped moving and—more importantly—talking. I could never go through with it, though. I am not a psychopath.

There was always the possibility of leaving him and starting a new life, but our marriage wasn't all bad. We managed to balance it out. My husband is a good man. He is just not great at handling his own frustrations. Near forty, he evaluates his life quite often, and the result gives him more grief than he can handle. I'm good at terrorizing myself emotionally, so I've become resilient to the emotional terror he inflicts on me. So our marriage works—more or less.

We don't have millions of dollars in the bank or a private yacht anchored in the bay at Newport Beach, but we have two beautiful and fantastic children, and we have each other. I thought that ought to count for something. But I was wrong. My husband loved money and himself more than he ever loved me. To my dismay, I had to find it out in the most twisted and heartbreaking way.

Sheriff's Sergeant Tom Long: How would you describe your marriage, Mrs. Johnson?

Sarah Johnson: Happy. Stable.

Sheriff's Sergeant Tom Long: What happened then?

Sarah Johnson: Something went terribly wrong.

Sheriff's Sergeant Tom Long: What went wrong?

Sarah Johnson: Everything.

14 DAYS TO DIE

The morning sun penetrates the double kitchen window that overlooks our mediocre backyard. The light brings out the splash marks and food particles on the glass that the kids and Mike manage to sprinkle all over the window when they use the sink.

Usually, I'd grab a cloth, wet it and clean the grime off, then polish the glass to perfection. But I won't do it now.

This morning, I turn around and lean against the sink with my back to the window instead, watching Mike eat his sunny-side-up eggs in the breakfast nook. His fingers are folded loosely around the fork's handle, a piece of egg white stuck between the fork's teeth. He's working on his breakfast absentmindedly, almost like a robot that is programmed to do the same routine every day. His iPhone is tucked in his left hand like an extended limb. On the screen, his thumb jumps around as if involuntary spasms control it. I know he's texting. I'm standing only a few feet away from him. The man has no shame.

I'd like to find out who invented smartphones and lock him up for the rest of his life in a room with nothing but a device and an internet connection.

I've always believed that humans are emotionally wired. We need everyday social interaction in person—not via electronics. Maybe my lack of social interaction is to blame for how my life turned out.

Mike wasn't always so addicted to the screen. We used to eat breakfast together sitting around the dining table. I'd make all kinds of fancy dishes with eggs like omelets loaded with veggies, scrambled eggs with spinach and Parmesan cheese, or the frittata I learned to make while we were living in Italy. Up until a few years ago, we would clink glasses before drinking our fresh-squeezed orange juice and wink, sending air kisses to each other. My father used to say that I had so much pride in my work that it wouldn't matter what I did or who I was—a corporate director, baker, or housewife—I'd always achieve perfection. I still make fancy breakfasts, but now I eat alone.

Mike's cell beeps again. I recognize the alarm sound his phone makes when a new text message arrives. He smiles. I frown, wanting to rip the phone out of his hand, smash it on the floor, and stomp on it until it becomes nothing more than a pile of glass and metal pieces.

I feel anger rising in my chest. I lead my eyes away, but not too far. No. This morning Mike has my undivided attention, and neither the broken eggshells on the counter nor the dirty skillet on the stove can draw it away.

I analyze his outfit, the way he hunches over his plate, his hair—shaved and combed to the side like the soccer star Cristiano Ronaldo's. *Oh, for crying out loud, you're almost forty,* I want to tell him.

When he got home from the barber's a month ago showing me his new hairstyle I actually liked it. It made him look younger, more

14

stylish. But since I found out that he didn't update his style for me, I just want to take a pair of scissors to his hair.

A cup of hot coffee steams next to Mike's plate—black with a hint of vanilla-flavored Nature Bliss coffee creamer. The smile still lingers on his face as he sets his phone down and sips at the coffee. Maybe it's that cute, sexy half-smile that ignites the spark that lights up the stacked-up logs of bitterness in my mind, I don't know, but as I witness his joyful reaction to the message, a fire starts in my head—a fire that I won't be able to quench until I follow through with my plan. I should have known. Wives always do, so I've heard.

The image of the three monkeys—one holding its ears, the other its eyes, the third its mouth—comes alive in my mind. I've been a fool. The bitter recognition rushes blood to my temples making me dizzy.

Only yesterday I was going through family photos of our three years in Italy. I organized them by trips we took: Pisa, Firenze, Rome, London, and Croatia. I convinced myself that in spite of the occasional yelling and blaming, we were a happy family. We had it better than most people did.

I clench my teeth, take the broken eggshells from the counter, and discard them into the trash. I desperately want to hold onto those memories—of me feeling happy about the pictures—but the harder I try, the more they slip away. That was yesterday. Today is a new day. Today I have to take matters into my own hands, or soon I will be six feet under with nothing but regrets.

Mike drains the orange juice—not fresh squeezed but store bought. He's lucky I even made him breakfast.

I stare at his glass for a while, some old memory or perhaps just a thought swirls inside the recesses of my mind. I pick up the container that is half full with country-style orange juice. Based on statistics most women choose poison as a murder weapon. Sounds appealing to me too. There would be no blood. I wouldn't have to watch Mike's eyes as his soul leaves his body when I plunge a knife deep into his chest.

I shudder. The thought of murdering my husband bothers me because I've been living a clean and humble life for over a decade. But I'm aware of the darkness is somewhere still inside me. I only need to find it and bring it to the surface. I need my old friend, madness, if I want to execute such an unforgivable sin, or I will fail. It won't be easy I know. I married Mike because I loved him. He's the father of my children. But he gives me no choice. No one that despicable deserves to live.

The awakening winter sunlight pours through the open window and touches my bare shoulders. The warmth embeds a pleasant feeling in me. I step away from the sun. When you're plotting to kill your husband, pleasant feelings aren't the ones you need.

I must keep my head clear and my mind focused. After fourteen long years of marriage, I won't end up in prison spending the rest of my life trading toothbrushes for candy bars. Patience, I tell myself, is the one thing that separates the smart criminals from the lousy ones. Mike will leave in twenty minutes to play a pick-up soccer game with his buddies (so he told me) and I'll have the entire morning to surf the Internet for ideas.

"Is there any more coffee?" Mike asks, pushing his empty mug towards me without looking up from his phone. There was a time when he used to say please at the end of every request. I can't even recall when he stopped using pleasantries with me.

I wipe my hands on a kitchen towel and take his cup. I pour him coffee from the pot then I add a special ingredient. No, it's not love. A good splash of creamer disguises my foamy spit. The cup overflows.

"Whoa!" he snaps. "Watch what you're doing!"

I don't respond to that. "When did you say your game was?" I ask.

"I told you like five times already. It's at eight-thirty." He scoops up the remaining morsels of his eggs, shoves them into his mouth and pushes the plate toward me. Then he takes a big gulp of his coffee. My face remains expressionless while amusement rattles my insides. So that's how it feels to have the upper hand. I used to be good at this game. Though that was a long time ago.

"Why? You have plans for this morning?" he adds, unkindly, as if I don't feel like a useless accessory to his fun life already.

"No, I'll be home." *I always am.*

I take his plate and drop it into the sink instead of placing it in the dishwasher.

His phone beeps again. I want to claw the walls.

I watch him leave the kitchen with his nose buried in the screen of that stupid iPhone.

I should leave the kitchen, too, take a nice hot bath with candles on the side and rose petals floating around in the water. I should stop worrying about my chores and enjoy the remainder of whatever life I have left. But the mess in the kitchen bothers me more than I can handle. I try to suppress the urge to clean up, but I fail. I don't have OCD; I just hate clutter.

With a sigh of defeat, I load the dishwasher, wash the skillet in the sink, wipe the stove and clean up the countertops. The kids will be up in half an hour, hungry and demanding, and I'll have to start the whole process all over again. According to my husband, that's my job. But if I do have a job, why don't I get paid? Why don't I earn retirement? Why don't I have health benefits? Why do I have to listen to my husband reminding me every day to get a *real* job?

I'm in the family room gathering the kids' backpacks when my husband runs down the stairs, sports bag in his hand, dragging a trail of Calvin Klein cologne after him.

"Wish me luck," he says and kisses my forehead.

Fuck you I think but say "good luck" instead.

He storms through the laundry room and leaves the door open as always. I hear the garage door roll up and the sound of the engine idling in his brand-new Porsche. He had been driving a Prius for five years to save on gas, but five months ago—just after we moved back to the States—he traded his energy-wise ride in for this new sports car. I was always under the impression that we couldn't afford to live luxuriantly, but I was also under the impression that despite our problems we had a good marriage and that my husband loved me. It turns out that I was wrong on both accounts. I should never have married a Gemini, a two-faced manipulator.

As I step in to close the laundry room door and keep the heat inside the house, my eyes get stuck on a pair of shin guards on the top of the washing machine. I snatch them up and burst into the garage to catch Mike in time. I don't know why I even care what happens to his shins during a soccer game when I'm about to end his life, but I guess old habits die hard.

When he spots me framed in the garage door, he rolls the window down. I hand him his forgotten-yet-necessary set of gear. "Oh, thanks, Honey. I love you," he says blissfully.

His breath smells of mouthwash.

My stomach constricts.

As he rolls onto the street in our quiet suburban neighborhood, I wave goodbye. Then I close the garage; a bitter taste lingers in my mouth.

Since the kids are still sleeping, the upstairs is ghostly silent. In my room, I sit down in front of the old hand-me-down Apple computer I inherited from my husband when he bought himself a new laptop. Now its software is outdated and its memory too slow.

It also stores all of our music, pictures, and documents. If I want to save a new file, I have to delete an old one to make room on the hard drive.

Every year around Christmastime I start dropping hints about how I need a new, faster computer for my blogging, but my husband never picks up on them no matter how obvious they are. His gifts to me are always the same: jewelry. Not the kind you can wear to soccer practices or school pick-ups, but the ones you keep in your jewelry box for a wedding or anniversary dinner. None of which we ever go to together.

Sometimes I play with the idea of taking all my jewelry to a pawnshop and using the money to buy a laptop for myself. Unfortunately, my collection has only sentimental value, not monetary.

While I wait for the system to boot up, a terrible feeling of betrayal and depression comes over me. I pull off my wedding ring and put it on the table. I stare at it for a while, until my eyes sting.

The computer rattles on, and I look out the window. From the bedroom slash office, we have a view of the surrounding mountains. Their silhouettes are stark against the pale blue sky. Despite being winter, the landscape is picturesque. Here in Southern California, the weather is hardly ever gloomy.

I strain my brain to remember the name of the mountains. *Idyllwild?* I'm not sure. We have been back in the States for only five months, and my smallest problem was bigger than finding out the names of all the landmarks around us. I had to sign the kids up for school, find them soccer teams, a physician, a dentist; get familiar with the local grocery stores, post office, and gas stations; find an internet, phone and TV provider; manage the re-carpeting of the house and the delivery of our furniture; then put everything away, clean out all the boxes, wash all the windows, clean up the backyard, get our dog settled in; and in the meantime, fight with my husband over why I haven't gone on any job interviews yet.

Surging anger rushes into my heart. My pulse beats out of control, and I have to take a few deep breaths before I'm able to start typing words into the search engine.

I use Google Chrome. I like the look of it. Just like I use Google Search.

My fingers are cold as I type out *best criminal TV shows*.

A list of web pages pops up on my screen. The second title is the one I'm most familiar with: *CSI*. Under the picture of the cast, it says that the show has been on since the year 2000. I used to be a fan back when I had the time to follow many TV shows.

For a moment I consider searching for ways to kill someone humanely, but I think better of it. Searches like that can be traced back to a specific computer. I've already established that I'm not going to prison. Orange is not my color.

As I take a few calming breaths and blow warm air onto my cold hands, I hear my daughter calling me. She peed her bed again. She needs me to clean it up.

I rise from my chair and walk down the hallway leading to her room. My son is already up reading a children's mystery novel by James Patterson. This year he picked the master of crime novels as his favorite author. I like to believe that my son inherited his love of reading from me. I usually read during soccer practices. Actually, I read or run. Mostly read because I hate running in the cold. According to my husband, it's just another excuse for me to be lazy. He might be right. I used to be a runner. I was very athletic. I also used to work 12-hour jobs. But I gave up my career long ago when I got married to an Air Force man who dragged me all over the world at a moment's notice.

I don't only read. I also manage a blog with reviews and

giveaways. But I don't like to talk about that because according to my husband, it's a waste of time. He might be right. I scarcely make a few hundred bucks a month from advertising fees. I keep thinking I could develop my blog into something big: team up with other reviewers, run literary award contests, and lots more, but to make those dreams come true, you need confidence. My self-esteem has hit an all-time low.

I nod at my son, who responds with a half-hearted good morning and slip into my daughter's room. She's six years old but still wets the bed a few times a month. I blame the constant changes in her environment along with the scary animated movies available for children nowadays as the cause of her occasional bedwetting. If I can bring myself to wake up in the middle of the night, I take her to the bathroom, but most nights I'm too exhausted to wake up. My husband doesn't understand why I'm so tired all the time. "I wish my job was to stay home and play with my kids all day." He never stops reminding me.

I strip the bed of the protective pad and the sheets. I find the mattress cover soaked with urine. I have a homemade remedy for getting rid of the stain, so I'm not mad. I already have four piles of laundry waiting in my room, but this takes priority. I should tell my daughter that it's okay; can happen to anyone, but I'm not in a very compassionate mood today.

While the washing machine is running, I return to the kitchen to make breakfast for my kids. I remember that I haven't eaten anything yet, but I don't have an appetite. I pour myself a second cup of coffee and add milk. My son wants oatmeal with cinnamon and honey while my daughter is begging for pancakes. I tell them it's not a restaurant but fix both foods anyway.

My phone rings and makes me jump. From the unknown number I know, it's a stranger calling.

"Aren't you gonna get that?" my son asks, taking apart the LEGO spaceship I just put together for him last week for the third time. Why can't he just keep his building sets together? Next time he asks for more LEGO, I'm going to buy him a bucket of mixed pieces on eBay for half the money. I've gone crazy. Why am I worrying about toys when my life is hanging by a thread?

"Aren't you *going* to get that?" I correct him while my eyes can't let go of the number.

It could be the police calling to let me know that my husband got into an accident and died. But I'm not that lucky. Never have been.

I answer it, my heart in my throat. "Yes." The sound comes out weak and vulnerable. I clear my throat and move away from my children. "Sarah speaking," I say more confidently.

"Do you have an answer for me?" the man asks in a low monotone with a notable European accent. The same guy who called me last night and told me that my husband hired him to kill me.

I rub my forehead the same way I do when I negotiate deals with Mike or my son's coach. "I don't have the kind of money you're asking for."

"Do you want to die?" he asks me flatly as if reading a message from a note.

What a stupid question. I growl inside. How could Mike put me in a situation like this? After all I've done for him and this family. My hatred for him sits intensely in my chest. I feel as if every cell in my body wants to burst. I'm not taking this guy seriously enough. Where is the fear? The panic?

"What I meant was that I don't have the money you're asking for right now, but I can get it in a month." My hand is moist, and the phone almost slips from my grasp. I press it harder to my ear.

"That's a long time. You get one week."

"Three," I negotiate. Before giving up my independence for a man, I used to run my own medical company. I know a thing or two about how to cut a deal.

"Fine. You get two weeks, but not a day more. After that, I'm coming for you. And don't forget, one word to the police, and I'll make you watch your children die before I finish you." He hangs up on me without a farewell. I hold the phone to my ear for a while, seeing stars in blank spaces. I have to use a dining room chair for support to keep me from falling.

"Are you okay?" My daughter's sweet voice penetrates the darkness in my head.

My eyes come back to focus, and I see her cherubic face staring at me. My son is by my side in a heartbeat and tries holding me up by my elbow. My knees buckle, but I manage to steady myself.

"I'm fine," I say, caressing his thick blond hair.

He's the most achieving little kid I have ever known. He deserves to grow up in a happy family. For a moment I consider the option of letting the hitman kill me and having my children live a wealthy and happy life with a new younger mom.

Then I think better of it. That young Italian girl who's got my husband completely wrapped around her little finger will never be the mother of my children. What could she teach them other than how to steal someone else's husband? How to ruin a family?

If my husband thinks badly enough of me to hire someone to kill me, maybe I am bad. I can be bad—that I know. I will show him just how bad.

My fingers roll into tight fists. "Finish your breakfasts. Mommy needs to take care of something."

.   .   .   .   .

Sheriff's Sergeant Tom Long: What was your impression about the Johnson's when they first moved in?

Carol: To be honest, Tom—can I call you Tom? You just have this Lenny Kravitz thing going on, and I feel like I know you. Anyway, so yeah, you know I looked up how much they paid for the house on Zillow.com because I knew it was a foreclosure. And I won't lie, yes. It made me mad. Most of us here struggle with our high mortgage payments while they snatched this beautiful home for almost nothing. Then they started doing all that remodeling. I know for a fact that many people in our cul-de-sac were very upset about that. Like they were rubbing our noses in their money.

Sheriff's Sergeant Tom Long: Were any of them mad enough to kill?

Carol: Oh, no, I didn't mean to imply that at all. God, no! We are peaceful people here. Everybody is so loving. That's terrible what happened. Those poor kids! I heard they are getting millions of dollars from the insurance company. Is that true?

Sheriff's Sergeant Tom Long: I can't share that information.

.   .   .   .   .

After a good ten-minute search, I find the family iPad under the covers of my son's bed. The battery is only at two percent. Most likely, instead of sleeping, he played silly pointless games on it last night. Mike bought it on a whim three years ago. I had no use for yet another smart device especially when I could have updated my closet with the money it cost. I'm still wearing the same jeans I bought years ago. They fit, so either I'm not as fat as I'm told, or I was never skinny.

It takes another few minutes to find the charger under his desk buried in the clutter. At last, I sit down on my bed and search for the *CSI* TV show on Amazon Instant Video. An episode costs a buck ninety-nine. Mike won't be suspicious if I buy one or two yet I hesitate to click. I do it sometimes to catch up on shows I started watching.

I own all the episodes of *The 100* and the first two seasons of *The Walking Dead*. Neither of those shows will be any help for me to find a way to kill my husband and make it look like an accident. If I plan to commit the perfect crime and get away with it, I need to educate myself about forensics, science, maybe even chemistry.

As the word *chemistry* imprints itself on my brain, I remember hearing or seeing somewhere that most of the poisons that are strong enough to kill will leave a trace in the body. There are also untraceable chemical elements in the periodic table that are deadly enough to kill humans. I don't remember their names. I only have this faint image somewhere in the back of my mind.

I start fixing my bed, running the ideas through my head. The more I entertain the idea of poisoning Mike the more I like it. I mean, what other options do I really have? We don't own a gun. I wouldn't even know where to buy one. I could tamper with his new car, but tools leave marks. I also learned that watching *CSI.*

I notice my breathing accelerate. I grab hold of the footboard of the bed before I faint. I can't believe I'm planning to kill my husband. *What's gotten into me?* I'm a respectable homemaker and mother. If a vendor at a farmers market makes a mistake and hands me too much change, I give the extra back. If we go to the community pool, I tell my kids to take quick showers because I don't want to waste the community's water.

A silver-framed picture of Mike and me standing in each other's arms under the canopy of a huge olive tree rests on the top of the dresser at eye level. We look happy and so in love—as if we were newlyweds. The photo was taken in Volterra, Italy. It was a surprise trip from Mike since he knew how much I loved the *Twilight* movies. Though we didn't find any vampires, we did find love again. We ate gelato while sitting on the ancient stone wall of the city overlooking the vineyards of rolling hills. We tasted each other's ice cream. We hugged. We kissed . . .

The coffee acid swirls in my stomach, and I barely make it to the toilet. I hurl into the bowl like a drunken college student.

My son appears behind me and pats my back. I tell him that I'm okay, and I'll be done in a second. He snatches the iPad from my bed and leaves. And here I was thinking that he was worried about me.

I step into the shower. I need cold water to become alert. A spider sits in the corner where the tile meets the wall. It's in the same spot as it has been for the past few days, watching me wash up. I'm scared of spiders, but I'm not afraid of this little buddy. She reminds me of Charlotte from White's classic tale. Lately, she's been the closest thing I have to a friend.

"What am I going to do? Tell me, Little Guy," I babble to the spider. It doesn't move.

Through the cascades of water washing over my face, I hear my cell phone ring. My heart begins to race. I burst out of the shower taking the curtain with me. I skid on the wet tile and go down on a knee. The impact is hard and sharp. Hissing, I rip a towel off its hanger and fight my way out of my room. Half-way down the stairs, I meet my son. My phone is in his hand.

"Who was it?" I ask with a rush of panic.

"Some dude. He asked me to tell you *tick tock tick tock*." He raises an eyebrow.

I can't breathe. "Gimme that."

"You mean, give me that?" he corrects. I yank the phone out of his hand. He looks at me, confused.

"I'm sorry. I'm not having a good day."

"Awright," he says.

"Please don't answer my phone. I believe I've asked you that a million times already."

"I heard you were in the shower. I thought it might be import—"

"Just don't. Okay?" I interrupt. I turn around and make it back to my room.

This was the third time hitman had called me in twelve hours. Yesterday I didn't even know he existed. Now he's managed to turn my entire world upside down.

The first call came in last night. After I had put the kids to bed, I sat down in front of my computer to edit a blog post when my cell started buzzing next to me. Unknown caller id at nine o'clock at night—had to be a telemarketer, I thought. I answered it anyway, to stop the ringing.

"Sarah Johnson?"

"Yes," I snapped. I finally had time today to sit down and work on my blog. The last thing I was in the mood for was to listen to a telemarketer from Asia telling me that I won the grand prize for a vacation resort I'd never heard of before.

"I need you to open your Facebook account."

Now that request earned my attention. "What?"

"I know you are sitting at your computer, so just do as I say."

A buzzing started in my chest. It had to be a prank; Mike's trying to give me the creeps.

"Mike? Is that you? Cut it out! It's not funny."

"No, I'm not your husband, but this is about him. Just open up your Facebook."

It was already open—always is—I just had to click on the tab.

"Good. Now search for your friend Kristen Miller. . . Good. Now check her wall."

The caller seemed to know what I was doing. I looked behind me at the dark wardrobe. I could feel a vein pulsating in my temples as I pushed the chair back, got up, and set my eyes on the hangers. The sight of the eerie rows of jackets and lines of shoes chilled my blood. Any of them could have been a person. I flipped the switch and light spilled over the clothes. None of the hanging jackets had a man in it. I turned the light off, closed the door quietly, and took my place in the chair at my desk, my heart hammering in my chest.

I lifted the phone to my ear. "Who are you? How can you see me?"

"You don't have to worry about that now. I posted something on Kristen's wall you need to see."

Kristen Miller and I went to the same school—Temecula Valley High. She befriended me on Facebook a few days ago. I accepted her request though we hadn't been in touch for over a decade. We weren't exactly besties at school either.

With a dragging speed that would test anybody's patience, her wall loaded. I noticed for the first time that she only had a handful of friends and no pictures. I should have noticed that it was a fake profile. I didn't linger over her list of friends long because my eyes were drawn to a photo of Mike taking a petite young woman from behind, his bare butt cheeks flexing. Strangely, the first thing I noticed was how white his butt was, like a big round peach that wasn't ripe yet. But as my eyes swept over the image, the shock came fast and hard. As if someone had sucked all the air out of the room I started hyperventilating. The striped comforter hanging off the bed looked like the kind hotels use. I could swear I've seen it before. The wallpaper was familiar, too. Without question, the photo had been taken in our room in Hotel Signorini near Pisa, Italy, where we spent a family vacation. Four happy and beautiful days. Mike's libido was at an all-time high. He made love to me every night until I was raw. There was no way Mike could have hooked up with someone when the kids and I were right beside him at all times. . . . When he was so gentle and caring towards me.

My head began throbbing as if someone had taken a hammer to my brain.

"It's fake," I whispered to myself. "Photoshopped." To prove my theory, I should have analyzed the photo thoroughly, but I couldn't see past the aggressive doggie pose as Mike plastered himself onto the woman's back, holding her hair back in a violent way that had to be painful. A memory crawled into the spotlight. Afternoon naps. Every day Mike asked me to stay on the beach with the kids for an hour or two, so he could take a nap in the room undisturbed. He needed rest owing to a long and exhausting month at work.

"Who are you?" I asked breathlessly.

"That's not important."

"What do you want from me?" My index finger hovered over the button on the mouse, ready to click *download* on the picture options menu bar.

"Your husband wants to get rid of you and start a new life without you."

"I don't believe you."

"You saw the picture?"

"This doesn't prove anything. Looks like a summer fling to me."

"She's here in California. He brought her here."

I felt the blood drain from my face.

"Don't faint now," the man on the other end of the line said.

He was watching me—saw my face. I put my thumb over the

camera of my computer.

"Clever girl," the voice complimented, almost admiringly. "Now remove your finger and listen to me, because I'll only say this once. I'm the person people hire when they want to get rid of somebody. Your husband wants you dead. But I'm not a fan of killing women, especially mothers, so I'm offering you a deal. If you double the price your coward husband offered to pay me, I'll let you disappear."

"Wait!" I stopped him with a wry laugh. "You expect me to believe that Mike hired you to kill me? Do you know how ridiculous that sounds?"

"Look, Sarah," I grunted when he called me by my first name as if we were friends. "It won't be so ridiculous when I put a bullet in your head." His thick, ominous voice made my blood curdle.

"If he's in love with someone else, why doesn't he ask for a divorce like normal people do?"

"Maybe a divorce is too expensive. Maybe Mike wants your life insurance. How the hell should I know? Ask your husband about it. But what I do know is I'm really good at getting the job done. So what do you say, Mrs. Johnson? Do we have a deal?"

"I need some time to think."

"Unfortunately I need your answer right now."

My blood pressure was skyrocketing. It made my eyes bulge. I couldn't form a serious thought. "How much is my husband paying you?"

"Fifty large. You'll hafta double that."

"A hundred thousand dollars!" I blurted out. I would never be able to scrape together ten percent of that. Who does this man think we are?

"Do you have any more pictures?"

A long silence. "Refresh the page."

I did. The naked photo was gone. I missed my chance to

download it. The new photo was of Mike and seemingly the same woman. It was hard to say because she was dressed and had her back to me. The picture had been taken from my office somewhere, from the same spot where I was sitting looking at it, and at a very close range. Although I couldn't see Mike's face, I recognized him. After fourteen years of marriage, you can identify your husband from every angle. They were standing on our master bedroom's balcony, checking out our view.

I'm always home. When could Mike bring a woman here? Then suddenly I knew. Mike got me a facial treatment and a sixty-minute body massage on an ordinary day—not even my birthday. As I took the envelope from his hand, my love for him soared to incredible heights. No husband is that nice to his wife. Finding out the real reason he bought me the spa-day surprise shattered my whole world.

I pressed download on the photo. The file burned onto my hard drive. In the days ahead, I would need to look at that photo when I was drowning in uncertainty.

"I'll get you the money. I just have to figure out how," I said through clenched teeth.

"I need you to say we have a deal."

"We have a . . ." I started, but he stopped me.

"Ah-ah. Don't rush into it. I need you to understand that once you make a deal with me, there is no turning back. No police. No games. Nothing. You give me the hundred thousand, and I let you disappear."

"I understand."

"You sure? Because if you try to run, I'll hunt you down and kill you. I won't even charge your husband for it."

"I understand. We have a deal."

"I'll call you in the morning. And don't forget. No games. I'll know."

I didn't sleep that night. Like a corpse, I lay on my bed staring at the ceiling and thinking of the life I had with Mike. How could we have ended up here?

.   .   .   .   .

Stacy: You know, I wouldn't say we were friends. I mean, we talked during soccer practices. I took my kids to their community pool a few times. We also went to see a movie with the kids in the cheap theater—you know by Kmart—but, no, I wouldn't say we were friends.

Sheriff's Sergeant Tom Long: Alright. So in those times when you *did* talk, did she ever mention anything about her marriage? Any problems? Abuse?

Stacy: You know, she might have mentioned that she was upset with Mike a few times, but you have to understand that I went through a nasty divorce recently, and my ex is a complete jerk. So mostly I was the one bashing him, and Sarah just listened. You know, he owes me a bunch of money, and I'm drowning in credit card debt. My life is a complete disaster.

Sheriff's Sergeant Tom Long: Who owes you money? Mr. Johnson?

Stacy: No. My ex. I'm sorry. I'm being very insensitive here. Mike? What a pig! He was a paramedic or firefighter or something like that. Seemed like a nice guy. Someone who helps people. What a liar. Sounds like my ex.

.   .   .   .   .

Wrapped in a towel, I'm on my back on my bed. So much to do.

So much to think about. But I'm useless. I've been feeling low for a while. I've been a pillar for everybody in my family while forgetting to take care of myself. My husband's career skyrocketed in the past ten years. I helped him make decisions. I supported him while he was gone for weeks doing training, taking courses, and acquiring new certificates. I did his laundry, ironed his uniforms, cleaned up after him, cooked his favorite meals, baked to keep his sweet tooth satisfied, did everything humanly possible to create a peaceful home environment. And now my husband's fallen crazy in love with someone else, and simply leaving me isn't enough for him. He wants to get rid of me completely and irreversibly. Is it punishment time? I thought I already paid the price for the mistakes I made in college.

I stare at the corner of the wall without blinking and barely even breathing because I can't wrap my mind around my situation. Mike and I have had our problems. *Who doesn't after many years of marriage?* But we have been pulling through. I had been upset with him for uprooting the family whenever it suited him and planting us in a new country, on a new continent wherever a promotion was waiting for him. But I found my way everywhere. I made friends. We had money. We got by. If there were signs of our marriage being in trouble, I didn't notice.

Since our return from Italy, Mike seemed to be stressed out all the time. I wrote off his behavior as a side effect of starting a new life once again. His sexual appetite died out, but I thought it was because he had so much on his plate. Actually, I didn't mind that he left me alone most nights. My own passion had ebbed. For years we only had sex to have an orgasm anyway. Most times the few seconds of pleasure weren't even worth the hassle. I accepted that. I learned to live with it. Besides, what wife can remain passionate and romantic when her husband stresses her out about money day in, day out? Every fight we had was like a broken record.

Mike always dragged his coworkers' marriages into our conversations. According to him, everybody else's wife was working, but me, or they came from wealthy families or inherited huge mansions or trust funds. But when I asked him who would take care of our kids if I worked full time while he was gone for days or weeks, he said I could figure it out like everybody else does.

The truth is that Mike was right. I should have gone back to work, and I could have figured it out, but after twelve years of staying away from real life, I was too scared to go back to work. Life had passed me by like a silver-bullet train while I stayed at the station. A fresh, younger generation of smart people had entered the workforce. They were eager, hungry, and talented. Who would hire me? A sour, boring housewife. I used to be hungry too. I knew how to play men. I had assets, and I knew how to put them to work. I lost my mojo years ago. This family—this marriage—sucked the magic right out of me. But I guess that wasn't enough for Mike. Now he wants to suck the life out of me completely.

I try to remember our last big fight. About two weeks ago Mike went through our family budget, and when the numbers didn't turn out as he expected them to be, he came looking for me.

"So let me get this straight," I told him after listening to his yelling about how much I'd spent on groceries. "You want to eat steak and salmon. You want me to buy organic food for the kids, but you don't want me to spend money."

"Stop being so dramatic. Of course you can spend money but not as much as you do."

"Just for the record, I never spend more than a hundred bucks on a grocery trip, while when you hit the stores for all your booze, sodas, spices, and delicacies you burn through three-hundred easily."

"So you're saying that it's me who spends all the money on food?"

"Whatever. You know what? Why don't you do the grocery shopping, and I'll cook with whatever you bring me."

"Shopping is your job. Or you want me to do that too?"

"Interesting. I thought I didn't have a job."

"You don't have one that makes money."

"Do you pay a babysitter?"

"What are you talking about?"

"When you hire a babysitter, do you have to pay her?"

"Of course," he snapped.

"How about a cleaning lady? Do you have to pay her?"

"What's your point?"

"My point is that I do dozens of jobs which I'm not getting paid for. But forget the money. I don't even get credit for what I do. You know how sick I am of listening to you bitching at me all the time?"

"Then leave."

"I should. And I would if we hadn't had children together."

"So what you're saying is that you're only staying with me because of the kids?"

"What else is here to stay for?"

"You're a spoiled bitch! You know that? You've lived in places other people only dream about. You haven't had a job for over a decade. And you complain?"

"You have a very short memory. As I recall, when I met you I was a successful businesswoman. You had nothing. I supported you through school."

"Oh, here we go again. Bringing up the past. Let's talk about what's happening now. The fact is we live off one salary, and the only reason we get by is that I'm good with money."

"I agree. You're good with money. Now. You weren't when I met you."

"Oh, shut up. You think you can hurt me by telling me what a big loser I was before I met you? Why did you marry me then?"

"Not for your money, that's for sure."

"If I'm such a bad husband, why don't you leave me? Find yourself a nice rich guy and suck his blood for a few decades."

"You're an asshole! You know that? I don't suck your blood. I have a full-time job taking care of your children and our house and you. The only job you have is to bring money home. I do my part. Now leave me alone, and you do yours."

He let out an exasperated sigh. "So when are you gonna get a job?"

"I had a job. Remember the medical business? It was just starting to pick up when I had to leave it behind to follow you to that fucking country again."

"You gonna cry over that for the rest of your life or are you gonna find a new job?"

"Leave me alone. I'm so sick of you and your mouth."

"So what's your plan? Sit here and cry?"

"No, I've been working on my blog. I'll earn my living with it one day."

"I won't hold my breath."

"You never support me with anything I do. Whenever I ask your help with something, you always say the same thing. *I know you can do it. You're just lazy.*"

"I've been supporting your ass for over a decade."

"I made some money too. You just don't look at it as a contribution to the family. You consider it . . . I don't know . . . like a down payment on the money I owe you for living with you."

"Stop being so dramatic, Sarah. We're not on Broadway."

"You know, my mother told me once that being a hardworking mom is the most underappreciated job in the world. After her nasty divorce from my father, I promised myself never to fall for a guy and give up my ambitions and independence. And look at me now. I fell into the same stupid trap she did. But you wanna know why I put up with your bad mouthing? Because my kids know what I do for them, and they always will. And that's all that matters to me. I don't care about having a big career. Been there, done that. And from all the impressive things I've done in my life, giving birth to my children was the most important of all. And you won't take that away from me. Or from them. So fuck off!"

. . . . .

Carol: They were fighting. I heard Sarah yelling. She had this hoarse voice. It was so annoying. Now that I know why I regret being upset with her voice. It's just so sad. Oh, those poor children. At least they don't have to listen to their parents fighting anymore. And the money that dropped into their laps will be enough for them to build a happy life. Do you know who their guardians will be? Just asking.

Grace: Whenever something like this happens, the media and the police always blame the mother. I have nothing to do with how Mike turned out. He was eighteen when he moved out. If you want to blame someone, find the crowd he hung out with after that. Not me. I'm sorry, but my puppies are hungry. It's feeding time.

. . . . .

The memory of our sadistic conversation unsettles me further. Getting started on my day seems like it might be the hardest thing I have ever done. The sound of Mike's goofing around with the kids downstairs is the only thing that makes me crawl out of bed. I check the time. This was the longest soccer game he ever played. I'm dressed by the time he makes it upstairs to see me. I can't even look him in the eye. I take the dog for a long walk. I order pizza for dinner. I say I'm not feeling well and go to bed early.

I listen to the ambient noises coming from the TV downstairs. I focus hard on making out words and recognizing the movie Mike is watching because this exercise is the only thing that helps me block out the image of the naked bodies of Mike and the Brunette.

When I don't find sleep due to the heat or a day at home without exercise, I toss and turn for hours. Now, I lie on my back heavy and dead like a log buried in the forest floor. I can almost feel vines wrapping around my body and roots growing into my organs. The pain is real, but I don't resist it. I imagine shame would feel the same way. How will the world react when they find out that my husband hated me so much he hired someone to kill me?

His mother would probably be happy at the news of my demise. She never took my side. At our wedding ceremony, she sat down beside me, holding one of her stupid little dogs in her arms after I specifically asked Mike to tell his mother not to bring dogs to the restaurant. When she showed up wearing white and toting three of her babies, I confronted Mike. He swore to me that he passed on my message. I believed him then, but I'm sure now that he was lying then just as he's been lying into my eyes daily ever since. I entered this marriage to redeem myself—my heart laden with secrets. I guess I wasn't the only one hiding my true self. Mike played his part in the same way.

I try to take a deep breath, but my lungs don't seem to have the capacity to hold all that air. My chest starts shaking. My breathing is choppy and broken. I don't know what to do, how to get out of this unreal situation, and I'm not in the state of mind right now to think of a plausible solution.

The TV goes silent. I hear Mike filling up a glass with water from the refrigerator. His footsteps are soft on the carpeted stairs. Like a paralyzed patient, I watch him enter the room from the corner of my eyes. He slips under the covers as he would any other night. I picture my fingers wrapped around his neck, my thumbs pushing down on his Adam's apple, harder and harder until his face turns from red to blue. It's a good thing he can't read minds because he wouldn't dare shut his eyes if he knew what I was thinking.

I watch my husband in his sleep. The curtains are drawn in front of the window next to my side of the bed. Darkness conceals me, but a sliver of diamond light forms a bridge over his face. The glow from the full moon shines through the blinds on the French doors that lead to a balcony we never use. The doors are old and worn, in sharp contrast to the rest of the house which we remodeled three months ago. All the hard work fell on my shoulders. I searched for contractors. I asked for bids. I negotiated the prices, but my dear husband picked the style for everything. If I had only known that he didn't spend all the money to make our home look better for us. He fooled me into preparing the house for his new bride. The combination of rising anger and disappointment nearly blinds me.

When we were at Lowes picking out the color for the carpet Mike wanted, I tried to argue the benefits of laminate, but Mike would have none of it. Now I know why he wasn't so gung-ho about pleasing me. Soon I'd be lying six feet under, sharing a tight coffin with maggots and beetles and the lingering souls of dead people, while my husband would be sprawled out on the soft carpet with his new wife, my kids and their kids playing Go Fish.

I shudder and feel my neck twitch. Requires all my strength to remain still.

The red 11:11 flashes on the clock next to my husband's head. He is so peaceful in his sleep, handsome even. One would think that hiring an assassin to kill the mother of your children would cause a few sleepless nights. Not for my husband. His face is smooth, his eyelids unmoving as he probably dreams about making love to his young, new wife. In his dream he's lying there on the bed, his head propped up on the down-filled pillow I bought for him at T.J. Maxx, and he's watching the pair of firm tits bouncing around as she rides him. Her slender weight pins down his hips, while she moans and claws his chest. How narcissistic can a man be?

We used to have sex like that too when we were younger, no kids, no mortgage. We spent our entire honeymoon in bed. We attempted to lie on the exotic beaches of Kauai and soak up the sunshine with strawberry margaritas in hand, but the gentle caress of the wind, the warm touch of the fine white sand, and the buzz from the alcohol made us horny. The tickling sensation of the waves as the salty water slipped between our legs, the cries of the seagulls, the sexually-laced music from a beach bar nearby. . . . All were there to trigger our senses. There was this burning desire in us that couldn't be quenched. Like a drug addiction, it kept us seeking a new high.

I hear a muffled fart that slips into the night. My husband turns to the other side. The moonlight highlights the strains of gray in his hair. I feel as if those years of youth, love, and happiness had never existed. I wonder when the last time was that I felt sexually aroused. I can't remember. We do have sex sometimes, but neither of us is there emotionally. It's only our bodies trying to hold onto something that isn't there anymore. I'm expected to do my conjugal duties— ten minutes sex or one hour yelling. Usually, I go with option number one. Pull the curtains, make it as dark as possible, jump under the covers. "Yes, I'm ready."

Stripping down to Eve's costume is only fun when you have the perfect body. It's hard to concentrate on working up to the orgasm when my eyes get stuck on my belly fat or the orange skin around

40

my thighs. It's hard to let my mind swim in amour when I know that I forgot to shave my legs and that Mike must have felt the spikes as he ran his hands over my legs. Or when my feet are on his shoulders, and I see the peeling nail polish. Instead of giving way to the feelings, all I can think of is that I should have redone my toenails days ago. Or whenever Mike buries his face in my hair. I wonder if it reeks of the chicken soup or garlic pork I made earlier in the day.

I'd touch his face but pull my hands away quickly as I remembered that an hour before he pinned me to the bed, I cleaned the toilets with Clorox wipes and the smell of bleach must still linger on my skin. Sex during the day can be a disaster.

Going at each other at night is not that exciting anymore either. We have to be quiet not to wake the kids. My husband used to hear his foster parents moaning. His stories are embedded in my mind. My kids won't lie in bed with hands over their ears.

I'm good at staying quiet, and if Mike lets out a sound, I just cup his mouth, hoping that the lotion I put on my hand didn't mix with the dishwasher soap smell, but eliminated it.

Despite needing to stay quiet, I prefer having sex in the dark. Although I'm usually tired and Mike is not at a hundred percent either, at least I don't have to worry about how I look. I'm braver at night. I roll on top and ride him like in old times, grateful that Mike can't see my sagging boobs. He tells me sometimes to get a boob job, jokingly, but we don't have money for it, so I don't bother to spend the time researching how much it would cost. Maybe he wasn't joking. Gravity is a bitch!

I touch my breasts. Yes, they could be firmer and perched higher on my chest, but they could be worse. Well, Mike doesn't have to worry about touching them anymore. I bet his girlfriend's boobs will never sag. *What an idiot you are, Mike!*

Since we got back from Italy, we rarely had sex. I didn't pay much attention to Mike's lack of interest. To be honest, I think I was actually happy about it. Yet, now that I'm confronted with the fact that he has a young girlfriend, I feel a pang of deep gnawing jealousy. Mike's interest in sex hadn't diminished, only his interest in me.

I have to take a few deep breaths to calm myself. I don't want to wake Mike. I put my hand over my mouth and nose, muffling the sounds that are aggressively trying to break out of me. For a moment I consider putting my hand over Mike's mouth and nose instead, but I know that I don't have the guts to do something like that. As soon as he woke up struggling for air, I'd let go of his mouth.

My fingers grasp my pillow. I sit up and pull it to my chest. It's king size, thick—dense with feathers. I press it against my face and try to breathe. It's difficult. I can put the pillow over Mike's face and hold it down. I think of how long it would take to suffocate him. Two minutes? Three? Would the pressure of my hands as I hold the pillow down leave a bruise on his face? I think I saw on *CSI* that bruises could show up postmortem on a body just in time for the autopsy. I put the pillow back against the headboard. It's too much of a hassle, and I'm not a cold-blooded killer.

I lean back, fully awake and thoroughly disturbed. A couple of days ago my biggest problem was picking lunchmeat for the kids and deciding between fried chicken and meatloaf for dinner. Now I'm thinking of ways to kill my husband before he kills me. A short chuckle escapes my mouth. Why am I even taking that phone call seriously? My husband doesn't have a secret affair. Despite his tantrums, he wouldn't hurt a fly. This is madness.

Mike moves again. This time he rolls toward me, his eyes are open.

"What are you doing?" he asks.

"I can't sleep. I think I'm gonna go downstairs and read for a while."

"Are you ok?"

You hired somebody to fucking kill me. No, I'm not ok, I think but nod instead.

Mike gets up and scrambles over to the bathroom. *He should get his prostate checked out.*

I slip out of bed. My head is so confused that I prefer not to face him when he gets back. I can't risk giving away what I know about his plan.

I shuffle my way to the kids and check on them. Mason is on his tummy. His bedcovers are crumpled up in the corner. I re-arrange them on him as carefully as possible, but he isn't deeply asleep. He starts banging his hand on the pillow as he falls back to sleep, the same way he's been doing since he was a baby. Some say it's because Mike and I had sex while I was pregnant with him; others say it's because I used to rock him when he was a baby; most likely his head is so full of new information that his brain has a hard time shutting down, and he uses this method to put himself to sleep. I don't think it matters.

I caress his face with the tip of my fingers and shush him. He goes back to sleep.

Tammy is sleeping like an angel, her blanket clutched in her hand, her thumb in her mouth. I'm tempted to pull her hand away. A callus has already developed on her skin. But I stop myself.

I close her door and slip downstairs. I have bigger worries to deal with tonight.

I pour myself a glass of water. It's freezing and goes down like sharp icicles. What am I supposed to do now? What's the wisest thing to do here?

The junk drawer is on my right. I pull out a notebook and rip a sheet out. I get a pen from the cup on the dining table where I do homework with the kids. I decide to sit down, write out my options, and go from there.

Mike has an Italian girlfriend (I'm almost 100% sure she is Italian. From Pisa)
The hitman offered me two weeks to come up with the money
I will be dead in 14 days if I can't find a way to pay him off
Questions to work out:
1) How could Mike meet someone while we were in Italy?
2) How come I didn't notice his changed behavior?
3) How did he bring her to the US?
4) Why does he want me dead?
5) Why is divorce not good enough for him?
6) What am I supposed to do now?

I lean back on the chair, the end of the pen wedged between my teeth. I go back three years and six months, to the day when Mike called to let me know that he received an assignment in Italy. The image is as clear as if it happened yesterday. I'd just gotten back from a successful meeting with the assistant of an orthopedic surgeon. After months of meeting her, bringing her cookies, finally, she had offered my company a chance. And if my services pleased her and her boss, they would have hired me as their prime vendor for durable medical equipment. With that contract, I could have made a decent income while my schedule remained flexible. Sounded like a dream.

Feeling glorious after my meeting, I burst into the kitchen and dropped the grocery bags on the table when my phone rang. I answered it and pinched my cell between my ear and shoulder so I would be able to put the food away at the same time.

"Are you sitting?" Mike asked, his voice laced with excitement.

"No. I'm putting groceries away. What's up?"

"Well, you need to sit down, because I have great news."

I put the milk container in the refrigerator, shut the door, and leaned against the cabinet. "I'm sitting. Go ahead."

"We're going to Italy!"

"What? When?"

"I don't know. A few months I assume."

"Where is this coming from? Can we even afford it?"

"That's the best part. I'll get paid to live there."

My back against the cabinet, I slipped down to the floor. "I didn't know you were asking for a new assignment."

"I didn't want to tell you until it was sure."

"We just moved back a few years ago. Why do you want to go again?"

I heard a sigh. "I thought you'd be happy."

"Yeah. Uhm. Italy? It's cool. But Mason just started school. And I just got my first contract today."

"Oh, your meeting. How'd it go?"

"It went really well. The case manager will start sending me referrals."

"Well, you don't have to worry about that anymore. In Italy our house and everything will be paid for. Plus, we get to travel all over Europe. How awesome is that?"

When I married an airman, I was aware that we'd have to move wherever the Air Force sent him. But we just got back to the States. Mike promised me we'd stay in one place for a few years. Apparently, he wasn't in the position to make such promises.

"I don't know, Mike. I think we need to talk about this in person. Not over the phone."

"Why do you always have to be like that? You always bring me down. Can't you be happy for my success?"

"Don't start that again. Of course I'm happy for your success.

But moving again? This will affect all of us. Not just you. We need to talk about this. I'm not sure the kids will want to go to the other side of the world again."

"Well, they need to go where I'm going. It's a huge opportunity, and I'm not going to let you spoil it."

The line went dead. The phone fell onto my lap. Once the orders picked up, it would be pretty good pay, and we could afford to put Tammy in a pre-school as we planned. But after four months, Mike became very impatient with me. He urged me to find a real day job and find it fast. But with his inconsistent work schedule, I had to think of the kids, too. I wasn't getting any younger, and I knew that even if I worked full time, Mike wouldn't help me with chores. This medical associate position was perfect. Once I got at least four or five setups a week, I would earn a full-time wage without the full-time hours. All I needed was for Mike to be patient with me. Unfortunately, patience isn't one of his virtues.

My eyes swept over the worn linoleum. I knew Mike wanted to replace it, along with a million other things in the house. I looked forward to updating our home, too, but I was unaware that instead of trusting me and giving me some time to generate a necessary second income he had been asking his superior for an overseas assignment. Again.

My stomach was in knots all day knowing that if I didn't support the move, Mike would never forgive me; but if I didn't put up a fight against the move, then the kids would never forgive me. Over the past decade or so, Mike moved us to a new country five times. I knew full well what living in Italy meant for us.

Mike was working a forty-eight-hour shift that week, so I had plenty of time to feel sorry for myself. My initial enthusiasm over my new contract evaporated. There was no need for me to make business calls anymore or feel achieved and important. What I had left were the long empty hours that needed to be filled. But instead of doing something useful, after I dropped the kids off at school, I plunked myself down on the couch to watch USA daytime shows. When Mike called, I lied about what I was doing all day. I made it sound like I had been busy. In reality, I didn't even do the dishes after breakfast.

Days passed before I recovered from my disappointment.

It took six months for all the paperwork to come through to get us on that damn plane and fly to Italy. That half of a year was the worst period of my life. The kids continually acted out their anger and frustration. The ink was still fresh on my contract with the doctor's office when I had to cancel it. Then I had to listen to my husband complaining that I wasn't making any money. Forever reminding me how he knew this whole medical business idea was a failed plan—like I didn't feel low enough.

"Well, thank God for you. Without you, none of us in this family would survive," I told him after the umpteenth time he cried about the bills he had to pay without any help from me.

"Well, thank God for this opportunity in Italy because without it we would go bankrupt."

"I could have earned money with my new business."

"Yeah, could have, should have. But you didn't. So stop bringing it up."

"I only needed some time. I had a contract with a doctor."

"And where is he now?"

"We are going to Italy. How could I run a business like that?"

"Whatever. We won't have money problems in Italy. You can stay at home or get a job. I don't care."

"I don't speak Italian. What kind of job am I gonna get?"

"I don't know. You're not a child. You just have to figure it out."

"I have a master's in business management; I won't flip burgers."

He rolled his eyes and perched himself on a bar stool in front of his open laptop. "You always shove your fancy education in my face, but I'm the one who puts food on the table. So what's your education good for? I gotta go to work tomorrow. Are you gonna get me something to eat, or do I have to do that too?" There is a full gourmet kitchen at the Fire Station and a grocery store nearby. Between gym time and afternoon coffee break, he would have plenty of time to pick up some food for himself. But he enjoys making me feel like I'm here to serve him.

On days like that, when the man I married for love puts me down, I always wish I had chosen career instead of family. As a mother, I work seventy hours a week; without pay, without sick leave, without vacation time.

As a corporate manager, I would work less, enjoy the benefits, and get paid. But I made the decision twelve years ago when my son was born, and now I have to live with it. Like my mother would say, you reap what you sow.

The funny thing is that the idea of my staying at home with Mason originated from Mike. I grew up in a stable family, but Mike had a harsh life as a foster kid. When I got pregnant, we made a pact that we would never let our kids suffer. As a woman and mother, it wasn't a question of whether I should stay home or not. It just felt right. I didn't realize how much I was giving up. Then my daughter was born, and one day I realized that being at home for a decade made me forget how to be anything but a mother.

I blew all my job interviews because I had no faith in myself. Who would hire a dull woman who's not up to date on daily economics and politics; who may know where the best deals for fresh vegetables and meat are in town, but knows nothing about the latest apps; who can schedule a whole family's activities seamlessly and manage to get everyone to their appointments on time, but has no experience on a conference call?

Kona, our dog, puts his head on my lap in the dark. I jump from fright. I'm off balance. More than usual.

As I pat him, I lean over to my notes.

How could Mike meet anyone while we were in Italy?

Simple. My husband used to initiate dozens of fights at home. Then with the statement, "I work all day, but I can't get any peace at home," he would leave the house and not come back for hours. I'd wait up until he got home, blaming myself for not being a more understanding wife. After all, Italy was beautiful. My son got to play soccer for a local team. My daughter joined the swim team at Palladio Sports. They even picked up the language and made friends with the locals. I only found one friend while working out at the gym, but Mike couldn't stand her husband so that friendship died out fast. I always figured Mike didn't have any friends because he never introduced me to anybody. When we went on a trip, it was only us— the family. As it turns out, he *had* found a close friend. Close enough to bring her back to the US, ruin our family—everything we had built together—and even hire someone to kill me for the sake of keeping their friendship. It didn't sound like Mike at all. Or maybe you think you know a person, but you don't.

I jotted down: *He met her in a bar in Aviano one of those nights when we had a fight, and he left.*

Or wait a second. There was another American base near Pisa somewhere. Mike came home one day from work, informing me that the station was short on men, and he would have to go down there for two weeks at a time each month and help out. He started that new job only seven months before we came back to the States. I remember being suspicious, because I offered to drive down with the kids and visit him a few times, but he always turned me down. He said the roads between Bologna and Florence were treacherous and there was no point for me to put the kids' lives in danger. Later on, when I ran into the wife of one of Mike's coworkers and complained about how much time Mike spent away, she said that it wasn't mandatory. In order to be assigned, he had to volunteer. I confronted Mike about what she said, and he didn't deny it. "I'm doing it for the extra money," he said, pulling a small jewelry box out of his back pocket. He opened it and showed me a necklace with a pendant. "Take a look. It's made of Murano glass."

With a forced smile, I took it from his hand and put it on, wishing that instead of another piece of jewelry I'd never wear he would give me more of his time.

I crossed out what I wrote about Mike's meeting the girl in a bar. He must have met her in Pisa.

My jaws clench painfully, and the pen falls from my hand. While I was at home with the kids, making sure they adjusted well to their new school and kept up with homework, Mike was romping around with a young chick on sandy beaches.

A surge of anger erupts in my stomach that I almost puke onto the table. I run to the bathroom and fall to my knees in front of the toilet bowl. I gag and spit, but nothing emerges from my stomach. I feel sick to the bone, like a cancer patient after chemotherapy. Maybe I wasn't the perfect wife. Maybe I should have lost those few extra pounds that stayed on after giving birth to Tammy. Maybe if I had a well-paying job. Maybe if I had been more active in bed. Maybe if I were nicer to my husband, then he wouldn't have gone looking for someone else.

My eyes well up with tears. I hear footsteps. Someone is descending the stairs. The thuds are heavy. It has to be Mike. The door opens behind me. I don't look, but I can sense him.

"Are you ok?" he asks me in a mere whisper.

"No, I'm not ok," I roar with enough harshness in my voice to cause Mike's eyes to enlarge.

I do get mad sometimes. I lose my cool when the kids fight all day long on rainy weekends. Indoor activities are not cheap, and I don't want to hear Mike's bitching about money, so I try to keep them busy inside our house. By Sunday evening we're all ready to lose it. But other than those rare occasions, I'm pretty good at keeping my cool.

I rip off a piece of toilet paper and wipe my mouth. I brush by Mike. He reaches after me, wrapping his fingers around my forearm.

"What's the matter with you?" he asks a lot louder now.

I snap my eyes toward the stairs, indicating that he needs to remain quiet. The kids have school tomorrow.

"I feel sick. I think you poisoned me." I spit the words into his face. I'm losing my cool; I can feel it.

He steps back, his face ashen. "What the hell are you talking about?"

I look into his face, at length and with disgust wondering if he suspects what I know. "Relax. I'm joking."

He gives me a glass of ginger ale—very uncharacteristic of Mike. He's being way too kind to me. My suspicion over his secret life grows with each kind word he utters. His behavior has always bordered on the bipolar—a real Gemini. Super sweet one minute. Stark raving mad the next. I learned to live with it, though. I'm not perfect either. Nobody is. I never tried to change him. But somehow, he's going overboard with honey now. I feel like I'm going to puke—for real this time. I glance at the black handle of the butcher knife in the wooden case. I picture it poking out of his chest, blood dripping, his face losing color.

"Go back to sleep," I say. *Before I stab you.*

How many nights when the kids were sick with fever or diarrhea, yet he wouldn't get out of bed to help me take care of them. It was my job to tend to the children. His job was to go to work the next morning. Tomorrow he'll have to work, so what the hell is he doing down here with me?

He yawns, rubbing his small eyes. "Ok, but wake me if you need anything."

How can he be so calm? My fingers curve into tight balls. I can feel the nails cutting into my palms. I watch him climbing the stairs. I think of standing on the top and pushing him down. Bad idea. He might only break a leg, or worse, fractures his neck or spine, and I'd have to tend to him for the rest of his life.

I open the refrigerator and stuff my face with everything I can get my hands on, including meatballs and a container of chocolate ice cream—the kind that has no added coloring or flavor. I've been worrying about my family's health while my husband's been plotting to kill me. I'll be the healthiest corpse in the cemetery.

I wash down the meatballs with the ice cream. My stomach wants to burst. Since my lifestyle lacks exercise, I try to stay away from late-night dinners and snacks. I stop eating at six. Now it's almost one o'clock in the morning.

As I return the container of ice cream to the freezer, I think of the note I wrote earlier. A cold wave sweeps through me as I realize that I left it on the table in plain sight.

A few long leaps take me to the table. The paper is still there. I'm as disappointed as I am glad. Would the outcome of my marriage change if I told Mike what I knew?

I don't sit down as I pick up the paper. The first question is answered for me. My husband met an Italian woman in Pisa, and they spent two weeks every month for seven months, making out and spending our money.

I put a check mark in front of the question, and my eyes slip over question number two. The words blur on the paper. I'm too tired to think clearly. If I want to find the right answers, I need some shut-eye.

I don't go back to the bedroom where my cheating husband's having dreams about his new life. I toss myself onto the bed in the downstairs guestroom instead. It smells like my mother-in-law. She just left two days ago after a short visit. She didn't care for Mike when she fostered him, but she cares to visit us now. When she is here, I hate how she gets in my way in the kitchen. She doesn't cook, doesn't clean. She is just a busybody—a master of criticizing those who actually do something.

I close my eyes, but sleep doesn't come. All I see in the dark are imaginary home videos of my husband with his new family. They are a lot like our home videos from happier times. I have to run to the toilet four more times before I hear sounds from upstairs. Mike is up, taking a shower. The coffee maker's alarm kicks in, and it starts grinding the coffee. Soon the warm, pleasant scent oozes into my room. On average days, it's the scent of coffee that wakes me up in the morning. This time it puts me to sleep.

. . . . .

Stacy: Look, I'm not like Sarah, okay. I wouldn't put up with anybody's shit like that. She was always carrying her kids' stuff—the chairs, the umbrella, the bags—like a mule. I told her to fuck it. Make them carry their own shit, but she said she didn't mind. If you ask me, Mike should have come more often to games and practices to help her out. My ex tried to pull the same bullshit on me, but I kicked him out before he could get comfortable. I'm nobody's slave.

13 DAYS TO DIE

Tammy's jumping on my belly wakes me. My head pounds intensely as if a windup toy has been unleashed inside my skull. I force a smile as I push my daughter off me. My day promises to be a complete disaster, I know. I can feel depression pulling its dark veil over my mood, a feeling becoming all too familiar. Tammy is hopping up and down next to me. The shaking motion rattles my body to the point where I'd rather get up than endure it any longer.

I peek at my watch. It's 7:48. I'm behind schedule to get the kids ready for school, but I'm an emotional wreck, and my bones hurt, making it difficult to move. With great effort, I remove the blanket and push my legs all the way to the floor. My mouth is stale, and my throat is dry.

The kids wonder why I slept in the guestroom. I tell them that Mommy didn't feel well last night, and I didn't want to keep their father up. They want pancakes. I feel more like cold milk over cereal—quick and easy. They insist. I oblige.

While Tammy storms out of the room, I stare at an enlarged framed photo of Mike and me at our favorite beach in Guam. Whenever I feel lonely or insignificant, I come to the guest room to see this photo. When I close my eyes, I can picture myself sitting in a beach bar under the umbrella, a cold fizzy cocktail in my hand, my toes tracing Mike's shin in front of me. He'd smile at me, tuck a sun-bleached strand of hair behind my ear and kiss my lips. I relish that memory because whenever I dig it up, I can almost taste the bitterness of my tonic, the cold touch of the condensation that rolls down on the side of the glass and disperses on my fingers. My life used to be exciting, unique, more than most people are privileged to experience. Now the ride is over. It's been over for a long time.

This morning I refuse to let my eyes linger on the photo. Mike has betrayed everything we were and could have been. I already feel I'm standing on the edge. I don't need a push to send me to my doom.

My mind is completely blank as I make sandwiches: chilled leftover bacon fat over rosemary olive sourdough bread, honey ham, and turkey breast. On the side carrots, radishes and slices of cucumber. I'm grateful for my state of mind. After last night, I couldn't bear another tableau of Mike with his happy new family.

I cut an apple up and slice some cheese. The smell of the burning pancakes crawls up my nostrils. The kids complain. I push the window open. Kona sits outside, looking at me, shivering. It's about forty-eight degrees outside, yet she acts as if we live in Siberia. I ask my son to let the chickens out and give them food and water. He grumbles as he puts his father's sweatshirt on and slips into shoes demoted for use in the chicken coop.

I flip the pancakes and pour myself a cup of coffee. The chickens fly out of the hen house and start pecking around Mason's legs.

Mike's decision to bring these stupid animals into our HOA home, where keeping animals apart from dogs and cats is illegal, borders on stupidity. I doubt his Italian bimbo dreams about taking care of chickens in her new, beautiful Californian home.

I watch Mason running back toward the house with the chickens in tow. I consider the idea that maybe Mike wasn't thinking about killing me four months ago when he showed up with a box of baby chicks. Maybe his greedy girlfriend talked him into this craziness. Get rid of the old and bring in the new. But why kill me? Why can't he just ask for a divorce?

I assume he knows me. Despite the tendency to keep to myself and sulk around quietly, I can be hotheaded. I hold onto my family with my claws. It wouldn't have been an easy fight. I would make him stay with me. I wouldn't go down smoothly. My children need their father, and he promised to be their father. You can't just walk away because your nose got the scent of a new piece of ass.

Of course, she is more attractive than a battered mother of two. How often can they see each other? Living with someone makes you see them in a completely different light. You spend time with your wife on her good days and bad days.

A mistress can put on a show for as long as she wants. She knows when her lover will drop by to spend time with her, and she makes sure her hair and nails are salon-perfect, that she smells like roses, that her place is clean with no toys and dirty soccer shoes to put away, only sexy lingerie. She might even leave a lace thong here or there—on the arm of a chair, next to her bed—insinuating that she always wears sexy pieces and putting images into the man's head about what's under her daisy duke and tank top.

But in defense of the faithful wives and mothers in the world, we are also aware of hot guys around us. Guys who don't fart up the bedroom by the time you get out of the shower. Guys who don't smell like a gym bag after mowing the lawn on a hot summer day. Guys who put the toilet seat down, close their sock drawer, and put their dirty laundry into the hamper instead of on the floor next to it. But we don't give up our family and run off with those hot guys. No, we have responsibilities, and we are bound by our marriage vows.

I cut my finger on the last piece of apple. Blood gushes out of the wound and drips onto the plate. I don't even care. My mind is miles away. The man I gave my youth and heart to wants me dead.

"Mom, your finger!" screams Tammy.

Two pieces of apple are getting coated with my dark, crimson blood.

Damn it! Why does this tiny insignificant part of my body have to bleed so much?

"It's okay, Honey. I'll clean it up."

The kids eat their pancakes; only six are burnt out of eleven. We are out of maple syrup. I replace it with honey. They don't complain. Thank God, because I'm not in the mood to take their whining today. My head is throbbing, and my stomach feels as if it's been ripped out of my body, left out in the sun all day, and put back in place.

In the shower, I make up my mind to go to the police station. I'm going to report what I know. My husband hired some European gangster (I can't pick out his accent, but I'm sure it's European) to whack me. He's already found my replacement. The police will be able to find proof somehow.

By the time I put on a pair of old jeans and faded T-shirt, I realize that even if the police believed me and found evidence of Mike's criminal premeditated act, it wouldn't do our family any good. He'd be arrested and taken into custody. Without his income, our savings would run dry fast. I'd have to give up the house. The kids might have to change schools again. I'd need to hire a nanny that would charge as much as I would earn working at a Barnes & Noble store as a bookseller or at J.C. Penney as a sales associate. The odds are not in my favor.

Thirteen days. That's all I have left to sort things out. Besides, if I don't pay the hitman, he'll probably kill me anyway. Call it revenge. No, putting Mike in jail is not going to solve my problem. I need a better plan.

The kids are fighting in the bathroom. We are late again. I yell at them to stop and order them to brush their teeth and comb their hair. The bickering doesn't stop. I don't have time to do anything with my hair or brush my teeth. If I ever hear anyone say that motherhood is easy, I'll punch that person in the face. I can't even figure out how to keep myself alive because I have to take care of everybody else first.

I drive to school with the kids arguing in the back seat over chess club points. As much as I can make out from the heated bickering, Tammy wants Mason to share the points he earned during the past few weeks from beating other kids at chess. Every activity they do together seems to turn into a cockfight. Sometimes I wish Tammy would do ballet and Mason would get into boxing. Then they would have nothing in common to talk about.

"Stop belittling your sister, Mason," I grunt, passing the fifth Toyota Prius just like ours on the road. In high school, I drove a red convertible Mini Cooper decorated with stickers and stuffed animals. Talk about becoming insignificant.

"She always wants what's mine," Mason complains.

"Mason never shares," Tammy whines in a tone that sets the hair bristling on the back of my neck.

I squint at them in the rearview mirror and catch Tammy as she pushes her brother on the shoulder.

"Stop being so mean," she snaps at him. I don't know what they teach her at school, but she apparently has no grasp on what 'mean' actually means, so I explain it to her for the hundredth time.

When I tell her that she needs to earn her own points and not bully her bother out of his, she puts on a pouty face. "I wish Dad would drive me to school, not you. You're so mean." I guess *mean* is her favorite word. Could be worse. She could always cuss. Still, it drives me crazy when she says it. Mean. Mean. Mean.

Mason drops five Chess Master slips onto her lap. "Here. Happy now?"

I don't feel like arguing any longer, so I don't intervene. Just one morning I believe I deserve some peace. I let Tammy's manipulative way win again.

Near the school, I slow down. I enjoy watching other poorly dressed, hunched-over mothers walking their kids to school. It gives me the satisfaction that I'm not the only one who gets up early yet has no time to make herself look presentable.

By the time I reach the drop off zone, I've seen enough fat asses in tight yoga pants and tangled hair put up in messy ponytails to feel slightly better about myself. But then, there she goes again, the idol of us mothers, walking toward the gate and holding hands with a boy and a girl. I take in her attire: mustard-colored ankle boots, black floral nets, black body-hugging dress and a waist-high red coat over it. Her shoulder-length blonde hair is blow-dried as always. This morning, her makeup consists of smoky eyes and nude lipstick. I wonder where she goes after she gets rid of her kids. I imagine her in a big open office with a great view, doing something creative, working as a marketing director at the Promenade Mall, or doing public relations work for Loma Linda Hospital.

I see her every morning walking her kids to school while most of us mothers don't even get out of the car to make sure nobody sees us. We hide our wet hair, our wrinkled T-shirts, and overly tight jeans, or our pallid half-peeled-off nail polish on display in a pair of flip flops that don't match our attire but were conveniently by the door when we rushed out to the garage.

She tucks her flat ironed and rectangular hair behind her ears. The morning sun reflects off her polished nails, long and red. My stomach tightens as I pull over by the curb and let Mason and Tammy hop out, praying that Miss Perfection won't look at me. My kids start hurrying toward the gate on opposite sides of the sidewalk as if they don't know each other.

Mason catches up with Miss Perfection and her kids. The contrast is startling. My kids are dressed in decent, school-appropriate clothes, their hair is combed, and their faces washed. The blonde woman's boy is wearing sweatpants that are short enough to flash his ankles, dirty tennis shoes, his face is sleepy, and his hair is a mess. With a few knots and splits on the back, the girl's hair looks as if she combed it herself. Her dress doesn't match the leggings, and it's so wrinkled as if she had just dug it up from the bottom of her closet this morning.

I feel slightly better about myself as a mother as I turn out of the busy school drop-off zone that, despite traffic control, is always chaotic. It's as if parents hate being directed, so they ignore the rules to defy the system. Rebellious.

I roll up to the turnout lane then I look back at Miss Perfection. Damn, I love those boots!

By the time I hit Golden Rod Road reality sets in. All of a sudden, taking my kids to school seems a treat rather than a duty; a luxury I might not be enjoying for long. I hate Mike. I hate what he's doing to us.

From the madness in my head, I become too distracted to drive. Once I pass the streets, full of walking kids and parents, I pull over in front of someone's house.

How did we get here I wonder, my head buried in my hands, but fate doesn't grant me much time for self-pity. A garage door opens next to my car. An elegantly dressed black couple steps out of the garage that is packed with junk to the brim and walks to their car in the driveway. Dad's holding a little girl. He pops the back door open, kisses her and buckles her into the car seat. I remember how Mike used to take Mason to the car and buckle him in when we went to mommy and baby playtimes, or grocery shopping. The past few years he hasn't even shown up at his soccer games.

I catch the mother's evaluating eyes on me. I feel awkward and start driving off. I'm angry again. All the suppressed complaints about my marriage and Mike are back on the surface, just floating there like a layer of trash in the ocean. Mike was never the perfect husband I had cataloged him as in my mind. I only lied to myself to paint a better picture about my life to myself and others. Telling myself that I had it better than most wives helped me get through my tough days. But like any other lie, my lies caught up with me.

Mike wasn't always so passive. He used to be fun and hands-on. Maybe I'm the reason our relationship is ruined. Was it something I said? Or should have said but didn't?

I catch my reflection in the rearview mirror. I'm ugly. I used to be reasonably good-looking with big eyes, a broad smile, and smooth skin. In high school, I was ready to conquer the world. I was prepared to show everybody what I was capable of all by myself. Somewhere between saying, 'I do' and today, I lost my spark. The fire is gone from my eyes, from my personality.

I pull over again; this time, to the side of LA Fitness. Not in the front, I'm not interested in seeing happy homemakers in tight pants and pink running shoes going to the gym, arms interlocked, holding healthy frozen yogurts and green smoothies in plastic cups.

Here on the side nobody can see me. A tiny hole in my jeans over my right thigh grabs my eyes. The blue fabric is worn and has lost its color. At some places, it's almost white. My T-shirt is lame too. I bought it from Old Navy about nine years ago. *What is it still doing in my closet?*

Judging by my appearance, it's easy to understand why Mike went looking for a mistress. I've been taking care of other people for so long, that I stopped taking care of myself.

But I have an excuse. I don't earn money, and I don't want Mike to think that while he's at work, I squander his hard-earned dollars at beauty salons and department stores. Maybe I should have. Would he still yearn for the company of other women if I were sizzling sexy and fun to be around?

I get out of the car and start walking toward Rite Aid. I want to test men, or should I say, test myself to see if I still have it in me to attract attention. By the time I reach the entrance, I passed five guys. None of them checks me out in the slightest. In desperation, I smile at a balding over-sixty dude getting out of his beat-up Chevy. He raises his eyebrows and looks away.

I burst into the store, tears pushing at my eyes. I can't breathe. I don't know what I'm doing in the store. My eyes land on a display of small bottles of red and white *Barefoot* wine. I need a drink but something stronger, and I need it badly.

In the rear of the store, I find a line of premixed cocktails. I pick up a four-bottle pack of flavored Smirnoff Vodka. My hands are shaking as I put it on the counter. I only come here when I need more shampoo or a box of tampons.

The cashier doesn't bat an eye as she reads the barcode on my booze. I pay and rush to my car.

Sitting behind tinted windows, I look around to make sure I'm alone in the parking lot. Two high-school kids are kissing next to a Redbox vending machine. They wouldn't give a shit about a depressed middle-aged woman who looks like she hadn't slept for days and is drinking in her car. I'm the woman we scare our kids with.

"You better study at school, or you're going to end up like her," we, flawless mothers, say. "You shouldn't eat that junk, or you'll look like her in ten years."

I am that woman true perfect moms point out as a bad example.

Music is blaring from the radio. I think it's Pink, but I'm not sure. I'm drinking and crying at the same time when I turn into our driveway. The garage door opens and allows me in. The neighbors won't see me because I'm not getting out of my car until the door closes behind me.

I had big plans for this week. I was going to start running on the treadmill. I have two book promotions scheduled for next Friday. Both kids made the soccer tryouts and will have their first practice today. All through winter, I've been planning to run around the park while they played soccer in the spring. From next week, I was going to start getting back in shape and reclaiming my old life.

I rip open the refrigerator and pull out a container of orange juice. I gulp a full glass of it. Then I finish the kids' leftover pancakes. I'm still hungry. My whole insides are upset. I stuff some lunchmeat into my mouth. I take a bite from the block of mozzarella cheese. Someone didn't close the plastic bag, and it's somewhat hard. I wash it down with more orange juice.

I find two pieces of chocolate chip cookies in the snack drawer. They are hiding in a Ziploc bag under a loaf of bread. Someone left this bag open too, and they turned dry and stale.

I open the second bottle of Vodka cocktail. I drink almost the entire bottle with one gulp. I cry some more, then finish the bottle. My body feels weak, and I stretch out on the couch. No TV, just stillness. I hear birds chirping on the pear tree outside our window.

Spring is approaching. Spring is beautiful. I feel dreadful. I want to die. I should let Mike kill me . . . or the hitman kill me . . . whatever. I'm not wanted. Why should I live? What is there to live for?

My phone beeps, but I don't move. I only get up when my tongue starts itching for another drink. I picture all those pills at Rite Aid. Which combination of drugs and alcohol kills?

If I'm up anyway, why not check my phone?

Mike sent me a message. **I left my laptop home. Can you close the screen down? Thanks**

I flip the screen off with both of my middle fingers. "Do it yourself, you asshole!" I scream. "Ask your girlfriend to do it, you cheating, lying sack of shit."

Then a glimmer of light pierces the cloud of misery in my head. I slam the bottle onto the counter so fast it spills. I leave it and bolt upstairs to the office slash bedroom. The laptop is on Mike's desk, open, just as he said. I press the space button, and the screen comes to life. His desktop picture is the family picture we took by Lake Skinner a month ago. We were so happy. Mike was teaching Mason how to fish.

A stab of pain thrusts into my heart. It was all an act. He even asked a stranger to take a picture of our entire family. I'm always the one who takes pictures, but he was snapping shots right and left that day. It's all a ploy. He must have been planning my execution for a long time. He's been covering his tracks, making sure if there were ever an investigation, every element of his life would lead to one conclusion, that we were happily married and that he was a model father.

I imagine him crying on a white plastic chair at my funeral. An expensive white orchid wreath with the message: *We will never forget you* written in stylish cursive golden letters on a white ribbon. He won't spare the expense. He will show the world how much he misses me.

My stomach turns.

I type his password with ease. He confided it to me before we got married. I had access to his bank accounts, emails, and personal files. I never snooped, though. I trusted him. I had no reason not to trust him. Whenever my bank card was declined at the grocery store, I called him. He called the bank and fixed my problem for me. So, I had no reason to check our bank accounts.

GUam1999—the place we lived for a year and got married. Two first letters are capitalized. No spaces.

The password is declined.

A layer of sweat settles on my face. I taste its salty flavor on my tongue.

I try the same password in different combinations: all lower case letters, all capital letters. Nothing works. *After how many tries will the computer lock me out?* No idea.

I shut down the screen. Mike must not find out that I tried to get into his computer.

Rocking back and forth on his rotating chair, I start chewing on my nails. I'm running out of ideas.

There's a yellow folder in the corner of his desk. I flip it open with little interest in what's inside. It's probably investment-property papers.

When my grandfather died, I inherited a house in Wisconsin. Mike persuaded me to sell it and use the money for a down payment on a home closer to us. We found this cute house in French Valley in a quiet neighborhood a ten-minute drive from us. Simple, with champagne-colored carpets and tiles, an open floor plan, four bedrooms, two baths, with a decent size backyard and a pool. I fell in love with it. I must hand it to Mike. Buying it was a terrific idea.

But it's not the rental-property papers that are in the yellow folder; it's a copy of Mike's life insurance. The policy is for one million dollars, and I'm the beneficiary. Since we are never sick, not even the kids, there was no reason for me to keep this insurance policy in mind, but I remember now. Mike bought it when he had to go to Afghanistan for a year and a half. He wanted to make sure that the kids and I were taken care of in case he died in the war. He worked as a fire inspector inside a safe zone. His life was never in any real danger; still, we both grew a bunch of gray hairs in those eighteen months. Once he returned home, he kept his life insurance, but as far as I was concerned, it only collected dust in his office somewhere. Why was he pulling it out now and putting it in plain sight?

My eyes linger on the number: one million dollars. Money that big would solve all my problems. I could pay off the guy Mike hired to kill me and help the kids and me to start a new chapter of our life.

I'd never leave this house, though. I put too much effort into turning it into our home. It is at the end of a cul-de-sac; quiet but close to the center, great views, big living spaces, four bedrooms, and a big yard. The place has everything we ever wanted. Although I love the house, if all that money fell into my lap, I'd rip up this freaking carpet.

However, I love Temecula—a hidden jewel of a city in an otherwise overlooked Riverside County. A clean and organized cradle of family and retired communities, surrounded with arid hiking trails, lakes, and parks. The beach is only forty minutes away, the mountains an hour or so. The weather is set to please—always sunny, never too cold. The kids have friends here. We all love living here. I wouldn't leave, not if I had a million bucks in my pocket.

My head feels heavy from the alcohol buzz. I go downstairs for a glass of water.

I pull out the note I wrote last night. I reread the questions. Most of them are unanswered. Some of them seem unimportant even. How did he bring her to the US? Who cares, really? The most interesting question is why divorce is not good enough for Mike.

Millions of people around the world get divorced and start over with a new partner. Nowadays there is no stigma or shame attached to being a divorcee. Some women even promote this lifestyle, saying that at least they can do whatever they want, and nobody can boss them around.

Before we moved to Italy, I met a group of independent women a few years ago in an Irish pub called The Shamrock. A family friend was visiting us, and Mike and I took him out for a drink. I was outside with a gin and tonic in my hand hustling some girls for a smoke. I don't go out often. Partly, it's because I don't like to spend Mike's money. The other reason is that as a mother I feel that I'm supposed to be an example for my children. I can't come home intoxicated and reeking of smoke. Mike doesn't share my opinion, and many of the fights we have are about how boring I've become. Maybe I should have listened to his complaints. Perhaps if I stayed a party girl, he wouldn't have hired someone to whack me…

So, I stood outside that pub, smoking, and drinking, and talking to a group of divorcees like we were best buds. Mind you, in a pub, everybody is your friend. We talked about the secrets of a happy marriage. I said it was making your man happy, keeping your role as a woman, and doing right by your children. In unison, they verbally attacked me. *It's me before you*, they told me. *There is no way I would be washing somebody else's dirty laundry or kiss someone's ass all day.*

I thought they were all bitter and ugly. The biggest mouth had at least fifty extra pounds on her. Her boobs spilled out of her tiny top. It was disgusting; although I'm sure she was going for the sexy look. I pitied them. But look at me now. I tried to be a strong pillar for everybody in my family, but all I've earned with my efforts is a price on my head. *Why doesn't he ask for a divorce?*

The warm glow of the sun invites me outside. I drop myself onto a patio chair and close my eyes. Kona's wet nose touches my hand. I doze off.

A sharp stinging pain arouses me. I jump out of the chair. A dead bee is on the concrete by my feet. A red bump rises on my right hand. *Great. Just what I needed.*

I get back inside, take a sip of my Smirnoff Vodka cocktail and drink more water. The sheet of paper with my notes lies on the chipped tile counter. Mike hates this kitchen, but after the remodeling, we had no money to replace the cabinets or the appliances.

Then it hits me. Why not divorce? It's because the hitman is right. Divorces are expensive. Mike knows that. So does every husband here in California. The court would award me the kids and a big chunk of Mike's paycheck as alimony. He would only see the kids every weekend or perhaps every other weekend when they play most of their soccer games; so there would be no more surfing and beach time for poor little Mikey. He'd have to sit on the sideline for hours and sweat it out in the ninety-five-degree weather like the rest of us.

Killing me would be lots easier. Mike would collect the fifty grand he insured me for, get the kids, the house, and keep the money. What a deal!

I wonder how long he plans to mourn me after my death before his girlfriend moves in. Mike has always cared about what other people think of him. He needs to keep up the appearance of a sad widower whose wife was taken in a tragic accident. What was the plan? A bullet to the head? A car crash? A car bomb? I should have asked the guy when he called me.

I do twenty-six sit-ups and hold a plank for seventeen seconds. From the surge of adrenaline, I feel invincible. I flip the switch in the garage and brightness spreads over my car and the pile of stocked up stuff by the wall. I look for the black plastic military containers. We keep old photographs and books—things we don't need on a daily basis—in them. I remember there's a box of *CSI* DVDs inside one of them.

With no small strain, I take down the first case and flip it open. I find Mike's childhood photos, old framed pictures, baseball cards, and other assorted garbage. I think of making a pile and torching everything. I'm not that petty though.

The next one has old scuba diving gear in it, still sandy and white from sea salt.

The third one holds my photo albums and yearbooks. I sit on the cold concrete with my legs tucked in and check out my eighth-grade yearbook. I wish I had a device to turn back the time and start over. With the knowledge I have today, I'd do so much better.

In one of the photos, I recognize an old friend of mine, Benny Simons. His chubby face is spread out in a huge smile. He was a tech genius. His dad used to bring him parts of radios and other electronic devices from the thrift store. Benny would take them apart and put them back together or build something entirely new. I believe after high school he went to an IT college.

Benny should know how to break someone's password. Only if I knew where he lived now or what he did for a living.

The last container holds the DVDs. The boxed set that includes four seasons of *CSI* shows sits between other TV series collections like *Lost* and *4400*. I read the episode titles. They don't give anything away.

I clean up my mess and carry the box inside. I put the first disc in while I take my iPad in my hands. It seems, after all, I've found a use for it. Facebook is what I need. I search for Benny Simons. There's a whole bunch of people with that name. Okay, maybe we have some mutual friends. Let's see. I keep searching while the first episode of CSI starts. The main story is about a dead girl in the desert. I switch to the next episode.

There are two people from middle school who I know for a fact are my friends on Facebook.

Elizabeth Shaw: no longer on the list. *Great, she defriended me.*

Sawyer O'Connor. He's still my friend. I scroll down on his list of friends with almost no hope at all. Benny and Sawyer weren't close at school. I gasp when I find Benny's name next to a face I recognize among Sawyer's list of friends.

I check out Benny's profile. His most recent picture was that of a car in front of his old house here in Temecula. I'm feeling lucky. It seems his family still owns the same home they did when we were kids. Even better, it's like only a fifteen-minute drive from where I live now.

I send him a friend request. He accepts it immediately. A surge of excitement jolts through me. In a message, I ask for his phone number. I'm too official and to the point. As soon as I hit send, I regret it. I should have led up with hey! How're you doing? Long time no see and such. Before I can conclude my chain of thoughts, Benny's reply flares up on the screen. He gives me his number without asking why I needed it.

I don't call him now. The kids will be out of school in less than four hours, and I have a bunch of crime investigation episodes to watch.

I only pause the show once when I need to grab a bite to eat. I should be cooking by now. The kids are always hungry when they get home from school. I find a long-forgotten box of macaroni and cheese and set it next to the stove. It will do.

I have ten minutes to leave the house and drive to the school to get there on time when I see something that catches my eye. A wife poisoned her husband with Selenium. The coroner pronounced heart attack as the cause of death. I need to watch the end of the show, but I have no more time. I'm already late for pick up. My hair is still not combed, and I'm wearing the same pair of faded jeans and the T-shirt I had on in the morning. My mouth is sour, and my breath reeks. I pop gum in my mouth. At least I have a pair of cool sunglasses—a little treat to myself on my last birthday.

The rest of the afternoon I spend whipping up the macaroni and cheese, doing homework with the kids, and taking them to soccer practice, all the time my mind wrapped around Selenium. What contains Selenium? Where can I get some? What's the ideal dose to make it look like an ordinary heart attack?

I need to find a place where I can search the Internet without the police being able to trace it back to me. The library? I could call Benny and use his computer. After all these years of not talking, getting him involved would be cruel and unusual. I haven't seen him since high school. I can't show up at his house and make him an accessory to murder. Saying those three tiny words, even in my head, sounds so wrong: accessory to murder. It's only self-defense I point it out to myself. That sounds a lot better.

I put the kids to bed early so I can finish the *CSI* episode about the wife who poisoned her husband with Selenium. It turns out to be a waste of time. As the story unfolds, I only learn that the woman used a brand of dandruff shampoo that contains Selenium, and to cover up the garlicky breath Selenium gave her husband, she fed him bagels with garlic spread. She doesn't say how she made her husband swallow shampoo and in what amount. I'm a little disappointed, although it would have been too easy.

The best part of the story is that the police never arrested the wife. *CSI* couldn't prove the poisoning. Selenium. That's it! It's time to do some digging.

I take a shower before going to bed. I feel dirty, and not from housework because I didn't do any today. I feel dirty because of the thoughts that manifested themselves in my mind. How did I go from an immaculate housewife and mother, who never cheated on her husband or even had an inappropriate thought about another man, to being a murderer?

During an hour of lying restlessly in bed, I go back and forth between decisions. When I think of Mike whispering sweet nothings into his new girlfriend's ears, the same words he used to whisper to me, I'm rock solid about poisoning him. When I envision myself in an orange suit, my hands in cuffs, my kids sitting across the table from me, their eyes red from crying, I banish the idea.

I should grab the kids and run away, far from this city, away from Mike and his sick mind.

But I know my husband. He's a nice guy. It would be so much easier to wrap my mind around what's happening to me if Mike were a drug dealer or a pimp. For a moment, I consider that it's not even he who wants me dead. His girlfriend is forcing him to get rid of me because she dreams about sleeping in my bed and showering in my newly renovated bathroom. I put the pillow over my head. I wish it would be that easy to stop the voices in my head.

A message comes to my cell. I jolt into a sitting position. I forgot to call back Mike earlier. He called around six from the fire station, but I didn't feel like talking to him, so I let the call go to voicemail, winning a night of peace. Then I relax back onto my pillow. Why should I care if he worries about me, or the kids? He's probably calling as part of his act to prove to the police that he cares about us. How long has he been playing this game? Since we got back to the States? Or did he already work out this plan while we were in Italy?

I check my phone. The message is from an unknown number. It says: **12 days sweetheart**

I know who that is. It's that sick European bastard who's been blackmailing me. I hate Europe. I hate all Europeans. I want Obama to send a nuke and blow up the entire continent. Who are these sheepshagger lowlifes who come here and steal my husband, my country, my city—my life?

Fuck off–I write back but don't send it.

I know thanks for reminding me–I send instead.

I decided on poisoning Mike with Selenium. This game has come down to two options. It's him or me. I need Mike's million-dollar life insurance to pay off this grease ball and start a new life. Otherwise, I'll be dead, and I'll be condemned to watch the people I despise to carry on with their lives, raising my children like a big happy family. No fucking way!

12 DAYS TO DIE

I'm standing in the kitchen when Mike confronts me. "Why didn't you answer your phone yesterday?" This is the first thing he said to me since he got home from work this morning. And he didn't ask me nicely. I don't remember when I gave him permission to treat me like a dispensable employee.

The kids are still in bed. Today is Saturday, the only day they can sleep in. We dedicate our Sunday mornings to the Lord. I wonder how many other hypocrites like us go to church and pretend to be honest people. How does that commandment go? Thou shalt not kill? It's the fifth one, I believe. Every Sunday I sit in my pew, worshiping God, yet when I'm faced with a choice, I choose the devil. Is it possible that we all have darkness within us; only some of us never have a chance to act upon it while others are left with no choice? And that's me now. I have no choice.

"I was jogging around the park during the kid's soccer practice,"

I tell Mike. "By the time I saw your call it was too late to call you back." I sense my eyes going in and out of focus. The image of me burning in the fires of hell keeps yanking me away from the present.

I do notice Mike's eyes widening. "Jogging?"

Actually, I was walking most of the time, but he doesn't need to know that my lungs and body are so weak that I was out of air after a few minutes. I'll let him believe that soon I'll have the beautiful, lean and muscular body other wives will envy. A sexy figure he won't be able to touch ever again.

The hazy memory of our last intercourse, which after more than a few cranberry vodkas was unusually wild and passionate, makes me smile. Though I don't remember a lot from that night, I remember Mike's glowing face the next morning. I'm glad I gave him something to dwell on while rolling on the ground from an induced heart attack and having white foam bubble up on his lips. What I didn't know then, but I know now, is that Mike most likely made love to his girlfriend the very same day. Rampant disgust grips my chest, and I can barely keep down my stomach contents.

"Yeah. I've been very stressed out lately over money and my blog, and I needed to release some pressure," I say with an enormous amount of self-control that makes me proud of myself.

His enthusiasm ebbs. I can tell by the way his shoulders drop. "Are you even looking for a job?"

I swallow hard before I say without batting an eye, "Actually I went to the new hospital down on Temecula Parkway to see if I could restart my medical business, and I got a contract. I'll be making a ton of money soon."

Suddenly intrigued, he turns around and leans against the cabinet, arms folded on his chest. "How much money you talking about?"

"I don't know, five maybe ten grand a month. It can be more if I hire some help." I feel my hands shaking as I fabricate all these lies.

I look for a distraction to avoid his eyes. The countertop is clean. There are no dirty dishes in the sink. I bend down to empty the dishwasher.

"You're kidding me?"

"Why would I kid? I just didn't want to tell you until it was for sure." I use Mike's phrase. The irony of it initiates a laugh that almost bursts out of me. It takes all my self-restraint to keep my amusement contained.

"Sarah, that's fantastic!" He pulls me up by my elbow. My neck flexes. I jerk away, a steak knife tightly in my grasp.

"Maybe you should calm down. Let's not spend the money before we have it. May take a couple of weeks to iron everything out."

His face broadens into a smile. "Calm down? How can I? A hundred grand a year? That's freaking awesome."

I watch him with disgust. Mike's love for me is measured by dollars I bring home. Bile burns the back of my throat.

He pulls me into a hug.

I press my eyes shut tight. *Easy, easy,* I warn myself.

"Let's celebrate tonight. I'll go and get some steaks and lobster."

"Don't you have a soccer game today?"

"It's just a pick-up game. I don't have to go." So that's all it took for him to ditch his new ladylove? Telling him that I found a way to make us rich?

"You should go. You know me. I don't like to celebrate in advance. Let's wait until the money starts rolling in."

He forces himself on me to kiss me, but I pull away.

"What's wrong?"

"Nothing." I shake my head. "I've had a tickle in my throat for the last couple of days. Whatever it is, I don't want to infect you."

My hands are moist and my pulse pounds against my eardrums

as I push him away from me.

He looks at me with eyes shrunk and filled with worry. "Can I make you a cup of tea?"

I'll fix you a cup of tea; one that will put you in eternal sleep, you despicable human being.

I shake my head no and resume my work on the dishes. I hear the kids running down the stairs. *Lab Rats* will be on all morning now.

Once the kitchen is clean, I go upstairs to check on Mike. Framed in the door, I watch him tucking his jersey into his shorts and pulling on his socks. I take in the almost comical way he peacocks in front of the mirror. His eyes are focused on his reflection while he hums to himself, oblivious to my presence. I'm like an old accessory in the room he's so used to, he would only notice if it were gone. Maybe not even then.

He must be satisfied with himself for how easily he has fooled me. But thanks to the hitman I'm enlightened about his lies at last. I have no doubt that he's going to see his lover instead of playing soccer this morning. I still want proof, so I decide on following him.

While Mike ties his shoes, I catch sight of his laptop sitting on the bed. The dirty secrets it may hold are calling to me.

Mike goes downstairs to fill up his water canister. I stay behind in our bedroom and call my neighbor Mary. I ask her to come over and watch my kids for a few hours. She's a middle-aged lady living with her husband in a pretty, well-organized, two-story home. They never had kids. I believe she had cancer in her uterus and it was surgically removed when she was in her early twenties. I'm not sure though. We aren't that close. I give her fresh eggs sometimes. In exchange, she watches my kids if I ask her, which is once in a blue moon.

She promises to come over in ten minutes. I don't want Mike to catch her while she's heading to our house, so I ask her to wait until I leave the house then come through the back door.

As I slip my cell phone into my bag and check my car keys, I remember how many times Mike left his shin guards home. When he got back after a few hours of a soccer game, I used to notice the lack of sweat on his jersey or grass stain on his socks. I remember finding it odd, considering that, when he works in the backyard or punches his bag in the garage, he always sweats like a horse. How many signs were out there for me to pick up on, and I stepped right over them. I feel angry and upset with myself. *Ignorant, gullible, foolish girl.*

When Mike opens the garage door, I'm ready to go. I grab my bag and tell the kids that Mary would be along in a minute. They don't care. *Lab Rats* keeps their eyes glued to the screen.

I don't have to worry about following Mike from a great distance. It's California. Toyota Prius is a trendy top-rated car.

After leaving our neighborhood, he takes Winchester Road north. As far as I knew, his games were south of Temecula, at Birdsall Sports Park. My heart is out of control as I follow him from a safe distance. I feel like those detectives who tail criminals in TV shows. Every traffic light we stop at, I wipe my sticky hands on my thighs. I keep in Mike's lane. I'm nervous. I've never done anything like this before.

He takes a right on Benton, which should give me a clue, but I don't realize that he's driving to our rental house in French Valley until he takes a left onto Antwerp Street. The garage door opens on our one story second home, and he pulls in next to a red Mini Cooper. I feel like I was tossed back in time. I used to drive the same car back in college.

I pull over to the side and keep the engine running. It might take Mike a while to handle business with the tenants. As the minutes roll on, a nagging feeling starts nibbling at my insides. We always respect our renters' privacy, so why would Mike pull into the garage; moreover, where did he get a remote to open the door? If something were broken at the house, the renter would have emailed me, and I would be the one handling the repairs. I don't remember any complaints from them for a very long time, but I check my phone just in case I missed it in the blinding chaos my life had become as of late. No emails from the Raider family.

After ten minutes of biting my nails at my stakeout position, I start worrying. Though I'm on the verge of losing my marbles, I'm pretty sure the renters have a black pickup truck and some insignificant sedan.

I start driving, passing our house. Then I take a left and come back to the main street. The house is next to a dog-walking park, so that's where I'm headed. I can't just walk up to the main door and ring the bell to check on Mike.

I park the car and rush to the fence that stretches unyieldingly between our property and the community park. I push through the line of hedges battling thick spider webs. Disgust and fear rattle my entire being as I rip the cobwebs off my skin like a mad woman. I manage not to scream, though, for which I'm proud of myself. Mike always says that I act like a child when I come in contact with insects. I can't tell him the real reason why I can't bear the sight of them . . . a corpse . . . a smell—copper . . . vomit. I push the images from my head. Not now. I can't think of that now.

I use a stick to clean out the wrought-iron fence that lines the edge of our property from the front and try to peek through the bars. The sun is reflecting off the windows on the front and the side of the house. I need to move toward the back to look at the yard. This entire area is overgrown with chaparral, which gives safe homes to nasty rodents. I must be crazy for wading through these shrubs in my flip-flops.

Once I find a great hiding spot between two eucalyptus trees, the vacant backyard opens up for me. The blue water glistens in the pool like a mirror. I spot a set of patio furniture with red cushions and blooming flowers in tall ceramic pots. The backyard (which is the renter's responsibility) looks great and well kept, very different than it used to be, but I can't get a look inside the house from this angle either. This whole ordeal of blazing my trail through spiky bushes was for nothing. Without a spy camera, I won't be able to see inside the house and find out what Mike's up to. Nonetheless, I stay on my post and wait. I don't know what I'm waiting for, but at the moment, staying seems better than retracing my steps through the painful path.

Only a few minutes could have passed (yet I got bitten by three ants) when the sliding-glass door moves, and Mike emerges from the house, wearing a pair of swimming trunks—white with gray and black stripes on both sides. I bought them for him at T.J. Maxx when I was looking for bargain deals on clothes for the kids.

He jumps into the pool; the water splashes onto the hot concrete. I can hear it sizzling. It's humid and warm today, unusual for February. Cooling off in a pool would feel refreshing. I only get to swim in this pool when I clean the place between renters.

I hear a woman's voice asking Mike if he wants lemonade. The accent is not American. Blood rushes to my face.

I start climbing a tree to get a better view over the brick fence that surrounds our rental property from the back and connects to the wrought iron fence. I get a glimpse of a tall, olive-skinned brunette in a tiny, black bikini carrying a tray of pink drinks with little umbrellas. I pull myself higher, my heart about to rip itself out of my chest. I should have brought my glasses. From all the work on the computer and reading books, my eyes have become nearsighted. I'm

hanging over a thick branch like an idiot when I notice her belly—
YIP YIP! A dog's bark startles me. My hands slip, and I fall to the
ground. My right hipbone is on fire. A woman pushing a stroller
glares at me. A little white, furry dog on a leash is barking, but the
sound comes out more like a comical yap.

They don't say anything. They don't need to. I feel humiliated.
Their stare is killing me.

I pick myself up off the ground and walk away without a word,
dusting off my pants.

I take a few deep breaths in the car. I can't push the image of the
woman from my mind—especially the bulging, perfectly round belly
that hung above her waist like a must-have accessory.

A mad feeling, like some locked-up wild animal, bursts out of me.
With screeching tires, I stop in front of our rental house. Yes, ours.
Mike's and mine. The house he bought with *my* inheritance. Why on
earth does that bitch need a four-bedroom home with a pool? Anger
blinds me to the point that I seriously consider ramming my car into
the front door. But what damage could a feather-light Prius do to a
sturdy building? I wish I drove a Jeep instead, or one of those
refurbished military Humvees.

An elderly gentleman walking his dog stops and watches me. He
seems to be considering whether it would be safe to cross the street
in front of my car. I don't move, only stare straight ahead of me. I
don't even care if Mike catches me here. He's been nagging me every
day about money, while he has given up our rental income and
moved his whore into my house, God only knows how long ago. I
should have checked our bank accounts more often.

I pull out my phone and the slip of paper with Benny's number.
I dial him up. He's at home. He can see me anytime.

I drive back to town and get lost in the maze of streets in the
Harveston community. I thought I remembered Benny's house, but

it appears that I didn't. I call him back for his address and punch it in the GPS. Two minutes later, I'm in front of his house with shaking hands and a messed-up head. It appears I'd been circling the same block for a good ten minutes.

I knock on the door with a series of fast raps. I can't think clearly. I don't just want to kill Mike. I want to kill both of them. But there is a baby now. Fucking bitch! Didn't she see the ring on Mike's finger?

I knock on the door again. I hear Benny yelling for me to come in. I find him in his old room on the right at the end of the hallway. The place smells like cat urine. I gag.

"Sarah Stevens, isn't this a nice surprise?" he greets from a chair in front of a line of monitors.

"It's Sarah Johnson now," I correct. I have to make sure people are aware of how happily married I am. Once Mike drops dead, nobody can suspect that I had anything to do with it.

"I know," he smiles. His face is much slimmer than I remember. "I just like your old name better."

I smile back and step closer to him for a hug. He used to help me with math. I would give him some of my lunch. We were that kind of friends.

He used to have BO, and I brace myself for the smell as we hug. His pleasant cologne surprises me.

"What's going on with you, man? I haven't heard from you for ages," I use the lines I should have sent in the Facebook message.

"You know, same o', same o'."

"You look great, buff," I manage to say through the haze of shock.

Benny's hair is a long cascade of black connected to a bushy beard and mustache that gives him a shaggy look, but his arms are lean and muscular, just like his legs. There's no jiggling belly pressing against his Comic-Con T-shirt or double chin hanging over his chest.

"An hour a day in a gym does miracles for you."

I purse my lips in admiration. I've never seen a nerd like Benny change his lifestyle so drastically.

"Good for you. You look great," I say amazed.

He blushes from my praise. "How about you? What brings you to my sanctuary?"

I open my mouth to speak when a crispy, faltering voice slithers down the hallway. "Who's in the house?"

"It's a friend, Mom. Leave me alone!" Benny shoots back.

"What friend? You don't have any friends."

"Shut up, Ma!" Benny drops his keyboard and shuffles to the door. He kicks it shut and turns to me. "Stupid old hag. She hasn't changed a bit."

"What are you still doing at home?" I ask and regret it at once. Asking a thirty-eight-year-old man why he is still living with his mother is like asking a middle-aged woman when she will get married and have kids. Not the subtlest way to start a conversation.

"Didn't you get a job in Silicon Valley?" I add quickly.

"Pa died . . . Cancer. . . Ma needed me here, so . . ."

I nod. It sucks. "I'm sorry. I didn't know."

He shrugs. "Can I get you anything? A soda?"

"Umm . . . No thanks. Look, Benny, I'm sure you're busy. I . . . I don't even know what I'm doing here." I feel lost. Maybe I should stop swimming against the tide and let the waves sweep me up and take me on a new journey. After all, I'm a Catholic. I should believe in life after death. I should allow the events to unfold. People die every day—some from cancer, some at the hands of murderers.

"You know me. I don't judge people. Just say it," he encourages me.

"Say what?"

"Just tell me what you need. Spare me the buddy-speech and the catching-up time. I know you didn't come here after twenty years to talk about old times."

"May I?" I point at the edge of his desk.

"Sure."

I sit down, my feet still touching the floor. "I'm sorry about your father. I should have come to his funeral."

He shrugs. "Don't worry about it. Nobody came."

My eyes lose focus as I think of my other high school friends. How many funerals and weddings had I missed by living overseas?

"What can I help you with?" He's not mad, or upset, only friendly.

"Can you break into someone's computer if there is a password on it?"

"Can you bring it to me?"

"No, I don't think so."

He laughs aloud, scratching his beard. "I could tell you how, but you sucked at math and everything related to technology, remember?"

I swallow hard. "I need to get into Mike's laptop. There's something in there I need to see."

"Well aren't you the sneaky little housewife?" I can tell he's amused. He was never a fan of Mike. I crease my forehead. The *sneaky little* part doesn't bother me; the word *housewife* does. I also went to a great college as Benny did. We both ended up disappointing our teachers who thought we would be going places.

"You wouldn't understand."

"Why? Cuz I'm not married?"

I crack my neck nervously. "That's not what I meant." I push myself off the desk. "This was a mistake. I shouldn't have come here. I'm sorry for bothering you." Had I completely lost my charm? Back

84

in school, I could get anything I wanted with a little honey. No questions asked. No begging. No prying.

"Wait!" His voice stops me at the door. I look back to see him ransacking a drawer in his desk. He pulls out a disk and tosses it to me.

"It's an invisible program that runs in the background. Install it when Mike's logged in—when he goes to take a leak or something and leaves his computer running. Then wait until he logs in again. This program keeps track of every character a user types. Then send him for a glass of water or the mail, whatever, open the program and read what he wrote."

"How do you install this program?"

"Just put the disk into the DVD/CD reader. You know where it is, right?"

I nod. I'm not that dumb when it comes to computers.

"A window will pop up. Press *install*. It takes about twenty seconds. When the next window pops up press open. Take the disc out. It will start running as a spy program in the background. Once Mike writes his password and leaves his computer unguarded, click *search*, then type *bigmac*. Then click *open* on the application file. A window will pop up with all the characters he typed. If you have time, go through the list of letters. If not, take a picture, and you can analyze it later. Once you find the username and password click X to close the program."

"Maybe I should write this all down. Sounds difficult."

"No, it's not. Besides, you won't have time to read while you're doing this."

He goes through each step with me again. Seems doable, but I can't help but feel awkward. Hacking into someone's computer, even if that computer is your husband's, is a crime. Moreover, it's like opening up a can of worms. You never know what you'll find. The prospect of my secret mission may leave me broken, more than I am right now standing in the door of my high school buddy's bedroom, trembling, feeling lost and alone. So alone.

"What's that? In your hair?" Benny asks, pointing.

I shake my hair nervously. Was it a leaf I missed pulling out of my hair before I knocked on his door?

While I run my fingers through my curls, Benny makes his way to me. He leans in to inspect whatever he saw. I get a whiff of his cologne. Spicy. Cinnamony. Embedding feelings of warmth and safety in me.

"Have you been going through Mike's stuff in the attic, too?" He pulls out a dirty little white cocoon and shows it to me. Looks like a fly wrapped in a web.

Shuddering, I start stomping my feet and shaking my head as if a nest of maggots had fallen into my hair. I use both hands to shuffle my hair. I hate spiders. I fear spiders.

Benny's arms steady me. His massive hands press against my back. I stop moving and look at him through a curtain of tangled hair.

"It's gone. You're good," he says, calmly, almost seductively. I run my hands through my hair again, pulling it all back, away from my face. I don't like the beard or the mustache. I'm not a fan of long hair when it comes to men, but there is something in his eyes that grips me. They're royal blue with spots of a lighter shade and white speckles like the ocean under a starry sky, or the vast universe itself. I'm lost. And I'm not sure if I want to be found.

I kiss him. My lips latch on to his with the coldness and precision of a spaceship when it latches onto a space station. The kiss is awkward. Not just because I haven't had physical contact with a man apart from Mike for over a decade, but because he doesn't return it. He lets me have my way but doesn't egg me on. Even the husky nerd kid from school who lives with his mother doesn't want me.

I don't release his mouth. No way I'm going to face him now. I feel a teardrop rolling out of my eye and trailing down on my cheek as I pull my arms out of my cardigan. No man walks away from a naked woman. My cardigan is on the floor when a pair of hands wrap around my shoulders. I feel a push, but it's not violent. It's gentle, like something my mother would do or my older brother, who died in a car accident when I was twenty-one.

Kyle was my idol. The best brother a girl could have. He kept me out of trouble. Made sure my actions weren't out of line. When he was gone, taken from me by a drunk driver, I lost my way for a long time. I was mean to everybody; especially to boys who drank excessively or partied too hard. For three years, I played a game of coaxing boys to fall in love with me only to break their hearts. All I wanted from them was to shatter their mere existence into pieces.

Benny searches my face. I look away. An old image with painful details flashes in front of my eyes. A pair of dangling legs in loose jeans. A bare chest. My initials are written on the inner arm with black ink. A rope around the neck.

I shut my eyes hard. I feel a vein throbbing in the back of my head. Benny knew me then too. We weren't close, but he knew what I had done. What the hell was I thinking coming here?

I bend down to pick my cardigan up and rip the door open. I bolt through the hallway and make my way back to the street to my car. I plop myself into the seat with one swift panicked motion. The CD bends in the back pocket of my jeans. I lean forward and pull it out. It's still whole, unscratched. I drop it next to me on the seat and storm out onto the street.

The past always catches up with us. There are no unsettled scores or unpaid bills in life. Everything has a price, and it seems the tab has been handed to me. The cost? The highest a person can pay.

Stacy: I don't know anything about a lover. Mike was a hottie. I didn't see him a lot. He only showed up at practices a few times, but I don't see why Sarah would be looking for someone else. He's not like my husband. A few years into our marriage, my ex turned into a pig. He got this fat beer belly. It was disgusting.

Benny: No, we weren't involved romantically. She was my friend. She was a great person. . . damaged. . . but great. She didn't deserve what happened to her. I have nothing else to say. Thank you.

. . . . .

The sight of the empty garage gives me a sliver of relief. *I've beaten Mike home.* I pull into the right side as always. Mary and the kids are still watching *Lab Rats* in the living room. The scent of fresh coffee still lingers in the air, and I can also detect the remnants of the morning's toasted bagels: blueberry and cinnamon.

The golden sunbeams penetrate the blinds on the window next to the refurbished fireplace. In every other circumstance, this would be the perfect image of a Saturday morning with my family.

I thank Mary for coming over on such short notice. We make small talk, and she tells me about her niece who dislocated her shoulder while skiing in Big Bear. I don't know the girl, but Mary's stories of her relatives make me feel as if I'm part of her family too. We hug, and she leaves. She didn't ask why I was so preoccupied this morning. I feel relieved that I don't have to come up with an inane lie for her.

After asking the kids if they need anything, I run upstairs and check Mike's laptop. It's gone to sleep, so I'll have to wait until he logs in again to install the spy program. I take the CD out of my bag and keep it in my nervous hands. I stare at the disc until my eyes blur, then I slip it under a pile of papers on my desk near Mike's computer.

To keep my hands and mind busy, I start ripping the sheets off everybody's beds. All I think of are the rows of computers at the library. I need to research Selenium in great detail, but it would be a mistake to use my own computer. It's traceable. I should go to the library right now instead of wasting time doing my housewifely duties.

Now that Mary's left, I would have to take the kids with me. It shouldn't be a problem. They love checking out books, whole piles of them. They never read them all. The excitement wears off after the first couple of hours. Maybe having it all, getting every book they want makes them tick.

Yeah, the library is a good idea. But when I picture myself sitting at the desk, Mason and Tammy nagging me for food or drink, I dismiss the idea. It just seems wrong to have my children beside me when I'm looking up ways to kill their father.

Mike finds me by the stove. He compliments me on the mouthwatering aroma of the hamburgers I'm making. He's got some color and looks very cheerful. Forget the poison; I'll choke him with my bare hands.

He doesn't come too close to me. He's smart enough to know that his skin must reek of chlorine instead of sweat. I wonder if he even cares enough to do a few push-ups and jumping jacks to break a sweat before he comes home from his lover.

He goofs around with the kids. They push him away. The TV is more interesting. I can't bear watching them together because the only thing I can think of is how they will do the same thing when

I'm gone, although it would be the Italian bitch, with the accent, cooking Spaghetti Bolognese in the background instead of me flipping burgers. Or maybe she sucks at cooking. Is that why Mike came home to eat?

While he takes a shower—I don't know why, to waste the water—the kids set the table. I stack everyone's burger. Mike likes his with everything on it. Mayonnaise, ketchup, onion, pickles, lettuce, tomatoes, jalapeño peppers, and I add something extra, something special. I lift the patty and spit lovingly into the mayo and ketchup mix.

I can't stop my inner laugh as I watch him eating his lunch with gusto, smiling and remarking how good it tastes. I haven't felt this good for a long time.

I've been taking Mike's emotional abuse for years. He took everything from me: my career, my youth, my beauty, my self-confidence. Well, if I want to be completely honest, I should say I gave up all those things willingly, along with a part of my soul, for this family and for him. But blaming him for every misfortune that's happened to me makes me feel better.

After lunch, he asks me to take a nap. I know what that means. He wants a little Hanky Panky. Why? Because his pregnant girlfriend doesn't spread her legs for him anymore? Or does he want to keep up the appearance of a well-oiled marriage? Does he want to tell the officers after my autopsy that we were a happy couple? *Her death was tragic. We loved each other. The coroner found evidence of recent intercourse to prove it, right?*

I must walk away from Mike because I'm about to puke again or stab him. I tell him that I'm coming down with something and it would be smarter if he stays away from me. Any other time he would complain, reminding me of my obligation to fulfill my conjugal duty. But now he meekly accepts it and goes upstairs. Usually, when he wakes up from his nap, he logs onto his computer. I need to be on the alert now.

The kids play with Nerf guns outside, and I use the time to check into three episodes of *CSI*. I fast forward through all three in less than twenty minutes. I don't even know what season I'm at now, not like it matters. I find two gunshot victims and one stab victim. That's not what I need. I want more poison. I don't own a gun, neither does Mike. Besides, guns are traceable. Ballistic specialists can match the bullet from a victim's wound to a weapon.

Stabbing doesn't seem like my kind of choice either. I'd never been able to walk up to my husband and say, 'here, honey, something for you' and thrust a knife into his heart. Besides, people sometimes slice their own hands while stabbing someone. Also, I can leave behind prints, DNA, skin cells, who knows what else. If I want to stay out of prison, I need to do this smart.

I hear Mike's footsteps upstairs as the floor is creaking under his weight. He was supposed to tighten the screws on the board before the carpet guys started working, but evidently, he missed every other one.

I turn the TV off and go upstairs. Our sheets are done in the dryer, and I make the beds while he is—as I predicted—typing on the computer. I need to get him away.

"Do you have some plans for this afternoon?" I ask stuffing the pillow into the case.

"I don't know. Maybe I should mow the lawn," Mike says, leaning back in his chair and stretching his arms.

"If you do that, I'll come and weed."

"OK. Tell Mason to do a quick poop patrol."

I yell down the balcony. Mason sends me back his perfected frown while Tammy chases the chickens back into the coop.

It takes another good ten minutes for Mike to change into his working pants and T-shirt. He moves so slowly that I have to clench my teeth to keep my mouth shut and not rush him. He even checks his face in the mirror, examines his nose. *Hurry up, goddammit*, I think to myself, eyeing his computer screen. Once it goes to screen saving mode, the computer will log me out, and I'll be doomed.

"Can you pick the hair off my nose?" he asks, and I feel a scream stick in the middle of my throat.

I take a deep breath and say, "Sure."

On my way to the medicine cabinet, I brush my fingers along his laptop's touchpad, buying myself some time.

He's joking with me as I pluck the tiny black hairs with a pair of tweezers. He makes faces. I want to stab him in his eye. I pinch his skin a couple of times instead. Mike is as strong as an ox, but he can't take the pain. He'd die in childbirth, which is funny because he always tells me that giving birth is not a big deal, millions of women do it every year, a rabbit can do it.

I don't know why, but images of my son's birth pour into my mind. After twelve hours of overnight labor, the doctor had to perform a Caesarian on me. The cord was tied around my precious baby's neck. When the doctor announced that we had a beautiful boy, Mike squeezed my hand and bawled his eyes out like a snot-nosed toddler. I wept with him. When the nurse took Mason away from us, Mike kissed my forehead and rushed to catch up with the nurse to keep an eye on our baby. We'd seen in movies that nurses sometimes mix up the nametags on newborns.

We were happy. The perfect family.

I have to strain my eyes to keep them from tearing up. Though I tried hard to deny it for years, I know precisely when Mike changed. The war in Afghanistan is to blame. Each time he came home for R&R he was more distant and colder. When I asked for his help with something, his answer was always the same, like a rehearsed line,

"You can do it yourself. You must have managed things around here when I was gone."

Mike hisses as I accidentally scratch the skin on his nose. "Ouch, that hurt!"

My eyes come back to focus. There is a tiny cut on the very tip of Mike's nose. "Sorry. These tweezers are very sharp."

I brace myself for a fight, but he leaves me without a word, rubbing his nose. No screaming. No giving it back. He's composed. Calm. So not Mike. The afternoon delight and frolicking in the pool seem to have done him some good. I feel an in-depth sadness gathering in my chest like storm clouds gravitating toward each other, joining forces ready to wash everything away. I want to take shelter, but I don't know where to look. Will I ever have the strength to kill the father of my children?

. . . . .

Carol: Look, all I'm saying is that beautiful people always get involved in scandals like this. Yes, ugly people too, but that's beside the point. They had it coming. I mean, you can't have it all just because you're pretty. It wouldn't be fair.

. . . . .

When I hear the lawnmower kick in, I pull out the disc from under the pile of papers. From the moment Mike left the bedroom, I stood by his laptop and kept it running. I push in the disc and install the program. All goes well, just like Benny predicted. Now I only have to wait for Mike to return and type in his password.

Down on my hands and knees on the lawn, I'm agitated and antsy as I pull dandelions by the root from the grass. They are everywhere.

Our neighbor doesn't take care of her backyard, and whenever the wind picks up, we are showered with seeds. Maintaining our lawn is a never-ending saga. Why even bother with it today? Soon I'll be dead or rich. In either case, I won't have to do this anymore.

Considering that I told Mike that I don't feel well, it seems odd that he finds nothing wrong with my being outside and working. I do feel horrible, although not from a virus. It's from my parasite husband who's sucking the life out of me. Well, my throat is bothering me, too. It must be from the stress.

The sun hangs low in a pool of pink and orange when he finally comes back to his computer. Luckily, he only sends a few messages to his friends on Facebook. As he gets up from the chair, he tells me that if I don't mind, he'll play FIFA on the play station with Mason. *How could I mind?* I've been waiting for this moment all day.

The shouting and squawking of the boys drift up from downstairs, giving me the courage to open the spy program and look for his password. Tammy walks by the office door, but she doesn't stop. Her momentary appearance still gives me the jitters.

The spy program's window appears on the screen, and I feel like I have three hearts, and they're all running off beat.

The first line starts like this: two spaces, then mjohnsonpisa2013facebook.........

It's not difficult to find the username and password in the first line of typed letters. What's difficult is to believe my eyes. Mike replaced the guam1999 password he'd been using for years with the city and date where he met the foreign bimbo. Guam was the place we fell in the most profound love one can have with another, where we got married, where our family started.

I can't breathe. I feel the blood draining from my head. The screen goes blurry. I support my head with my hands. I want to allow myself to cry, to feel sorry for myself over what's happening to my life. I can't crash now. I need to keep digging. It's my opportunity to check his files and pictures, maybe even his emails and Facebook account, but I need to come out of the shock first.

I half-walk and half-stumble to the bathroom sink. The boys' yelling at the virtual referee pierces the air. I lean against the sink, and I'm not sure if I'm going to vomit or if I just need some air. I splash cold water on my face. My eyes come back into focus. The entire weight of the situation overwhelms me. My husband isn't just having an affair, a meaningless fling. He's in love with someone else, and they are starting a family together. Only, I'm in their way. Divorces are messy and cost a lot. With me out of the picture, they'll have the house, the kids, and the fifty grand from my life insurance, both cars, even my personal belongings—not that it's worth doing anything more than dropping it at a thrift store.

It takes a few minutes to compose myself and return to the laptop. I open Mike's Gmail account. There are dozens of emails from someone called Emanuela Ghiotto. Undeniably Italian.

All the emails are short, half Italian and half bad English. She professes her love to my husband in each message I open. Who names their daughter Emanuela? Sounds like a catchy name for a prostitute. That's what she is probably, a girl for hire.

Most of the emails from Emanuela have attachments, pictures of her in sexy lingerie posing on a bed or chair or table. They look professional, well composed, sharp, staged. Mike used to take pictures of me, too, when I had a body worth immortalizing, but they were all slightly out of focus, or poorly centered. We shot them for fun, on the spur of a passionate moment. These photos are too good, too professional. The worm of suspicion wriggles its way into my brain. This girl is onto something. She's going after my husband to trap him. Men are stupid. They think with their dicks first. Always.

A dart of panic urges me to do something to put an end to this scam. I need to tell Mike that he's being played. I must warn him. This girl is a professional scam artist. She's after US citizenship and Mike's non-existing money. I need to do something. I close the email, and I'm about to stand up when a lone blue folder on the desktop catches my eye. It's titled *work related*. Call it a woman's instinct, but I click on it.

In the pop-up folder, I see that all the files are JPEGs. I change the view so I can see them in the sidebar. The first one is a selfie of my husband with Emanuela. The image is small and of low resolution, but I recognize those eyes on my husband. I haven't seen them as of late, but for years he looked at me with those same passion-dazed eyes.

I feel like I'm losing weight just by sitting and staring at the picture. I feel my legs shrink, the fat on my belly disappear. Something deep inside me pulls the rest of my body in. Like a big black hole, it sucks me in until I'm nothing.

I only have the mental strength to look at one more picture. The happy couple is lying on beach towels on white sand. I bought those beach towels at Target four years ago. Suddenly all I can think of is that I used that towel too when I took the kids to the pool. Does bleach remove semen? It doesn't really matter, because I don't use bleach when I wash beach towels. I probably didn't even wash them after Mike brought them back from Pisa.

I need a glass of water, or rather, a shot of Vodka. I picture the cabinet above the refrigerator where Mike keeps his hard liquor. My mouth is dry. My throat itches for a shot.

"Sarah, come down! You have to see this awesome goal I shot!" Mike's calling startles me. I need to answer to keep him downstairs, but I can't. My voice catches in my throat.

I close the folder and click X to get rid of the spy program window. I walk disoriented from wall to wall, yet somehow, I make it back to the bathroom sink in one piece.

"Are you coming?" The voice bounces off the walls all around me, making my head spin.

My muscles disobey, and I stand stationary, the reflection of my face frozen in the mirror.

I've heard about marriages falling apart, about cheating husbands and wives, but I've never imagined one day I was going to be one of those victims. I'm not even being given the chance of becoming a bitter divorcee. I'm not wanted at all.

Mike and I used to talk about his co-workers in Afghanistan who instead of going home for vacation went to Thailand to do drugs and cheat on their wives with fragile tiny Asian girls. Their families back home lived their everyday lives in sweet oblivion. They thought their husbands were going through unimaginable hardships to earn money in the war zone to support their loved ones.

Maybe those stories were about Mike and not his fellows. The irony of it cuts my heart in half. I should have given Mike more credit. He's one smart son of a bitch. He probably shared all those stories about cheating husbands with me to make me believe he was a good guy.

If I had a potion of Selenium at home right now, I wouldn't hesitate to put it into Mike's evening beer. As my fingers fold over the edge of the countertop, my eyes find the electric toothbrush on the charger. I change the heads. I put mine in the case and put Mike's head on. I dip the entire head into the water in the toilet bowl. Then I turn it on and make sure it scrubs the inside of the pedestal well. Without rinsing it, I put it back on the charger.

11 DAYS TO DIE

Mike's cursing assaults my ears in the morning. His voice, which is only halfheartedly muffled since he's never been the one to show sympathy for others' comfort, penetrates my throbbing head. My eyes need some time to get used to the dimness that still hangs over the bedroom. Even when my eyes are fully open, my vision is blurry as if I were trying to look at something underwater.

I toss the blankets off me. The heavy, moisture-infused air rises under the covers and settles on my face. The faded Old Navy T-shirt clings to my back. As I prop myself up on my pillow, I start jerking on the thin material to vent my chest. I stink, but it's a good stink now. My odor will keep Mike at bay.

"Fucking hell!" The grumbling continues unabated in the bathroom. I rub my eyes sleepily.

"What's going on?" I ask with a yawn, clawing out the crusted morning rheum from the corner of my eyes. Another sleepless night.

Another day passed wasted. While I'm not any closer to finding a solution to my problem.

He doesn't answer, but I hear him gargling and hissing at the same time.

I crawl out of bed and drag myself to the bathroom to see what his problem is at this early hour. He acknowledges my presence with a sideways glance. He spits the foamy mouthwash into the sink.

"Look at this!" He leans closer and pulls down his lower lip with his index fingers. I press my fingertips into his left temple and push his face under the light. I don't even attempt to be gentle.

A big, red sore perches on the inside of his bottom lip and numerous small puss-colored bumps dot his pink mouth and tongue. The toilet water infused toothbrush head has done its job!

"Looks like a mouth infection to me," I observe with borderline irritation. I wasn't expecting such a severe result, and I'm shocked. It's my first genuine accomplishment for a long time.

He clicks his tongue and turns back to the mirror, leans in so close that his breath fogs up the glass. He examines the deeper areas of his mouth. "From what?" he babbles.

I bend down to the faucet and drink some water, "I don't know," I answer snidely. " Maybe you should watch what you put in your mouth."

"Very funny." He frowns at me and wipes the remnants of his shaving cream off his face. "Thanks for caring."

Fuck you! I think, yet look at him with the most concerned face I can muster.

"You want me to look up how to treat it online?" Which is what I would do if everything were perfect between us.

"I gotta go. Just send it to me in an email."

In your dreams, buddy! My stomach tightens as I suppress an evil grin.

While he dabs on his cologne and fixes his hair, I watch him lean against the wall next to the shower. Ever since the hitman called me, I've been scrutinizing Mike's face, his behavior, for any sign of pity or regret, but I found none. If it weren't for my recent discoveries and the hitman's stories, I'd say this whole kill-for-hire is no more than a prank, a chapter in a bad piece of pulp fiction.

In eleven days, my existence will be nothing more than a memory, yet he's upset about a little pain in his mouth! How can it be that I mean so little to him after fourteen years of marriage? Come to think of it, Mike showed more distress over his ever-increasing gray hair than over the lump I discovered in my breast two years ago. It turned out to be nothing, yet he wasn't even the least bit worried about when I first mentioned it to him. So why am I surprised?

He brushes past me to get to his closet. I peek at my watch. He needs to leave in five minutes, or he'll be late for work. His department at March ARB is almost an hour's drive from our house.

I cast my eyes over the bathroom counter. The toothpaste cap is missing, and some toothpaste has oozed out onto the white Carrara marble. I guess Mike has no idea how hard it is to remove stains from natural stones. There is a drop of blue shaving gel beside the sink, next to a couple of pieces of black facial hair. All that eye-catching clutter lies there as if it belongs, claiming a spot in my otherwise spotless bathroom.

He must have seen the mess he left behind, too. He also must know how much the disorder bothers me. His razor lies face down on the counter, lying in a pool of hairy and foamy water. A comb, a pair of boxers, and a T-shirt are hanging off the edge of the counter. The toilet seat is up, and the toilet paper has been all used up yet not replaced.

Normally, I would rush to pick up after him. I've been trying to do the right thing, serve the needs of others to atone for my sins.

Now I only shrug, leave the mess behind, and go back to bed, hoping the sores will bother him for at least a few days.

.   .   .   .   .

Stacy: I guess they had a nice house. But as I told you, we weren't really friends. I've been to her place only a few times. Yeah, it was clean, I guess. I mean who cares really. I don't try to sound unsympathetic, but she didn't have a job, so she had all the time on earth to clean that place. Not like me. I work two jobs, got two messy kids, and a worthless ex. Actually, I hated to go to her place because when I did, I always had the feeling that she was showing off how organized her house was, you know what I mean? Like she wanted me to see how a home's supposed to look. I hang with messy bitches now. They don't make me feel bad about myself.

Carol: I've only been inside their house a few times, but it wasn't spotless. I saw shoes scattered all over, bags, even books. I don't think she was as perfect of a housewife as she tried to paint herself. Look, Tom . . . I know, I know, you already asked me that, sorry. Well, Detective Long then, don't think Sarah was an angel. I've seen a thing or two. Oh, I can tell you. Can I just call you Tom?. . . I know I said it before, but did anybody else ever tell you that you look like Lenny Kravitz?

Benny: I don't know anything about a mouth infection. Maybe you should check his computer files and online habits. You might find the reason he got sores all over his face. The guy was a pig.

No, I didn't hate him enough to hurt
him. You already asked me that. And
please, no more questions.

.   .   .   .   .

It's late in the afternoon and Mason and his friends are flipping their Kendamas in the backyard, or whatever the name is of this new toy any kid would kill for. I can picture a balding fat man laughing as he checks his toy making company's financial statement. A piece of wood and a string for twenty-five dollars! Ridiculous.

Tammy is out on the street in front of the house, riding her bike with a neighbor kid.

Mason had a soccer game earlier today, but I didn't take him. It was only a scrimmage, so I don't feel bad about it. We skipped church as well. The mere thought of me sitting among religious folks while thinking of ways to torture my husband before I give him the final lethal dose of Selenium seems blasphemous.

I lie in front of the TV with a bag of caramel and cinnamon popcorn beside me. A layer of yesterday's dust and last night's sweat glows on my skin like a latex second skin. I already managed to spill coffee on the T-shirt I was sleeping in, and now two brown circles stare back at me from my chest like the eyes of my damned soul.

I believe I'm on season four of *CSI*, but I can't be sure. The DVDs are not organized in the box, and they come to my hand randomly. The only clue I have is that the actors are still young and still play their roles with passion. I almost believe everything they say. In the episode, 'Bloodlines', Sara is caught driving under the influence. I go through a whole spectrum of emotions as I watch Grissom stand up for her.

There is no one to stand up for me. My brother is dead. My

parents slowly distanced themselves from me when I went rampant after Kyle's funeral and preyed on dozens of party boys to get my revenge. The last honest conversation I had with my parents was over the phone after the incident that eventually forced me to pull the parking brake of my life. My mother told me that my brother Kyle would have been ashamed at how I dishonored his life. I wasn't there to honor his life. How could I? He was dead. I was damning my own life, thank you very much.

Kyle was the responsible one of the two of us. On the night of the accident, he was on the road trying to find me at a party. I was well aware that my parents were expecting me to be back home hours earlier, but I was having too good a time to leave. Besides, I wanted to show my father that he didn't own me.

That college frat house party was the last time I laughed and behaved frivolously. I still laugh with my children, but it's not the same. Every fun thing they show me, a new bike trick, climbing a tree, going all the way to the end on the monkey bars, makes me think of the same thing: Kyle was just as happy a child.

A gang of boisterous kids bursts through the patio door just in time to see Dr. Robbins removing a gunshot victim's brain.

"Gross," Mason yells. I pause the movie. The image of an open skull freezes on the screen. I quickly turn off the TV.

As I make the kids sandwiches, I feel Mason's eyes on me. He must be embarrassed in front of his friends about my just-out-of-bed appearance. Well, if they don't like what they see, they can go home. Since when was our house turned into a free day-care center and all-you-can-eat buffet?

Sundays are always busy days for me. I get up early. I put the blankets out on the balcony to air them out. We go to church. I bake. I cook. I watch a movie with the kids, or take them to the playground, to Get Air Trampoline Park, or go to the kids' soccer games. I won't do any of that today. I refuse to spend my remaining days doing chores.

I tell the kids I'm not feeling well and fall back onto the couch without cleaning up the kitchen after them. The way my day is going by drags me deeper into depression.

Another few hours pass with crime shows. I cry when CSI Nick Stokes is buried alive in a coffin. I hear the bottle of tequila above the refrigerator in the cabinet calling my name. A strawberry margarita sounds damn good right now. But I can't drink. It's too early. What if something happens to the kids, and I have to drive them to the hospital? What if one of the neighbors drops by to borrow an egg, and she finds me tipsy.

On second thought, I barely have any time left to drink. By the twenty-third of February, I will either be dead or a rich widow—most likely the former. Why even bother keeping up appearances?

I feel sluggish and too comfortable on the couch to dig out the blender and fix myself a drink. I do manage to drag myself to the cabinet and take out a bottle of red wine. I pop it open and pour myself a healthy glass. I fill up the rest with Sprite, hoping the buzz comes fast to my head when I drink on an empty stomach.

Back in front of the TV show, which is supposed to help me find a method to commit the perfect murder and get away with it, my eyes start to blur. It's warm inside the house, just like my wine. The humming of the heater and the voices of the conversing kids work in unison to lull me to sleep.

I should be at the library right now, looking up the side effects of Selenium poisoning, then be off to Rite Aid to buy some gloves, more bleach, anything I might need to cover my tracks. I haven't felt this worthless since Mason was four months old, and I had to stay at home with him for two weeks because I had a nasty cold and a sore throat. Mike was in Afghanistan, and I was stuck at home with no help at all.

By the beginning of the second week, I refused to answer my phone, cook real food, or even take a shower. The baby cried, the house was a mess, and I fixed my tired eyes on the screen to pass the time. Although, back then I followed the TV show *Lost* instead of crime shows. I haven't enjoyed the luxury of being sick ever since. Twelve years without a fever or a sore throat.

I feel the same hopelessness now. Deep down I know that I must kill my husband, take his insurance money, pay off the hitman, and start over, but I don't think I have it in me.

Mike calls. I don't answer. I'm just not in the mood to listen to his complaints about his oral problems. His foster mom can help him out. She knows everything better than I do anyway. I should never have married a control freak momma's boy.

"So what do you think, should we go for it?" I'd asked Mike when we found our house on the market.

"I think I'm gonna call my mom and ask her what she thinks." *Sure, you do that. We aren't mature enough to decide for ourselves.*

*   *   *   *   *

It's dark outside when one of Mason's friends' mom texts me. She wants her son home in fifteen minutes. She doesn't offer a thank you for feeding her kid and watching him all day. I mean, I wasn't really watching him today, but he was still in my house all day and eating out my fridge.

Come to think of it, most of the kids who hang out at our house have the same type of self-absorbed parents. Saturday morning, nine o'clock the doorbell rings. One of the neighborhood kids at the door. He or she came to play. By lunchtime, I get half a dozen kids in my house, keeping Mason and Tammy from helping me around the house. What an idiot I've been for allowing all these people to take advantage of me! I can almost hear what they say. She doesn't work; I'm sure she doesn't mind having all those kids.

My phone rings again just when I get off the couch to open a new bag of chips. The morning started out with three half-eaten bags in my pantry; now I'm going for the last one.

Fuming, I reach back to pick up the phone from the ottoman, thinking Mike is calling me again. My stomach shrinks to the size of a kidney bean when I see the caller id. I answer.

"Just a reminder that I didn't forget about you," the man with the European accent says.

Just kill me now, and let's get it over with. All I need is a couple of hours to take a shower, wash all my dirty laundry, and clean up the house, so once the crime scene investigators show up, I won't have to roll over in shame in my grave.

I picture them going over my bed with their blue lights, picking up all the semen stains. *Or, wait a minute! I changed the sheets yesterday. OK, I'm good there.*

But still, they will check the bathrooms, the kitchen. I need to empty the trash cans all over the house. Oh no! That stupid pair of cheap Chinese gray flats I picked up at K-mart stinks like hell. I must get rid of them. I've also got to go through my closet and throw everything out that stinks or has a stain on it. I need to wash out the refrigerator too. I also need to ask Mary again to watch the kids because Mike won't be home until tomorrow afternoon. Well, the police will probably call him and ask him to come home, but, still, someone needs to watch my kids until then.

As I sit back down, I knock over my second glass of Spritzer. A thin crimson trail spreads out on the floor all the way to the shag carpet. I roll my eyes. *What the hell is going on in your head?*

"Are you there?" I hear the man ask.

"Yes, I'm here." I draw in a breath that brings calmness and relief instead of turmoil. "You know what? I don't have the money. I don't know who told you that we have money but that person lied," I blurt out. I hear some background noises. A car drives by. People talking.

"Your husband says to me if I kill you all the money will be his alone." I detect frustration in his voice. It's the first time I identify anything but confidence and threats.

"What money? We're an average middle-class American family who lives off one income."

"You have two houses and cars. You live in a nice city."

"Yeah, and we also have mortgages and daily squabbles over money. I have to get a job just to be able to afford the kids' soccer club fees." I sigh, pick up the glass and drain the drop of wine that sits unyielding on the side of the glass.

I almost enjoy this casual conversation about murder and money with a criminal as if he were my friend. Only there is one problem. Everything I say makes my life sound so depressing that by killing me, he'd be doing me a favor.

If you believe Christians, I'll be in a better place after death. Well, maybe not me. I've sinned too much. Is a decade of servitude enough to buy my way into heaven?

"How about your life insurance. One million American dollars."

I laugh out loud. I'm too numb from the warm wine to care about what will happen to me tonight, tomorrow, or next week. "Mike has a million-dollar insurance policy, not me. Mine is only what? Fifty grand?"

I hear murmuring on the phone as if someone put a hand on the speaker while talking to someone else. I can't make out any words. I can't even say if the other person is a man or a woman. I push the phone harder against my ear. It doesn't help.

"Get me my money, or I kill you both." The line goes dead, leaving an unexpected blow to my chest.

Kill you both? What's that supposed to mean? I thought Mike and the Italian bimbo wanted to get rid of *me*. And *me* alone. That was the only thing that made sense in this madness. Mike wants to save money on divorce and collect the money from my life insurance. Fifty thousand. Kill us both? That doesn't make any sense.

The kids show up at the door, asking for the remote. It's their turn to watch TV, they tell me. I can't focus my eyes or my mind on them, so I push myself off the soft leather cushions and make my way upstairs. I head straight for the office where I begin a thorough search on Mike's desk. I yank open every drawer. I shuffle through every folder looking for my life insurance policy.

Mundane stuff is all I find: contracts for our properties, insurance policies on the cars, a dental estimate for the work Mike needs to get done, letters from the bank, a few notes, but nothing suspicious.

Feeling dizzy and lightheaded from the sudden move as I straightened up, I steady myself at the doorframe. Why can't I find either of our insurance policies? A couple of days ago Mike's was right here on his desk. Where did it go?

The blue binder with our essential documents: marriage and birth certificates, etc., sits tilted on the shelf. I flip through the papers. Everything is in there except the insurance policies. *If I were Mike, where would I hide them?*

The next hour finds me turning every closet upside down and ransacking every drawer. I only find frustration. I wipe the beads of perspiration from my forehead and air out my shirt. I won't turn the heater down, though. I want Mike to have to pay the high gas bill.

I drink water straight from the faucet before I start searching

Mike's closet. I take down each pile of clothes and look between his folded T-shirts and pants. I put my hand into his pockets. I frisk his dress shirts and jackets.

Angry and frustrated, I bolt down the stairs. Adam Davenport is cracking a joke on *Lab Rats,* and the kids laugh as I pass the living room and burst into the garage. There, between rattraps, to and buckets of paint, I find a brown folder wedged between tubes of silicone in the bottom cabinet in the corner. As I lift it out, I know that Mike's hiding something. He knows I'd never go near his workbench. When it's time to paint the house or rip up old linoleum or tile, I'm right there beside him to do so. But fixing leaks and broken sprinkler heads has always been his job.

With numb, nervous fingers, I open the folder. Both of our life insurance policies are nestled inside. At first glance, nothing seems unusual about them, other than Mike keeping them with his tools.

I sit down on the dirty concrete, cross-legged, and start analyzing Mike's policy. I run my eyes over every page. Seems the same as I remember. One million dollars goes to me in case of his death. I put the documents face down next to me and take the insurance policy we took out on my name years ago in my hands. The first thing that grabs my attention is the date that has been changed on the contract. This is not the policy I had. This one was signed two months ago! With a racing heart, I flip to the part that shows the amount payable. One million dollars is typed with numbers in black and white. The figure is also spelled out to eliminate any doubt that it could be a forgery. There's only one thing in my new policy that's the same as the old one. The beneficiary is Mike!

I get back to my feet and reach for the flashlight next to his red toolbox. I need air, but mostly I need to see better. I lift the sheet of paper in front of the light and check the signature. It's mine. No trace marks. No dents on the paper. I look at the numbers again. Just as perfect as my signature!

Wine doesn't help me figure out this mystery. I need a clear head, which, considering how much I have been drinking today, I won't have for at least a couple of hours.

I lie down on the dusty concrete with my legs and arms spread, sharing the room with dead spiders and ants. If I don't see them, they don't bother me. My arachnophobia is only in my head, triggered by a traumatic event. I remain still, my eyes closed, and summon memories of Mike making me sign documents. I heard it in the movie *Under the Tuscan Sun* that sometimes it's easier to catch ladybugs if we let them come to us. I'm allowing the memory to come to me.

And it works. I remember the last day of school before Christmas break when I was working on the computer in the morning. Then later, when I was heading out the door with the kids late, as usual, carrying their backpacks, Mike pushed a stack of papers in front of me. He asked me to sign them quickly because he wanted to get them in the mail that morning. When I asked what they were, Mike said something about changing the management company for our rental. I had no reason not to trust him and scribbled signatures and initials on the pages he showed me.

I move my fingers and toes to restore feeling. A storm of anger and disappointment brews inside me. All the numbness that kept me on the couch—unwashed, uncombed, unkempt—has disappeared. My husband didn't hire an assassin to execute me because he wanted to save money on a divorce. He wants me dead because one million dollars will drop into his lap. What a splendid life he and his new young wife will have once I'm out of the picture!

I put the policies back into the pocket as they were, then I push the folder back between the tubes of lubricants and sealers. I reorganize the tools and everything else I might have moved on

Mike's workbench. Crazy thoughts invade my head as I make my way back to the house. Will Mike even take care of my children when I'm gone, or does he want a complete do-over?

I need to go forward with my plan. Poison my husband, get the money and pay off the hitman. But I'm a wreck. The day was a disaster—meaningless hours spent on doing nothing productive. My legs feel like lead as I drag them to the kitchen.

It's past ten o'clock. I send the kids to bed. They whine, begging for one more show on TV, but I don't have the patience to argue with them. I unplug the TV and tell them if I hear one more word, I'll smash the screen, and there will be no more watching TV in this house.

Since this day has been wasted anyway, I drink vodka out of the bottle before I go back to the bedroom. I stand under the shower of water for the longest time. I can't bring myself to care about the drought or saving money. The vodka hits my bloodstream hard. It makes me feel horny the same way it used to when I was getting ready for a party in college—a couple of shots of hard liquor to gather courage for teasing a boy for hours until he became lost and mesmerized, followed by days or weeks of teasing. Then I moved in for the kill. Most of the boys took it hard. They, too, loved the game, only they didn't like to lose. Then came the yelling, name-calling, pushing, shoving. We all have to pay for the kind of life we choose to live. Only, there was one boy I underestimated.

Water dripping from my body I stand in front of the marital bed—the bed I've been sharing with Mike. I always thought that having your husband run away with a man could be the most horrible and humiliating thing that could happen to a wife. But no, this is much worse.

We were so much in love. We lived in our own little world. We knew secrets about each other nobody else knew. Maybe you need to burn down the old before you could rise anew from the ashes. I needed to be erased, like a poorly written essay, a first draft.

I wander toward my kids' rooms. I can't stand staying on my feet. The alcohol makes my head spin. I drop on my daughter's bed and curl up in the corner next to her unnoticed. Though I feel warm and comfortable, sleep doesn't come. After fourteen years of marriage, caring, cleaning, dirty laundry, cooking, love, kisses, and hugs, all I'm left with are two options: kill or be killed. Who could remain sane with a dilemma like that?

10 DAYS TO DIE

The sun on my face irritates me to the point that I can't take it anymore and sit up. I start massaging my face to get the muscles working. A foul combination of burnt milk and blackened toast sits heavily in the air. I reach back on the bed to touch Tammy's legs behind me, but my fingers find only empty sheets. Though the haze in my head tries to keep me under, I manage to come back to my senses.

I bolt down the stairs, still wobbly and clumsy from yesterday's wine and last night's agonizing sleep. Laughter drifting from the kitchen brings some relief. The kids haven't burned the house down or suffocated from CO_2 poisoning.

I find Mason spreading butter on a slice of burnt toast. A pot of thick, dark oatmeal is begging for mercy on the stove. Tammy stoops over her math homework on the breakfast nook and scribbles numbers in silence, without bickering with her brother. They're both dressed. Their hair is combed. My kids are ready to go to school without my help.

"Oh, gosh! I'm sorry, guys," I offer, but my apology doesn't make me feel better. "I don't know what happened." I yawn, no matter how much I try to hold it back. My jaws click from how wide my mouth opens. I pour myself a glass of water and send it down my parched throat. I hope it will help ease the throbbing in my temples.

"S'okay, Mom, I got this." Mason smiles, patting me gently on the back.

I lift the pot of oatmeal to my nose and take a whiff. I know it isn't salvageable.

I cup Mason's head in my hands. "I'm so very proud of you."

Tammy expresses her disappointment with the *patented* grunt she recently invented. That girl will be an actress someday. It'd be nice to be around to see her perform.

"I'm proud of you, too, Tammy. Look at you. You're all grown up."

I kiss Mason's forehead, and on my way to get a new pot, I lean against Tammy and plant a kiss on the top of her head. Surprisingly the emotions rising in me aren't warm and kind; instead, they're violent and cold. A cloak of intense hatred towards Mike drops before my eyes, like a thick velvet curtain that blocks out the smallest shred of light. He doesn't deserve us.

As I start on a new pot of oatmeal, my cell phone chimes at the charging station. I know by the sound that it's only an email—a junk, most likely, from an online store that wants to make sure I don't forget about them by sending me five promotional emails a week. I ignore the email on my phone. I want to enjoy this special moment with my children without any interruption and disturbance.

I stir the food with rapid circular motions, the handle of the wooden spoon pressed into my palm. I tune in to the kids' conversation to assuage my nervousness. They can't wait to leave for school. Their day is brimming with plans. They never liked a place we lived before as much as they love it here.

After I set down the two bowls of oatmeal, flavored with the usual cinnamon and honey, I pull Mason into my arms. His soft hair touches my nose, and its fragrance triggers old memories: days infused with the scent of baby powder and fruit and vegetable purees. I promised my children that I would always take care of them, that I would never allow anything bad happen to them, yet for days I've been weak, wallowing in my own sorrow and self-pity. I may have lightheartedly planned to poison my husband to save my life, but I wasn't doing anything to make it happen. I was beginning to accept that after seventeen years of servitude my tab still hadn't been paid and the time has come to balance my account. One soul was lost because of me, and now my soul will be taken for it. An eye for an eye.

I look at my kids—they are ambitious, full of life—and I can't stop thinking that accepting my fate is wrong. They need me. If I die, I'll be taking their futures with me, too. And for what? So Mike can start fresh? How selfish can a man be?

It's been seventeen years since a boy with a broken heart hanged himself because of me. I've been nothing but a good girl ever since. I've changed. I don't play with people's emotions anymore. I don't say things I don't mean. I don't tease. I don't make empty promises. I've been trying hard to stay on the right path even though my new sympathetic way of life won't bring him back to his family. But I've been living with guilt for so long that it's time I allow myself to see the other side of the coin.

After my brother Kyle was murdered by a drunk driver, I devoted my life to shattering the souls of guys who lived recklessly. I played with the hearts of at least two dozens of guys over a period of two years. When I dumped them and crushed their dreams, they were enraged. They tried to make me pay. But all of them were strong enough emotionally to move on and eventually accept defeat and get back on track.

Only this one kid was different. I don't want to say his name or even think about it. I need to be strong. I can't allow myself to fall back into the abyss of despair again.

Today, for the first time, I permit myself to think the unthinkable. He killed himself. Yes, but I didn't drive him to it. That poor boy took his life over a failed summer romance because he couldn't process his emotions; he couldn't accept failure. Which tells me that he might have killed himself for another girl, or a flunked test, or a lost job. But, unfortunately, it was me.

As I watch my kids eat their breakfast, I wonder where the boy's soul had gone. To heaven perhaps, where he's laughing at my predicament right now. "It's your turn, bitch!"

I'm not going to talk to Mike about his heinous plan. I won't try to solve our problems. I'm through with mentally weak men. I'm going to the police instead. I have proof to support my story. I can show them the phone calls, the insurance policy. They will believe me. Mike is going behind bars. Let's see how long his lover will stand by him when all they get to see of each other is a half hour every other Sunday, where they will have nothing in common to talk about. She can cry about money to him while he talks about racist gangs and the vicious hierarchy of the inmates.

After a cold shower, I slip into a black skirt and a red form-fitting blouse. I pull on a pair of high-heel ankle boots. I braid my hair and put on some mascara and lip balm. I haven't looked this good since our anniversary dinner last year: a table, candles, a mariachi band, a platter for two. The memory makes me shudder.

The kids are chasing each other around the dining room table, their backpacks bouncing. They are having a happy and peaceful morning. An unusual but welcomed event.

After I drop them off at school, I drive to the Temecula Police station. I wish it was located farther than a ten-minute drive. Then I'd have more time to think about what to say.

In Temecula, even the police station is reasonably new and beautiful. The sand-colored three-story building stands distinguished against the pale-blue sky dotted with white, puffy clouds—a picturesque, commercial image for the city. Wide driveways lined with slim palm trees lead me to the front of the building. Only a few parked cars are spread out over the large lot in front of deep green lawns. I guess the city isn't required to save water during times of severe drought.

I pull into a spot next to a white sedan. I feel less alone that way. A small plane reflects off the elongated turquoise windows as it passes over me. I can hear the echoing engine sounds. I wish I could just fly away.

The main door opens, and two uniformed officers step out of the building leading a skinny young woman with hair half-black half-white like Cruella de Ville's from the Disney movie. I don't belong here. Yet, here I am.

I check my phone. The hitman called me three times from the same number. Even if he used a disposable cell, the police should be able to track it. I see in the movies how law enforcement nowadays has the technology to pinpoint people's locations with foot-length accuracy.

I snatch my bag from the seat next to me and open the door. But before my foot touches the ground, I freeze up. Can the police arrest Mike for a crime he hasn't committed yet? I'm not sure. This is real life, not some Hollywood movie. This isn't Tom Cruise's *Minority Report*. In real life, premeditating a murder isn't' a crime until someone dies otherwise half the country would be in jail for inappropriate thoughts. It's a *he said, she said* crime, which is difficult to prove.

My enthusiasm ebbs as I process my options in my head.

Only if I could prove at least the premeditated part, the hitman would be arrested, perhaps even Mike. Would a phone number and a story be enough to charge someone? What do they call that kind of evidence? Circumstantial evidence, yes, that's it. How many criminals have gotten off the hook because the police hadn't collected or cataloged the evidence properly, or because the so-called circumstantial evidence wasn't enough for the jury to bring in a conviction?

Besides, how many years can they possibly get for planning a murder but not executing it? Once they were released—maybe even early on good behavior—I'd have to be on the run and live in constant fear for the rest of my life.

There was another aspect I had to consider. What am I going to do if the hitman finds out that I went to the police? What am I going to do if they arrest him, but some sleazy lawyer manages to get him off?

I guess it's a risk I have to take.

I shut the car door behind me when my phone starts buzzing in my hand. I jump as if I'd been shocked by electricity. It's a number I don't recognize. The area code is out-of-state. I don't want to answer it because nothing can be more important than putting an end to my nightmare. But if it's business-related, I can't ignore it. Once Mike is arrested, I'll need money.

"Good morning, Sarah speaking," I say, trying my best to sound professional.

"You got two seconds to get back in your car and drive home. Tick-tock." The line goes dead.

An entire hive of bees breaks loose in my chest. Less than two minutes later, I'm on Highway 79 driving back to the city center. I'm not hurrying home to get the hitman's money or disappear without a trace. No. I'm not willing to leave my children behind so I can live. What kind of life would that be? Instead, I set my mind on killing Mike and this time for real.

My decision is severe and final. This is it. With the one million dollar insurance money, I'll pay off that aggressive waste-of-space hired gun. Then the kids and I will live a low-key life, so he doesn't get the notion to come back and blackmail me for more money.

On the way to the library, I make appointments to get my hair and nails done. I'll either be a leaving this earth in style or be a good-looking widow.

I rack my brain to remember the last time I enjoyed the company of other people, friends, and neighbors. Did I gripe about Mike? Our marriage? I think I might have told Stacy that things hadn't been so dreamy between us lately, but I don't think I said anything that sounded too serious. But just in case Mike gets a sudden heart attack at his prime age of forty, I need to ensure that my friends won't suspect I had anything to do with it. They must tell the police that I was perfectly satisfied with my marriage.

I make a plan to hit Macy's and T. J. Maxx to stock up on new clothes after my trip to the library. Spending Mike's money will make me feel a hell of a lot better. Hopefully, I'll have time to max out his credit card before judgment day comes. Then I stop myself from daydreaming. If I'm able to take Mike out in the next ten days with Selenium, I don't need a maxed-out credit card on our record. The police might think that we were experiencing financial troubles.

I carefully avoid the cameras at the library as I make my way to the computer tables. I'm not at Grace Mellman where I usually go with the kids. This morning I drove all the way to the main city library on Pauba Road.

I feel the excitement tingling the toes in my boots as I sit down. It's early, and only two other people are using the computers: a young kid with messed-up smudged tattoos on his pale neck, who should be in school right now. As I take in the ear-dilating ring that makes his earlobes sag, I consider asking him if he was interested in doing a job for a quick fifty grand. He looks like he could use the money. He also looks like he could get the job done. Shame overtakes me. I can't drag anybody else into my sick twisted life— especially not a high school kid.

I fix my eyes on my monitor without giving a second glance at the middle-aged man who sits a row in front of me to the right.

I open Google search and type in *side effects of selenium poisoning.*

Over three hundred thousand results in 0.40 seconds. A surge of excitement rushes through me. I click on the third link. I always click on the third link when I search the Internet; not because I'm superstitious but because I don't trust the leading companies in any area. A website opens up with the following information.

Signs & Symptoms of Selenium Poisoning

Last Updated: Aug 16, 2013 | By Owen Bond

Selenium is a mineral that's essential to the body in trace amounts, mainly for synthesizing enzymes, but it can be toxic in large amounts. According to the "Doctor's Complete Guide to Vitamins and Minerals," the tolerable upper intake level of selenium is set at 400mcg daily, with 800mcg daily potentially causing toxicity and a dose of 5mg is considered lethal for most people. Selenium poisoning has no known antidote, so recognition of the signs and symptoms is essential for survival.

Main Sources of Selenium

Selenium is used in some photographic devices, gun cleaning solutions, plastics, paints, anti-dandruff shampoos, vitamin and mineral supplements, fungicides and some types of glass. It's also used to manufacture drugs and as a nutritional feed supplement for livestock and poultry.

Exposure to Selenium

In some regions of the U.S., especially the western states, the soil has naturally higher levels of selenium. This can build up in the plants and injure the livestock that feeds on them. According to the Agency for Toxic Substances and Disease Registry, people who consume crops, vegetables or animal products in these regions could be exposed to too much selenium. Additionally, excessive supplementation of selenium is a growing cause of toxicity and poisoning, sometimes because selenium levels are given in micrograms and some people mistake it for milligrams -- a thousand-fold difference.

After reading the entire article, I know I'm onto something. *CSI* doesn't lie.

I find another website that will help me calculate the dosage I need to induce Mike's heart attack.

800 micrograms per day (15 micrograms per kilogram body weight) but suggested 400 micrograms per day to avoid toxicity.

The Chinese people who suffered from selenium toxicity ingested selenium by eating corn grown in extremely selenium-rich stony coal (carbonaceous shale).

This coal was shown to have selenium content as high as 9.1%, the highest concentration in coal ever recorded in literature. A dose of selenium as small as 5 mg per day can be lethal for many humans.

Symptoms of selenosis include a garlic odor on the breath, gastrointestinal disorders, hair loss, sloughing of nails, fatigue, irritability, and neurological damage.

An interesting article about an Australian man who died from Selenium overdose grabs my attention next.

After ingesting 10 grams, some 250,000 times greater than the tolerable limit suggested, the man became very ill. He took the selenium at 7:00 am, was in the hospital by 10:30 am and despite the best efforts of the medical staff, was deceased by 1:00 pm.

I check out a dozen other articles and websites, but I don't learn anything new. I already got everything I need to start, so I'm not disappointed. I fold up my notes and put them in my purse, delete the browser history, and log out. I'm startled when I realize that the computer tables had filled up around me.

Keeping my head down, I walk back to the street and get in my car. I search my phone for nearby pharmacies. I'll need to purchase several bottles of Selenium to achieve the dose I need for Mike. I drive back to Navy Federal Bank by Nicolas Road to withdraw some cash. On my way to Murrieta, driving by Ralph's makes me realize that I need to buy food so that the kids have something for lunch tomorrow. I feel like a complete psycho who makes a quick grocery-shopping run on her way to buy poison. I don't feel sick, though; I just laugh. If destiny wants to twist my life in this sick way, then I'm gonna go with it.

Back in the house, I put the food away, grab my keys and get back on the road. In the *CSI* episode I've been using for guidance, the two women used a dandruff shampoo that contained selenium to poison their husbands. I decide to stick with pills instead because I don't think I can make Mike swallow shampoo. Though I'll need to mash up a ton of pills to reach the fatal dose.

I hit two pharmacies in Murrieta, and one in Wildomar. I then drive back home. I spread out all the containers and pills on the kitchen countertop and read the labels carefully. I decide to add the selenium to Mike's food in two and a half milligram doses twice a day. For that, I'll have to smash up ten pills for each treatment and stir the powder into his food.

I bought beef and potatoes to make Mike's favorite food: beef stew. I'll add tons of garlic to account for his breath. Good thing Mike eats garlic like it was candy.

It's nearly three o'clock when the stew is done. I scoop some out into a smaller pot for Mike. He'll gobble it down tomorrow when he gets home from work after a forty-eight-hour shift. When I'm about to drop the fine white powder in, which I spent a good twenty minutes to smash and grind, hesitation kicks in. Will I really go through with this?

Mike has always trusted me. Whenever he was sick, I brought him pills, and he took them without question. He never had a moment's doubt in me when it came to his food and health. Feeding him poison will be as easy as breathing.

I draw courage from a shot of Bacardi. I send down a glass of orange juice after it. With a sudden move, I drop the poison into the stew and stir it thoroughly with a big wooden spoon. Then I drive to the school to get my kids.

*   *   *   *   *

The blanket of the night has already descended on the house when the kids go to bed. Ever since we got home from school, I kept my mind off the stew by helping with homework, picking up books, toys, and clothes, putting away laundry. Yet more than a few times I stood in front of the kitchen sink, holding Mike's pot of stew over the drain, ready to dump it, but each time, the image of Emanuela and Mike in my bedroom stopped me from pouring the food down.

When upstairs quiets down, I take out the faithful bottle of Bacardi. I've been longing for a cigarette for hours. One would go well with my Mojito. Only bad moms leave their kids at home and slip out to the nearest gas station to buy smokes, but that's what I'm about to do now. What does it matter if I'm a good mom or not— if I refrain from drinking and smoking in front of the kids, if I gave up on partying once they were born—when, in the end, Mike will be the one who turns me into a corpse or a murderer. Howsoever I end up, I'll do it with my head held high. This is my story now, and I'll write it as I please.

· · · · ·

Stacy: I didn't notice any changes in her behavior. She came to practices. She even started running around the tracks, which bothered me because I had so much to tell her about how Calvin, my ex, took the kids to Disneyland, but he refused to pay for our son Nick's medical bill. But I couldn't tell her because she was gone running. Running isn't my thing. I'm more of a Pilates-kind of girl. But I'm not doing that either. I don't have time.

Carol: Look, Tom, I'm sorry, Detective, we didn't talk much because she was this stuck-up kind of woman, but I remember her mentioning it to me once how healthy they live. No drugs. No medication. No GMO. You know, tree-huggers. So if there was any Selenium in his body—what did

124

you say Selenium was? Oh, okay—as I said, if he had any drugs in his system, then you should look into it because it sounds very suspicious to me.

Benny: She wasn't good at chemistry. I had to tutor her in math too because it wasn't her strength either. She was more like a street-smart kind of girl, you know. If she had given any pills to Mike, and I'm not saying she did, I'm sure she had no idea what she was doing. What? Wow! That's a lot of Selenium. (Clearing throat). No, I don't think she has anything to do with this. Mike was kind of dumb when it came to numbers too. It wouldn't surprise me if he overdosed himself.

9 DAYS TO DIE

After I drop the kids off at school, I once again find myself at the Rite Aid down the street on Nicolas Road. I've been tapping into Mike's stash of wine and liquor, and although he couldn't care less about household items or the kids' wardrobe contents, he does keep a close inventory on his booze. I need to restock his bar before he notices that somebody has been looting his stockpile. I also need to make sure I have something to reach for when my brain needs a few hours of numbness. It's not like I care what he will think of me as a wife—or as a mother—when he realizes that I've developed a sneaky drinking habit. I want to keep my secret because he can't know that something is off with me.

I've been running through my married life like a horse with blinders, my eyes fixed solely on the road ahead. I never peeked to the right or left, considered my options, changed any of my routines. No need for me to stray. Frankly, I had no desire to get out of my comfort zone. I had a husband, two children, a house, and my daily visits to Organic Roots. What else was there for a homemaker to wish for her happiness?

At times, a desperate yearning gnawed at my insides, yet I was too much of a coward to act on it. Would I have been more fun and desirable if I flirted with men occasionally to keep the fire in me glowing? Would Mike have been more interested in taking me passionately in bed if I hadn't given him everything he wanted without asking?

When I was a teenager, there was this guy Tommy living in the house next to us who seemed to hold the answers to all my questions. He used to hang out with my brother Kyle, fixing bikes, bungee jumping off bridges.

One day while Tommy was eating a grilled cheese sandwich in our kitchen, I sneaked up on him. It was one of those rare moments when my brother left me alone with one of his friends.

Kyle was in the shower; his eyes being pounded by water instead of being set on my every move. For years, I believed that he made every guy who passed the threshold of our house take a vow of staying away from me. All those hot guys in our house, yet none of them talked to me, hit on me, or showed any interest in me. The more they resisted me, the more I wanted them. Winning the attention of at least one of them became a game to me. A challenge I was desperate to win—desperate enough to make a fool of me.

On this particular day when I stepped into the kitchen to pour myself a glass of juice, I found Tommy alone, his motorcycle-toughened hands clenching his sandwich. The opportunity I'd been waiting for a long time. As I passed behind him, I ran my hand over his shoulders. His back stiffened under my touch while his eyes snapped in the direction where Kyle might be expected to enter the room. I enjoyed the power I had over Kyle's friends. In spite of their vows, they did sneak a glance or two behind my brother's back whenever I opened my legs for them in my short skirt. I got off watching the beads of sweat pearling up on their foreheads from how dreadfully they tried to divert their attention away from my panties. In those early high school years, I fed off their suppressed desires. Most likely, I developed most of my self-restraint watching them.

I still tap into that self-restraint each day of my married life.

They wanted me so badly, but they couldn't have me. Having so much control over others was empowering. And I teased and teased shamelessly to feed my ego because Kyle made it easy for me and hard for his friends. One inappropriate comment or one move toward me would terminate those boys' friendship with my brother and perhaps even earn them a broken nose.

So on that particular day in the kitchen, my fingers were tracing the muscles on Tommy's arm causing him to drop his food and straightened his back, pushing against the chair in what I believed to be an almost painfully forced motion. I leaned over the countertop, so he could see my young tits just enough to make him sweat.

"Stop that, Sarah," he snarled through clenched jaws. His eyes stole another glance at the staircase.

I started tracing the mound of my right breast with my finger. My nipples were tucked safely in my blouse, but my décolletage allowed a great view of the small mounds that looked so delicious, like Hostess' Snowball candies.

Tommy folded his arms, watching me. The tip of his red tongue wetted his upper lip. I pictured his handsome face buried in my chest. I imagined what he would do to me if Kyle weren't home. Still a virgin physically, my mind had been fucked a hundred times. Nowadays teens' lives are drenched in erotica and sex through music videos, movies, books, and the Internet, but when I was young, we found a way to learn about sex too. Back in my time, my friends and I read books written for teens by Ph.D.'s instead of horny housewives. *Dear Doctor, my question is can I get pregnant from oral sex?*

I laugh at the memory now, but when a Q&A book that was read ragged by students at school landed on my lap, I drank up every word. None of the questions looked stupid or unimportant to me.

Tommy squirmed in his chair, looking away from me. I emitted a low moan. He picked up his plate and slipped off the barstool.

Driven by anger and humiliation, I leaped to his side and pulled him back by his arm.

"What's your problem? I'm not pretty enough for you?" I barked into his face. He closed his eyes hard as if composing himself, or at least ransacking his brain for an appropriate answer.

"You're a beautiful girl, Sarah, so sexy and desirable that no man will be able to say no to you. And that's exactly why you need to stop teasing guys."

I let go of his arm, a frown embedded in my face. He must have noticed my disappointment or was just afraid of any possible retribution, because he continued, "You know what men like about hunting?"

I shrugged at his stupid, apropos-of-nothing question.

"That the prey doesn't come easy. The hunter has to track it, use clever games to find it, and at last take it down. All this tracking takes time—time full of excitement and anticipation. Killing the prey feels glorious only if the hunter has enough time to build up those feelings of excitement and anticipation."

I made a face. "I have no idea what you're talking about. You know what? If you don't like me, just say so. You don't need to come up with a stupid tale about the fox and the rabbit."

He shook his head with a sigh. "You're a beautiful doe, Sarah. Now you only need to allow hunters to track you down. You are the prey. Let the guys be the hunters."

I flipped his plate making his grilled cheese drop to the floor. It landed greasy-side down. Why do they always have to land greasy-side down? "This has to be the stupidest analogy I ever heard in my life," I hissed.

"Just think about it." That's all he said. He gathered up his food and walked out to the patio. I didn't follow him. I also refused to waste another second of my life thinking about his sexist comparison. But come to think of it, that was the last time I ever teased anyone like a cheap whore.

When I first started dating Mike, I still lived by the prey-and-hunter rule. I kept the game going for a few years. Then the anticipation and excitement of being chased were gone. The prey in me got tired of the same old same old. So our sex life fell in line with the statistics. The appellation *trophy wife* shouldn't be used as a status for the young, attractive wife of an older man, because it fits better for a tired housewife who has been taken down after being hunted for a long time and mounted on the wall—a lifeless, defeated creature.

Emanuela is still a prey for Hunter Mike. Not for long, I assume. She's pregnant and an alien in a strange new country. The only comfort I find in this bizarre situation is that her surrender will come even faster than mine did.

As I near the entrance of the Rite Aid, I smile at my logic. I hope I'll be around to witness the bimbo's downfall. And when it happens, *trophy wife* will apply to her in both meanings. She will become a double trophy wife.

My smile soon vanishes when a poster on the drugstore's sliding door displaying a woman on the beach drinking her cocktail out of the bottle catches my eye. With only nine days left for me to live or die, I should be taking a vacation to Bali, partying with sexy strangers with hard, tanned bodies in clubs where the air is dense with smoke and body vapor. If I must die, I should go out with a bang. At least I'm lucky enough to know when I die, like someone with a terminal illness.

"Mrs. Johnson, I'm sorry to tell you this, but you have less than ten days to live. I suggest you take care of your business, spend some time with your loved ones, and prepare yourself mentally for the final good-byes."

"Thank you, doctor, for telling me the truth. It's much better knowing how much time I have left on this earth than living as if I never died; as if I were immortal."

"Your welcome, Sarah. May I call you Sarah?"

"Sure, doctor, why not? It's never too late to make new friends."

I laugh at my idiocy as I enter the store and head towards the back where identical refrigeration units line the wall like the guards at Buckingham Palace. I like to stand in front of the first unit and look down the entire row. Organized. Disciplined. Perfect. I love that.

The store is near vacant. Only one grandma-aged woman squints at me as she ushers her little toddler along in a ridiculous Cinderella outfit probably made of recycled plastic in China. Staggering about in a pair of see-through plastic high heels (instead of glass slippers) the girl whines for candy. The whole getup looks toxic and very uncomfortable, but hey, whatever your little princess wants.

I envision Emanuela and Mike's daughter being brought up the same way—growing up in a selfish, self-centered environment where she gets everything she wants.

"I said I want that man, mama."

"But he's married, my darling."

"I don't care what he was before he met me. I want him, and I'll have him."

"Whatever makes my princess happy!"

This foolish imaginary conversation fires up my inner laugh, and for the first time in a long time, I'm enjoying myself.

The little girl with a finger in her nose pokes her tongue at me. I stick out mine back at her. She bursts into the most ridiculously phony cry ever and starts pulling on her granny's skirt.

"What's wrong with you?" the lady calls out to me.

What's wrong with you? I shrug and keep walking.

Submitting to the advertisement on the door, I pick up a four pack of Bacardi cocktails but having a change of heart I put them back. I need something stronger.

While most people with terminal illnesses spend their last days enjoying peaceful dinners with family, telling their kids and husbands how much they love them, and how they expect them to be strong once they are gone, I'll spend my remaining days drinking, smoking, and deciding between killing the father of my children or letting him kill me.

A tall bottle of vodka winks at me. I take the hint and lift it from the shelf. I put more bottles of liquor and wine in the cart. I'll need to replace the ones I already drank.

On my way out, I pick up a bottle of MiraLax. It'll come in handy if Mike gets home from work this morning with any funny ideas about being too intimate with me. Not like it has happened lately, but with his bimbo being pregnant and what not, he might need a quickie after lunch like old times. No way, Jose!

As I try to navigate my way through the laundry room to get into the kitchen, my phone rings in my pocket. Mike's calling to let me know that he has to stay for a few more hours at work to cover for someone. I couldn't care less. Since deciding to let go of my decade-long guilt, I feel renewed as if a tumor has been removed from my lungs so I can finally breathe.

With the extra few hours Mike has granted me, I'm going to be able to drink my Vodka orange at my own pace. No need to rush and be jumpy whenever I hear a car passing in front of our house.

A text comes in. It's from Benny. A pang of guilt stabs me. After my short visit to him, he most likely expected me to keep in touch.

R u OK?

I don't feel like typing, so I ring him up.

"Oh, hey. Yeah, I'm OK. Thanks for checking up on me."

"Yeah, no problem. So how'd it go? Could you install the program?"

I clear my throat, not to get my voice back, but to win some time. "You know, I never tried. Hey, Benny, sorry for the other day," I say it quickly. "I don't know what got into me. I want you to know that Mike and I are fine."

The line goes silent for an awkwardly long time.

"Benny? You there?"

"Look, Sarah, I did some checking on Mike. There's something I think you should see."

From the embarrassment, I feel the heat breaking out on my neck and face. "What? Why would you do that?"

"I don't know. You seemed . . . lost. Do you have time to grab a coffee with me?"

It's too late for excuses and lies. If Benny did some research on Mike, he must have found something out about Emanuela. "Meet you at Starbucks in ten? The one on Winchester? Next to the I-15 ramp?"

"I'll be there. And Sarah . . . you may not like what you'll see."

"Just be there, Ben."

My thoughts run wild as I put the Vodka in the freezer—I read somewhere that that's where true Russians keep them. I also make room for the carton of orange juice on the top shelf in the fridge.

Where could Benny do his research on Mike? Hacked his Facebook account? His bank accounts?

I pull out of the garage so fast that I almost run over a neighbor kid who just flashed behind my car on his bicycle. My stomach contracts to the size of my fist. Why isn't he in school? Stupid homeschoolers! I need a few calming breaths before I can proceed out of the cul-de-sac.

Winchester is backed up. I go from red to red. When the traffic light stops me at the infernal Margarita-Winchester intersection, I know I'll be late.

I don't know what type of car Benny drives, and because of those awful tinted windows on the Starbucks building, I can't be sure if he's already made it here or not.

I pull into a spot quite a distance from the entrance and walk on the smooth new asphalt, watching the bumper-to-bumper line of cars on the I-15 on-ramp merging onto the freeway, but I don't see cars. I see a horde of sheep trying to get to the water. Nobody honks the horn or offers a shaking fist to other drivers. People who commute hours a day to work have already accepted their fate in silent resignation. Although Temecula's population has grown from 25,000 to over 100,000 in twenty-five years, we're still called *a bedroom community*.

I guess being stuck in traffic two-three hours a day was part of what prevented me from looking for a job. Still, tens of thousands of people drive to San Diego and Los Angeles every day.

Though today isn't as warm as it has been the past few days, the sixty-five-degree air-conditioned air still loops around me as I enter the depressingly brown building. When the interior designer came up with the plan to decorate this coffee shop, I'm sure he had tranquility and harmony in mind. When my eyes sweep over the shades of brown that dominate the walls and furniture, I get boredom and depression on my mind.

I find Benny stooped over two white paper cups in the corner. I take my place across the table from him. On the way here, I replayed conversations over and over again in my head, preparing myself mentally for what I would say—how I would make him believe that whatever he found didn't mean a thing, but when I'm here face to face with him, all the rehearsed lines vanish from my head.

"Is that for me?" I ask. Inane question.

He pushes one of the cups toward me. "Coffee latte with extra cold milk and three packets of sugar."

We'd never gone to Starbucks together, but that's the way I always made my coffees in high school. I offer him a smile with a slight nod and take my seat.

"You know I'll just cut to the chase and show you what I found. Then you can decide if you want to talk about it or not." I watch his neck where an excess of loose skin hangs like a limp rooster wattle. I wonder if he ever considered plastic surgery after losing all that weight.

"Why are you doing this?" I lean back instead of forward. I should keep our conversation to ourselves but there are only a few other people in the shop, and they are all immersed in their own problems. Nobody cares what anybody else is talking about at nearby tables. Besides, I need to show Benny that he has overstepped his boundaries this time.

Every guy I liked in high school became the target for one of Benny's private investigations. He dug up pictures and emails about everybody I got close to emotionally. At the time, I enjoyed the flood of information, and the superior feeling that I was holding all the aces. Now? Well, now I believe that sometimes not knowing is better than knowing it all. Life is too short to worry about ex-girlfriends and previous minor, or major, altercations.

He pushes his coffee aside and bends down for his laptop. "I know we've barely kept in touch in the past twenty years, but my beliefs haven't changed. I can't stomach liars and cheaters. But what I can't stand the most is when someone tries to make a fool of my friends."

Friends? He tutored me in math. I bought him a coffee for it.

"Let's see what you have there."

His laptop comes alive from sleep mode. He turns it toward me with the screen facing the wall and not the store. I lead my eyes to the browser bar: adultfriendfinder.com

"Do you know this site?" Benny points his finger to the title on the homepage.

I shake my head as my heart picks up speed.

"It's a site where people hook up for sex. Mike has a profile here."

I thought there was nothing new I could learn about my cheating husband, but this news punches me in the guts.

"What do you mean?" I swallow hard. "Can I see it?"

After a few clicks and typing, a page loads with Mike's profile picture, a description of himself, and what he's seeking. Could be an old account. A little fun he had before he got married. But when Benny shows me the dates of his recent messages, I have to admit to myself, no matter how painful it is, that I'm wrong. Fifty messages line up on a single page, and there are a bunch of pages.

"Did you read them?"

"A few."

"Is it a fantasy or the real thing?"

"Well, according to these messages it's real. Dates. Names. Places. They're all here."

"How long has he been doing this?"

Benny sips at his coffee. I stare at the foam ring that stays on his bushy mustache.

"He always has."

I press my face into my hands. How many times had I had yeast infections during our marriage that I attributed to community hot tubs, pools, or cheap underwear.

I feel Benny's hand on my arm, cold and moist like the rags I put on the kids' foreheads to take down a fever. I don't want to look up and face him. What am I gonna say, that I married a douche bag who managed to pass himself off as the catch of the day?

I need to keep my face down before the urge to explain my marriage escapes my mouth. The proof of Mike's infidelities and lies glares off the screen between Benny and me, so what's the point of telling him that Mike is a great father and husband anyway? As inane as it sounds, I believed it myself for so long. Or perhaps I just accepted the life I thought I deserved.

On every trip we took as a family, an adult friend was waiting for my husband. Arranged. Free. Secretive.

Why had I never come across that website? Damn! Mike is a great liar.

"Have you ever considered getting married?" I ask Benny through the wall my hands keep around my face.

"No . . . not really."

I'm a victim here. I need to come off as a victim even if the truth may come back and bite me later.

"I think Mike wants to get rid of me," I blurt out. I look out of the window, but I can't see much because my eyes are misty with tears.

"You'd be better off without him," Benny offers, pushing the cup of coffee into my hands.

"You don't understand." I fix my eyes on his. My voice catches in my throat. "I think my life's in danger."

I notice his bushy eyebrows lower over his small dark eyes. Despite his weight loss and cool computer-geek getup, I still don't find him attractive, at least not appearance-wise. I always loved his persona. Chilled. Easy-going. Smart—crazy smart.

"You can't possibly mean what I think you mean."

I shake my head and push the tears from my eyes.

He grunts, leaning back in his chair and folding his arms. A part of his long black hair gets stuck in his beard.

"Did you go to the police?"

I wrap my fingers over the paper cup. The heat is comforting on my skin. Sometimes when I think I've lost my ability to feel, even pain can be pleasant. I eat hot peppers with my food because on some days the burning pain in my mouth is the only proof I have that I'm alive and can still feel.

Teardrops run along my cheeks. "And tell them what?"

We remain sitting at the table nursing our fancy coffees for half an hour. I tell Benny about Emanuela and the house she's living in on our expense. I mention Mike's life insurance, and I even say that if someone would help me get out of this situation, I'd be more than willing to share the insurance money with that person.

I cry about the lies Mike has been feeding me. I complain about the servant life I've offered my family for over a decade. Benny thinks I'm being irrational. He urges me to go to the police, but I make him understand that there is no point. He offers me his help to disappear with my kids and start anew somewhere far away. But he's got an invalid mother to take care of, and I have no money. I leave out the part about the poison. He doesn't need to know that I'm a psycho.

He doesn't want to let me go home, but I tell him that a heap of laundry is waiting for me. He thinks I'm crazy. I believe that too.

All the way home, I bang my palm against my forehead for letting him in on my secrets. Once, when Benny was only ten, four fifth-graders jumped him on the school grounds. Although he took a severe beating, he broke the nose of one of the boys. He got suspended for a week. Now I have to worry about his showing up at our house and punching out Mike's teeth.

This story just gets better and better.

. . . . .

> **Benny:** This is a crazy accusation. Do you have any proof, Detective? Or are you just fishing here? Well, then I believe we are done here. On second thought, I wish to add one more thing to my statement. If you want to find out what happened, you should check out their rental home in French Valley. No, I don't know anything. I'm just saying it would be an excellent place to start.

. . . . .

The house is a complete disaster. The dirty dishes are piled up in the sink. Both hampers overflow with laundry, but I spend my morning on the couch, again, watching *Downton Abbey*.

After my second drink, I doze off and dream about the divorce of my childhood best friend's parents. They turned it into a nasty affair. The whole street listened to them fighting all the time. I never knew what triggered it, but her dad started to get wasted during the day. When I was over at their house, he'd drool on the couch, a cluster of beer bottles on the floor stinking up the house. I hated the place, but Ashley always called me and begged me on the phone to come over and take her away. How could I say no to my best friend?

Once while I was there, her dad started yelling at her, calling her names because of the clothes she was wearing. Ashley talked back to him, which he didn't take well. With his big sweaty hands, he pulled her hair, dragged her upstairs and forced her to change. He kept yelling that he would make sure she didn't turn into the kind of cheap woman that her mother was. I ran home crying all the way.

Finally, they sold the house, and Ashley moved with her mother to Montana. I lost touch with her. I did see her father in town a few times. He was always dirty, reeking of cheap wine and beer, his hair matted.

I was a senior in high school when someone told me that he hanged himself in a dingy motel room where he had been living since the divorce.

Years later, I found Ashley on Facebook, but I decided not to friend her. She looked like drug addict trailer trash with sleeve tattoos on both arms, on her neck, and piercings in her lips and nose. In every photo she shared publicly, she was curled up on someone's lap with a bottle or drink in her hand laughing. Sometimes I felt the urgent need to reach out to her, but I was married by then and had Mason. Mike would never have approved of my friendship with Ashley. What a hypocrite!

My face is lying in a pool of saliva when I wake up. I feel cold and hungry, my mouth stale. I stagger into the kitchen to eat a protein bar when I realize that I'm late for my hair appointment.

I run upstairs to rinse with mouthwash while I jump into a pair of jeans. They look baggy on me. *What the hell?* I grope in the closet for the old skinny black jeans I haven't seen for ages. Last time I tried to put them on was three years ago for Mason's birthday party. They only reached the middle of my thighs. Now those same pants fit me perfectly as if they were molded to my legs. I can button them up all the way, and none of the buttons are ready to pop off and shoot the mirror. Some belly still hangs over the waist, but I tuck it in quickly.

I yank my T-shirt off. I smell. No time for a shower, I wash my armpits at the sink, pile on the deodorant, and slip on a loose, embroidered, champagne-colored blouse. The wedges look ridiculous on me, so I put on a pair of flats instead.

I finish chewing my third piece of gum when I arrive at the beauty salon. Nobody knows me here, because I usually do my hair at home, trying to save money. Even though I'm fifteen minutes late, the girl with hair like Amy Winehouse's and long nails is still not ready for me. I pick up a *Vogue* and flip through the pages. I check out all the beautiful women in the magazine with envy. I tried to keep up with my appearance when the kids were still young, but it was too hard. I used to get up early to run on the treadmill, but the thumping noise of the treadmill woke the kids.

Then I signed up for a group exercise at the gym—just another short-lived attempt at getting fit. All the classes I liked were in perfect sync with the kids' sports activities.

Then Mike started to pick on me every day for not having a job, and all I could think of was how to make money.

Maybe if I stuck with the gym and had my hair done once a week and paid closer attention to how I dressed, Mike would have found me attractive longer. Maybe my kids would have been prouder of me if I looked like a *Victoria's Secret* model instead of a worn-out soccer mom.

While I pretend to read an article in the magazine, I listen to the conversations of women around me. Everybody looks younger than me, though I don't think they are. Confident. Happy. They seem to know what happened at the Grammy's, the new features on the latest iPhone, the best apps for online shopping with price comparison. I only know that organic milk is twenty-nine cents cheaper at Winco than at Sprouts.

When it's finally my turn, I tell the girl to do something crazy with my hair. I want to look younger, and sexier. She raises one eyebrow as she measures me up with a grimace then tells me she'll do her best.

Big chunks of hair drop to the floor all around me. I start to feel lighter with each snip.

In twenty minutes, I have side-swept bangs, hot-ironed hair that is shorter in back and gradually longer toward the front. I look like, I don't know, like Taylor Swift. Well, not really; her face and mine look nothing alike, but our hairstyle is similar.

I love how I look, though, the reflection I see in the mirror doesn't seem to belong to me. Other customers in the shop express their approval, and I walk to the cashier bathing in praise and glory.

I hand over a big tip, and I don't feel guilty about it. Soon a million bucks will land in Mike's lap or mine. Strangely, I'm not scared but feel amused by the whole situation. Although yesterday after a few glasses of wine, I was ready to accept my fate, allowing grim thoughts to invade my head: I don't have a purpose on this earth; I don't have a job; I can't support my family; nobody will miss me when I'm gone. With my new haircut, flatter belly and a whole new attitude, I feel determined to live.

Mike is the cheating, lying, and devious mastermind of premeditated murder. He should die and go to hell, not me. I wouldn't hurt a fly. I can't even kill the ants that come into the house for water on hot summer days.

I enjoy another hour, getting pampered at the nail salon. My feet bathe in warm, fragrant water. The unflattering, rock-hard calluses on my heels make me feel embarrassed, but I get over the feeling quickly.

A middle-aged Asian woman comes and settles down by my feet. She barely speaks English, yet a series of lousy plastic surgeries announces her desire to look more American. Her lips are overfilled, swollen, and bright red. Her hair is dyed a light brown. She must have gotten her eyes done too because they are unnaturally stretched and—despite her age—there are no crow's feet lines or saggy bags under her eyes.

She offers me a smile that reminds me of the Joker from *Batman*. She has good hands, though, and I enjoy her fingers pressing deeply into the soles of my feet. I lean back, the mechanism of the massage chair rubbing against my back. I feel relaxed and beautiful. I wonder if I had been more comfortable and hungrier for intimacy during my marriage—if I'd undergone this pampering more often, might things have turned out differently. Had I spent more time nourishing my body and soul instead of covering my ugly heels when Mike was taking me from behind, would things have worked out better between us? The obvious dawns on me. I messed up. I messed up my marriage big time.

I go with French nail designs on both fingers and toes. I don't feel bold enough to go with bright colors and motifs like the women on both sides of me. Maybe on my next visit— if there will be one.

Ten minutes until the kids get out of school, but I'm already in the parking lot. As I walk to the entrance, I feel people's eyes on me. Just last week, I stared at an exotic young mom in high heels, tight jeans, and a loose satin blouse feeling utterly jealous. She was eye candy even to me. Dads rushed to catch up with her, chat with her, impress her. I walked around them, invisible like a middle-school kid desperate to blend in. I stopped by the bicycle racks to stand alone like I usually do.

But, today, I'm the center of attention. I can almost hear them talking about me, wondering who I am. I straighten my posture and lick my lips, knowing that even my kids won't recognize me.

But I overestimated my children's interest in their mother's makeover. Mason merely asked if I had a job interview today as the reason for my wearing makeup. I tell him yes. I don't know why I choose to lie. Maybe I want him to stop questioning me.

As I pull into our driveway, a swarm of kids runs alongside the car, yelling for Mason and Tammy. I swear these kids sit by the window waiting for us to come home. I park in the garage while my kids take their bicycles out. I walk to the mailbox; just a routine thing to do, not like it matters anymore if there is a bill in there. I'm not planning to pay bills till I see the end of my story.

Across the street, our new neighbor Bruce is washing his car. His bare chest attracts my eyes like a magnet. He notices my stare and straightens up, squeezing the foamy sponge in his hand. I don't move my sight away as I've always done before. I don't consider myself married anymore. After what Mike has done to us, I don't owe him my loyalty.

Bruce makes no attempt to talk to me, and our stand-and-stare becomes awkward. I slip into the garage with an idea blossoming in my head. There's no better way to show the world that my marriage is excellent, that Mike and I have no problems than to have a party with the neighbors. Since we started our remodeling, I bet half the neighborhood is dying to see what our place looks like inside. They would be thrilled to get an invitation and show up for a night of drinking and eating.

That's it! We'll have a block party where we can show the world that our marriage is running like a well-oiled machine. Mike will love the idea, too, because I'm sure he's been thinking of ways to convince people around us that he had no reason to get rid of me.

And after the party, I'll kill my husband.

*   *   *   *   *

Expecting Mike to come home from work at any moment, I'm

in the kitchen heating up store-bought fried chicken in the microwave. The stew laced with Selenium is in the refrigerator, tuned up with a heavy dash of cayenne pepper. A warning sign on the lid tells the kids not to eat from it. I can't serve it to Mike for dinner tonight because I need him to be alive for the party. I'm not even sure how long it will take for the Selenium to induce a heart attack in him, but I don't want to take any chances. What if my calculations are off, and he drops dead after dinner? First, the neighbors have to have a chance to see us telling each other how much we love each other.

I'm leaning over the counter, writing down the menu on a sheet of paper when Mike steps into the kitchen and slaps at my butt. I jolt upright, my hands in fists.

"What the hell is wrong with you?" I grunt.

"You got some great ass," he says, smiling. "Did you lose weight?"

I move to take dinner out of the microwave, upset with myself. I should have changed into sweats and an oversized T-shirt before he got home. Despite his pretty little girlfriend, he's never stopped climbing over me here and there. The thought makes me feel disgusted. I promised myself not to dwell on his unfaithfulness, but I'm unable to block out the images of him putting his dick in various holes of that young chick.

"Are you pissed or something?" he asks, looping his arms around my waist.

I glance at the set of knives on my right. One of them looks particularly tempting. The black and silver handle would look stylish poking out of Mike's eye.

"No. I'm still not a hundred percent yet. I think the flu's gone to my lungs now." I fake a smile, and it must have come out teasingly because he presses his lips against mine. I want to headbutt him, knock him to the ground and kneel on his neck until he stops breathing.

"You look fantastic today. Did I miss an important occasion?" Mike says, his breath touching my face.

On any other day, I'd find him irresistible, charming even; now I have to grab hold of the edge of the oven to anchor myself before I poke his eyes out with my thumbs.

"What do you mean?" *Be charming. Play your part*, I tell myself.

He buys into my sweet face and tucks a strand of hair behind my right ear. His touch repulses me.

"New hair." He lifts my hand. "Pretty nails. Is this a new top?"

"Well, our anniversary is coming up next month. The fifteenth. It was time for me to update a little."

He takes a deep sniff at my hair. "Let's go upstairs right now," he breathes into my ear.

There were times when his warm breath on my skin would trigger a series of tingles in my body—when my breasts yearned for his touch. But with this terror in my head, I can only think of how to get out of his clutches. I should have changed into something dirty and unattractive I tell myself, once more gritting my teeth. Then my eyes catch sight of the bottle of laxative I bought earlier at Rite Aid. My face splits into a huge smile.

"What's so funny?" he asks, tracing my collarbone with gentle touches of his index finger.

"Nothing," I say, hypnotizing him with my eyes. "Nothing at all."

. . . . .

Carol: It's not like I want to start a train of gossip here, but our new neighbor Bruce—over there—took a liking to Sarah if you know what I mean. If Mike was upset with his wife, then he

146

had every right to be. Poor guy. He
worked a lot. Always gone. He didn't
deserve a cheating wife like that.

Bruce: Who told you that? Yes, I wanted
to kill that worthless piece of shit for
what he had done to Sarah, but it wasn't
me. Yes, you can look around. I have
nothing to hide. But I want to tell you
that you are wasting your time with me.
You should be out there looking for who
is responsible for this. She . . . she
was . . . special.

.   .   .   .   .

Only the bedside reading lamp casts light over our bed. I'm lying in the pool of a warm glow, my hands folded behind my head. I've been keeping track of Mike's bowel movements all evening. It's the ninth time he's had to run to the bathroom.

A classy woman would move to the room downstairs and offer privacy to her husband. Only Mike doesn't give a rat's ass about privacy. The bed stands a few feet away from the toilet, and since the door isn't soundproof, I can hear the splashing sounds, as if he were drowning a kangaroo in the toilet bowl water. And men have the nerve to complain about their wives' few extra pounds of post-baby weight! I feel like I'm watching a hilarious comedy. I should write a comedy.

The evening was otherwise quiet. After dinner, the kids did homework, took baths, and went to bed.

Mike has been walking around the house, sulking at times, cooing at others. The house is a mess, but I refuse to clean it up. Luckily, Mike didn't want to start a fight tonight, not when he was expecting to get into my panties. He grossly miscalculated one factor though: Hell hath no fury like a woman scorned.

My hands must have slipped a little when I poured the laxative into his beer at dinner. Perhaps a little too much because soon after we finished eating and I started gathering the dirty dishes from the table I heard his stomach flip. By the time I brought the kids home from soccer practice he was sick as a dog.

Watching Mike spend the rest of his evening shitting his brains out and cussing instead of face-timing his girlfriend gives me indescribable pleasure.

"I don't know, Honey. We all ate the same thing, and we're fine. Maybe you picked up the bug from someone at work." A wicked laugh threatened to break out of me as I said these comforting lines repeatedly all throughout the evening.

I don't offer him tea, not even a glass of water, so he goes downstairs and gets a ginger ale for himself.

His hushed voice travels upstairs on the night air. I can't make the words out, but I'm pretty sure he's on the phone, asking sweet Emanuela if she is OK. So they spent time together today. It seems the morning's unexpected-overtime story was a lie. Probably most of the overtime stories he's been feeding me are lies.

Around ten o'clock at night, I ask him to move downstairs to the guest bedroom because he's keeping the kids up and they have school tomorrow. The irony of the situation is that he used to tell me the same thing when I was breastfeeding my babies. He's overcome by my lack of sympathy and grumbles all the way downstairs to the toilet.

I stay up for a while, reading an article on my iPad from People.com about a mother who stabbed her kids to death then killed herself. No, pal. I'm not going to let you put an end to me and make my children's lives miserable. I'll end you first, and the kids and I will go on in peace. The money will be enough to help us bridge over the next period of our lives; until I find a decent job, or my blog takes off.

Wouldn't that be awesome? My mind buzzes with ideas and dreams, and for the first time in a very long time, I'm not worried about money, about Mike, about my future. Soon I find myself going under, and I sleep like a baby all night.

8 DAYS TO DIE

Once the kids are off to school, I gently open the guestroom door to check on Mike. The moment the poorly furnished room opens up for me, I can smell the sour and sweet scent in the air. I feel suffocated and nauseous from the heavy odor, and I stop and press my hand against the doorframe allowing my eyes to grow accustomed to the dim light.

Mike's arms lie draped over his legs. The thick, blue winter blanket is on the floor, and only a white, cotton sheet with tiny blue flowers tucked between his legs and tossed over his left shoulder warms him. His mouth is open, and his face appears pale and hollow.

I close the door because I can't allow myself to feel sorry for him. After everything that's happened in the past few days, after the hostile emotions I've developed for Mike recently, he's still my husband, the man I used to love, the father of my children. But even though we once had a good marriage, I can't approach this situation with any level of sensitivity—his actions have destroyed any chance for our marriage to survive.

Blocking out my feelings is easy at times and extremely difficult at others. I feel this emotional pull again. But I can't slip now. Not today, so I summon an image of Mike making love to Emanuela. That always does the trick.

I climb the stairs to the office and sit down in front of the computer. I log onto USAA Bank website using Mike's new secret password. It works. (No surprise there. Mike could never come up with a smart way of creating passwords for different sites. He predictably uses the same password everywhere.)

I check the bank account because I'm curious to see how much money we have in savings. I'm not planning to run away, not anymore, but it's good to know how tight we're going to be financially between Mike's death and the date the insurance company wires the money to me.

I discover there is $2,458 in the checking account and $8,944 in the savings. With the mortgage and car payments, we still should be okay for three months or so, unless the hitman hustles me for an advance on his fee.

I fold my arms over my chest and lean back on the chair. My eyes get lost in the blurring image of the computer screen. I could still take this money and disappear. If the police found me later, well and alive, would draining our joint bank accounts be considered a crime? If I don't want to end up looking like a wife who's on the run with her husband's money and children, I'll need to prove that my husband's been plotting to kill me.

It wouldn't be easy, and if I failed, I might very well lose custody of my kids. I won't let that happen. Mike isn't stupid. I'm sure he has a Plan B in case something goes haywire with my assassination attempt. I can't risk thinking that I'm smarter than he is.

I open up Microsoft PowerPoint and design a block party

invitation. I have a creative side. I'm good at designing flyers, brochures, and all kinds of promotional materials. Even back in high school, I volunteered to do the designs for our class events.

I press 'print' to make a dozen copies. After the second page, a warning pops up on my screen. The printer is low on ink. As it happens, I'm up to date on our office supply inventory just as much as I'm up to date on our pantry contents.

I open the desk drawer and take out a new box of ink. I replace the empty cartridge and finish printing. Then I set out to place invitations in all the mailboxes along our cul-de-sac.

I descend the staircase as stealthily as a cat. I'm a girl on a mission who doesn't need her husband to stop her now. Like a thief, I go through the laundry room to access the garage. Once there I use the side door to get to our yard and out to the street without alerting the dog.

Three doors to the left a neighbor is stuffing her brood of three into their expensive minivan parked in front of a double garage packed to the brim with worthless junk. Before she notices me, I start toward the opposite side on the sidewalk. I plan to leave an invitation for all the neighbors without having to explain why I'm putting together a block party when I have never organized one before. With one or two exceptions, I don't even talk to the people in my neighborhood. Staying out of each other's business and refraining from getting caught up with the local gossips have been my choice. Nobody seems to mind. Don't we all living in single-dwelling homes to be able to live isolated and undisturbed? Thinking about all this I conclude that it would be a shame if nobody showed up at the party.

I hit the first cluster of mailboxes. I slip in the first invitation. I'm feeling glorious already. I'm about to get into the second mailbox when the garage door next to me rolls up. The roar of a powerful engine as a car inside is starting up startles me. I feel like I want to run home and hide, yet I stay.

An old, poison-green Mustang pulls out of the organized and clean garage. I know very little about cars, but I was somewhat familiar with the driver, with whom we had a nodding acquaintance. Ever since Bruce, our eye-candy single neighbor, moved in, the only thing Mike could talk about was that Mustang. Before this cool American muscle car made its appearance and started attracting attention, Mike used to wash and polish his Porsche every week. But since then, the pampering time he allotted his car was reduced to once a month. I wondered if Mike regretted buying a sports car instead of a classic car like Bruce's; but if I asked him, it would have only confirmed what he was already thinking. He'd get angry and blame me even though I had nothing to do with his choice of cars.

Come to think of it; Mike always had a bad habit of blaming me for everything. He's always been a bully. Maybe subconsciously I married him because he offered me the punishment I believed I deserved for driving that foolish boy into suicide. Fool me once, shame on you; fool me twice, shame on me.

I stand stiff as a statue in my dark-grey yoga pants and a thin champagne-colored tank top for Bruce to pass. Any other day I would have averted my eyes and scampered off to avoid contact, but today I smile. I'm not twenty, but I consider myself okay looking in my athletic getup. After my morning shower, I even managed to comb my hair and make it look almost as good as it did yesterday when I left the salon. This morning I also spent more time putting on makeup rather than fighting with the kids to read. I think my laid-back morning attitude made all of us happier.

The red brake lights flare up on the Mustang as the car comes to a stop next to me. Heat burns in my chest as I watch the car door open. The mystery man nobody in our neighborhood knows, in spite of his living here for months, steps out of his car, dressed in a sharp black suit, black shirt, and black tie. I sense my nipples harden. I know they must be poking through my sports bra and the thin material of my top.

I catch Bruce's eyes sweep over my breasts. I can't breathe. I'm too excited and horny. So this is how it feels when you make eye contact with others instead of sulking around with your head down, living invisibly.

I spent my married years eliminating chances for an affair. I preferred to dress down and stay away from men rather than risk losing Mike and the family we built together over a fling or an inappropriate look or comment. Lately, I feel delivered from those obligations.

"Hey, neighbor," he greets in a gentle purring voice.

My smile widens, and I nod. "So how's the new house?" I ask, watching him intensely. His eyes keep jumping between my chest and my face as if he were a horny teenager who just saw something exciting.

"Love the view." He winks. I blush. *Oh, gosh, that dimple is so cute.*

The heat bursts out of my chest setting my entire boy on fire.

"I'm having ... I mean, my husband and I ..." (Remember you're here to make the neighbors vouch for your happy marriage. Don't blow it now.) "We're having a block party. You're invited, too."

He accepts a flyer from my hand and runs his eyes over it. I examine the creases between his eyebrows as he considers the info as seriously as if it were a life or death contract. *Life or death contract! That came out pretty good. How comic!*

"I'm sure you got better things to do than hang with a bunch of us old folks and married people, but if you got noth. . ."

"I'll be there."

My heart almost leaps out of my rib cage.

His hair is dark and slick, smoothed back with a ton of hair gel. I don't like a bearded man, but his facial hair is trimmed and sexy. I love it.

"Oh. Okay. Sure. We'd love to have you," I babble. I know I should get going, but I don't want to just yet. I enjoy the rush of adrenaline that's been missing from my life. I used to do all kinds of dangerous activities like copiloting for my crazy rally car driver friends—but not since I became a mother. Now I just try to keep safe and stay alive to be around for my kids.

With a flick of my hand that makes me look like a loved-dazed fool, I turn away and start walking toward the next collection of mailboxes. I don't get far when I stop and glance back at my sexy neighbor. That spawn of Aphrodite hasn't moved. I watch him slip the folded invitation into the inside pocket of his jacket.

"Where are you going dressed so fancy?" I ask, wanting to prolong our moment together. I feel like one of those desperate housewives on TV.

He smiles slyly. "I'm the floor manager at Pechanga. I must look the part."

Mike and I have lived here long enough to visit the casino, but we never have. What a shame! What made us become so boring?

"Come by and see me sometime." He nods and gets into his car and pulls out of his driveway. The motor's sound is thrilling to my ears. I watch him until he disappears around the corner. Allowing my imagination to run wild, I absentmindedly slip invitations into the remaining mailboxes.

Back in the house, I put the morning dishes away. After not cleaning for a few days, the house is taking on the look of a home for a family of ten. I wonder when Mike will jump down my throat over the mess.

Whenever I feel depressed or tired, and I don't feel like doing the same chores over and over again like a robot maid, Mike never lets it slide. Just after we moved back to our house and the moving company delivered our household goods, I spent countless hours cleaning, unpacking, and putting stuff away. Not just my junk but also everybody else's. The kids were at school and swamped with homework and after-school activities. Mike had already started back on his job, which he never missed a chance to remind me of frequently.

It took me a good week and a half to get the entire house in order.

When all was done—and done quite well—I crashed. I felt a flood of profound exhaustion come over me. I couldn't wait for Mike to go back to work, so I could spend a day on the couch and watch a bunch of episodes of the second season of *The 100* on the DVR.

At some point, I think between episodes five and six, my conscience started to nibble at me. The move was hard on all of us, yet the kids were at school learning new subjects, and Mike was at work doing whatever he does there all day while I lazed about the whole morning. I turned the TV off, did some laundry, and baked a huge batch of chocolate chip cookies—I ate at least half a dozen before they could cool off.

Then after an overnight shift, Mike came home the next day with a pissed-off attitude as he often did. Before long, he started to take his anger out on me. He complained about the few boxes that still lay in the garage and the dirty dishes I left in the sink. The trash was also overflowing—an unacceptable mistake by Mike's standards.

Wrongly I thought I had the right to ignore my duties for a day or two. But I miscalculated the boundaries I had with Mike.

"What are you doing all day?" he had asked, stuffing the dishwasher with swift, angry movements to make a point. The dishes clinked and thudded. The silverware rattled in the cage.

I stood behind him for a moment, watching him, detesting my existence. I refused to help him. He was already angry with me anyway. Sometimes it's better to let the storm blow over than try to fight it. I had every right to sign off on a lazy day for myself. The kids have weekends. Mike has his days off. I guess I'm the only one who never deserves a break.

Today I don't care about chores or what I'm expected to do at home or if Mike is going to yell at me or not. He already made his choice. He wants to get rid of me and live with another woman. I don't owe him a damn thing anymore.

I don't feel a bit uncomfortable over the dirty dishes that await me as I enter the kitchen where I find Mike leaning against the sink and sipping a hot cup of tea he made for himself. I don't offer him a comment, nor do I ask him how he feels or if he wants me to fix him a bite to eat. My days of blind servitude are over. In marriage, you need to give not just take. Mike broke that rule.

Without a word, I open the refrigerator and take out a cup of yogurt for myself.

"What were you talking about with that dude?" Mike asks in a faint whisper as if even these few words have pained him.

I left the only remaining invitation in the form of a wrinkled paper under my keys on the dresser. I pull it out and show it to Mike.

"I was giving him this." I shove the invitation into his hands.

The utensil drawer is open, and I pull out a spoon. Then I leave the drawer open. If Mike doesn't have to close it, neither do I. The yogurt is delicious. Usually, I gobble my food down because I'm always in a hurry, but this might be my last one, so I savor every bite—coconut, dark chocolate, and almond. Chobani sure knows how to awaken the taste buds.

"You're organizing a party? Why?" Mike's eyes are sunken and dark, rimmed with saggy black circles. He doesn't look scary at all, more pathetic than anything. Before my time's up, I'll use the laxative one more time. Why should I be the only one that has to suffer?

"Yes. For tomorrow," I answer, turning to throw the empty yogurt container into the trash can. I bang my hip against the open utensil drawer. Frowning, I slam it shut.

"On a Thursday?"

"Yeah. Why not? It's a four-day weekend. Presidents' Day, 'member?"

He finishes his tea and places the cup gently on the counter. Every movement he makes appears to be raw and agonizing to him. I find it interesting how there is no remorse in my heart for being the one who caused him all this pain.

"Don't you think you should have talked to me about this first?" he asks with rising fury in his voice.

I know he wants to yell and show me who's the boss of the house, but he's just too weak to do so.

To make up for the sins I committed when I was young I devoted my marriage to please my husband. Since we only have a little over a week to live together, I will spend this precious time annoying the life out of him. Sounds like a great plan to me.

I scrape the cabinet door with my nails. The screeching sound makes a cold shiver run down my spine, which I can't stand, but it also irritates Mike, and that I love.

"Will you stop that!" he grunts.

I give him an evil eye but then tuck my hands into my pockets nonetheless. "It was a sudden idea. I thought you'd like it. We can show the world how happy we are." I couldn't have said this more lackadaisically if I tried.

His brows sink deep over his glazed eyes. "Why would I want to show the world how happy we are?"

"It's just a figure of speech, Mike. Lighten up a little."

I thought he'd be all for the idea of laying a strong foundation for his lies. We both were playing the same game, although he had no idea I was playing, too.

He buckles over; a hand on his stomach. His face twisted in pain and impatience. "You need to cancel it."

"I won't. This is the perfect time to have a block party. You already called in sick. There'll be no school for four days." I wave my hands around like an Italian. He doesn't pick up on the hint. Or he doesn't want to let me know that he did. "You always say we don't have any friends. Now, this is your chance to make some."

He drops his head and for a while massages the back of his neck. When he looks up, his eyes are bloodshot. "This is the stupidest idea I ever heard. I don't want to be friends with anybody here."

"Well, I do."

"Is that right? Who's gonna finance this party? You?"

"No. But neither will you. It's a potluck party."

"What's your new boyfriend gonna bring? His charm?"

"Now you're the one who's being ridiculous." I put my hand up, as if I were offended, and, as such, storm out of the kitchen and rush upstairs.

Mike follows me, his grumbling intensifying with each step.

"Are you having an affair?"

"What? NO!" *The nerve of some people!*

He pulls my shoulder back. "What are you doing when I'm not home and the kids are in school?"

I jerk away angrily as if I were offended by his assumption, although my real plan is to push his buttons until he explodes. If he attacks me, I can take him down and claim self-defense. No need to experiment with poisons.

"What do you think?" I bark into his face. "I usually sleep in, and then drive the kids to school without breakfast. After that, I take an hour-long bath, get a massage, a manicure and pedicure, then Pedro comes and we tear up the sheets all day. Then I go get the kids from school and watch TV the rest of the afternoon."

"Very funny." He pokes his bony fingers into my chest.

"Stop! It hurts!" I scream.

My voice seems to make Mike freeze. I want him to charge at me, but he retreats instead. Probably the importance of the big picture just dawned on him.

"I won't be here for your fucking party," he says in a manner that's composed yet despicable, then he turns his back to me and lumbers away.

My eyes follow him to the bathroom. "We'll see about that," I whisper to myself and fold my arms.

An hour later, I offer him a placatory bowl of chicken soup laced with just enough MiraLax to keep him home tomorrow.

·   ·   ·   ·   ·

> **Stacy:** No, I've never seen a bruise on her. I can't believe she was a battered woman, and I didn't notice it. As I said, Mike had a job where he helped people. He must have seen many abused women and children. It just blows my mind. I guess he knew exactly where to hit her without leaving a mark. Just like my ex.

·   ·   ·   ·   ·

Due to budget cuts, Wednesdays are modified days at school, and by quarter past one I'm back home with the kids. The homeschoolers are already out on the street riding bicycles, and my kids beg me to let them join. No school tomorrow, so I don't see why I couldn't let them play. Besides, I have plenty to do if I want to be ready for tomorrow's party, so I appreciate that they are out of my hair.

In the garage, I'm balancing the kids' backpacks and a pile of mail when I notice a shadow crossing over mine. With kids screaming on the street, cars driving by, dogs barking, I don't even know how I noticed it, but I did. A shuffling sound. A strange smell. I can feel the hair on my arms stand on end. I'm not alone in the garage. I hear someone breathing, and I turn around in panic.

"I thought you didn't have money." The croaky voice and thick accent startle me. My cargo drops from my hands. The letters skid all over the garage floor. One of the kids' metal water canisters lands on my big toe. I hiss from pain. I recognize that voice even though I've only heard it on the phone until now.

A hand grasps my throat from behind and starts dragging me back until I reach the inner wall next to the open garage door. I hate this spot because that's where all the black widow spiders hide: in the aluminum bars, on the wood panels, on the ladder I just tripped over. The back of my head smashes against the plywood, and I spread my legs to find my balance. While I look into the eyes of my assassin, his elbow pushes against my larynx.

He looks nothing like a murderer; more like a photo model in a bike magazine, or perhaps even like a professional soccer player. But I know who he is. This is the man Mike hired to kill me.

I swallow hard, searching deep inside me to find the guts I need to reply.

"I know who you are," I tell him while my fingers try to pry his arms off my neck.

He puts an end to my attempt at breaking free by slapping away my hands. We struggle silently for a while like children, or rather like lovers who are building up for hate sex. Eventually, he wins as he pins me hard against the wall in a part of the garage that's obscured from the street. He could thrust a knife into my heart while my kids are having fun with their buddies a few yards from us. *What happened to my heart? Did it just stop beating?*

"Congratulation for figuring that out, genius." His face is expressionless, ice-cold.

"You gave me time till next week. What are you doing here?" I struggle to speak as his arm is pressing hard against my neck.

"I've been watching you, *Sarah*, and I can't say I like what I see. I don't think you're taking me seriously enough."

"Mom, are you there? You want me to close the garage door?" I hear Mason's voice and the tires of his bicycle screeching on the concrete in front of our house as he brakes. I can't let him see us.

"Go back to play. I got it." I want to yell, but my voice comes out a panicky shriek. I swallow hard. "Go, watch your sister, please," I manage to say with more composure.

The hitman's arm loosens around me as he leans out of the shadows to have a look at the street. I step back and knock over Mason's skateboard that was leaning against a concrete pillar. It rolls all the way to my car and smashes against the tire. Mike will be bursting through that laundry room door any minute now to check on what happened to his precious car. Then all the cards will be out on the table.

I'm not ready to die yet. I've been counting on these eight days I have left. I didn't wash my laundry. I need to go to confession. I want to hug my children one more time.

"I do take you seriously," I say almost breathlessly. I'm showing vulnerability, and I hate myself for it. My children whom I'm supposed to be protecting are right here. They are so close that I worry about their safety. Does Mike even know what a dangerous man he has unleashed upon us? This isn't a game anymore, a story for a new episode of *CSI*. Mike is jeopardizing the safety of his entire family, his own children. I can't allow him to move me out of the way. My children will never be safe with a father who doesn't shy away from murder for money.

I find it very difficult to wrap my mind around this new perspective since I have been under the illusion that Mike loves our children more than he loves his own life. I don't know of another father who shows so much interest in his children and spends so much time with his kids as Mike does.

The hitman pounces at me again and grips my arm. "Look, bitch! Stop spending my money!"

"I d. . . don't," I stutter, pulling away. Funny thing is if he'd hit on me in a bar, I'd fall for those eyes in a heartbeat, especially after a few Mojitos.

He flicks my hair. "You are going to die. Do you understand?" His fingers sink into the flesh on my right temple.

"I don't want to die." I'm crying now. I don't want to, but there's nothing I can do to stop it from happening.

"Then pay up, bitch."

"I don't have the money you're asking from me." My knees are buckling up. I won't be able to stand much longer.

He yanks my hair back hard. I screech in pain. *Mike should be here by now. Where the hell is he?*

"You're not fooling me. Look at you. Look at this house. Your husband told me you have money." I think I recognize his accent now. It's Italian, like Mario Balotelli's. I haven't heard enough foreigners speaking English to develop the knack of distinguishing accents, but I recognize his accent now without a doubt.

After a Liverpool soccer game, I listened to Balotelli's interview. I couldn't make the connection before because Balotelli has terrible

English, and he mumbles, while my attacker speaks fluently. For a moment, I wonder if there's any connection between Emanuela and this guy.

"Look, everything you see here is mortgaged up to the hilt. I don't work. My parents can't support us." (I omit the part that they could support us only we aren't talking.) "We don't have the kind of money you're asking for."

He kicks the same pillar the skateboard had been leaning against, and this time the end of an extension cord jumps off the nail from where it was loosely hanging.

"I don't believe you. Your husband promised me fifty grand if I take you out." There's a touch of panic in his voice. Maybe it's my time to capitalize on his confusion.

The extension cord is dangling in front of me. I calculate my chances of pulling it out long enough to wrap it around the guy's neck and choke him. Then I take a moment to evaluate whether I'm even capable of doing something like that.

I shake my head, watching him through half-shut eyes. If I'm not strong enough to take this hulk of a man down, at least I can intimidate him with my stare. "Maybe he wants to pay you from the million dollar insurance money he'll get when I die. But he only offered you fifty grand to kill me! That doesn't sound fair if you ask me. Think about it."

"You told me on the phone that he only gets fifty thousand if you die."

"Yes, I know what I said, but I did a little search around the house, and I found a new policy. He raised the amount payable." I don't emphasize the million dollars again, because I don't need him to get any ideas. "But look, I know for sure that there is a policy on Mike, too. And you told me that you aren't so keen on killing a woman."

He lets go of my arm, leaving bleeding cuts on my skin where his nails cut into my flesh.

"What are you saying?"

"Look, what if I get rid of Mike on my own and make it look like an accident. Then when the insurance pays me off, I'll give you two hundred thousand, and you can keep the house in French Valley as well." I throw the part in about the house to make the rabbit jump out of the bushes.

His brows crease. I bet I surprised him. "I don't know. My sister needs Mike for the baby."

The shock arrives fast and hard, like a blow to the stomach. I feel every syllable strike against my guts. I should have known that there was a connection between a hitman with a heavy accent and Mike's Italian ladylove. If I hadn't allowed self-pity to consume me, I would have figured it out long ago. I have a 156 IQ for Christ's sake, or at least I used to have.

As I search for the right thing to say, I catch his confused expression, the way his eyes look at me yet don't see me; how his upper lip wrinkles up the skin around his nose. I got him off balance. This moment I created may be my only chance to gain control over him and our deal.

As my pain transforms into rage and hatred, I understand what I must do. I'm going to kill Mike and pin the murder on these 'exemplary' Italian conspirators. You just don't come to my country and act as if you own the place.

"Or how about this?" I step closer to the mountain of a man and talk straight into his face with a measured voice. "I'll fake a car accident where my kids and I *die,* but we don't. (I use air quotes when I say the word *die,* just in case he's as dumb as he looks.) When the insurance pays Mike the money, I'll hack into his bank account and withdraw as much as I can. Then I split the money with you. Also, your sister can have Mike all to herself. With me completely out of the picture. What do you say?" I press on.

He touches his chin while his eyes seem to get lost in Mike's neon advertisement collection over the workbench. "It could work. But why not just kill you and get the money from your husband instead?"

"Because Mike lied to you. He's gonna get a ton of money when I die, but he isn't willing to give a shit to you or your sister. Trust me; I know how selfish my husband is."

At the latter statement, he makes a funny face overshadowed with doubt. His expression irks me to death, but he's right. I don't know my husband at all.

"How do you know he won't hire someone else to kill you? A million bucks should be enough to do whatever he wants to do to cover his tracks." I strike the iron while it's hot, but he remains unresponsive. Maybe I should slow down with the offers. They might be too much for him to comprehend. "Look, I'm offering you something here that can help you start a new life back in Italy . . . or here in California, whatever you want," I add it as a side note.

"What makes you think I'm not drowning in money already?" he blurts out all offended.

I'm beginning to see past his act. He's a fake. I've seen enough assassins on TV to know how they look and act. "I've done lots of jobs before you." He attaches his statement at the end like punctuation.

"Yeah, I can see that you're a professional all right," I flatter with both voice and gestures. "But ask yourself this; can there ever be enough money?"

He hesitates. I need to press on.

"Fifty thousand versus two hundred thousand; how much is that in Euros?" I pretend my hands are part of a scale, indicating that it's time for him to pick a side.

"Alright. I feel you." Oh my gosh! He's learning English from rap videos.

"Our deal is still on? Eight days?"

He looks at his watch. "Seven days and ten hours."

Geez, at least he can count. I'd better keep that in mind when I hand over the money to this lowlife.

7 DAYS TO DIE

People's chatter and occasional laughter drift into the kitchen. A motley group of neighbors has gathered in the street in front of our house. They are here for an afternoon of fun and gossip. My head is still heavy with worry, but the chaos and clutter somehow manage to make me smile. Maybe instead of the cemetery or the exotic beaches of Spain, I'll end up in a nuthouse.

Before retreating to the safety of my kitchen, I spent the last hour getting familiar with my neighbors, circulating among them and dropping hints about my happy marriage. Were it not for struggling with my internal tug of war this little get-together might have been an enjoyable event. Maybe all I needed to be happier were friends; warm bodies with opinions and laughs and smiles. I should have made more effort to befriend my neighbors. Friends are the glue that holds a marriage together my mother used to say. Friends are the reality check to keep us sane. But again, wasn't it my parents' sexy best friend that almost caused their divorce?

Betty was an obnoxious and self-absorbed woman who also happened to be the wife of my father's business partner. As a kid, I was oblivious to the way my parents' marriage worked or didn't work. That is, until one day Kyle and I saw our dad and Betty making out in our kitchen. Kyle suggested we not tell mom what we witnessed. She found out anyway. I still remember the yelling and name-calling. It was quite ironic that dad was the first one to turn his back on me when my behavior after Kyle's death didn't measure up to *his standards*. I guess it's human nature to offer criticism yet not be able to take it ourselves.

The knife moves in my hand in perfect rhythm as I cut up a ripe, juicy pear. The fruit salad was the first dish that disappeared even though my neighbors went above and beyond with their food contributions to the potluck. We had homemade pasta salad from Chrissie and her family, a seven-layer dip from Trish and her husband, mini sausages wrapped in bacon and dough from my next-door neighbor Carol.

Mike had chosen Pink Martini on Pandora and connected it to his Sony Bluetooth speaker in the family room. From the soothing music, my hips start swaying as I work on the fruit absentmindedly.

All morning I'd been inexplicably blissful. My sweet dreams about Bruce, the Mustang-driving, handsome neighbor, may have had something to do with my mood. I should cut back on late-night drinking. The hitman assaulted me in my own house yesterday, yet I spent the night after dreaming about making love to a stranger. Mike is right: I have to get my head examined.

A candle is burning on the mantel in the living room: orange blossom. From the window, I see the kids kicking a soccer ball in the backyard. I'm alone in the kitchen. All the guests are outside in front, snacking and drinking. Mike is out there with them, effortlessly blending in with the crowd like strawberries in a margarita. Once he realized that the party meant loading up on local gossip and cold beer, he gave in to my plan and turned from a grumpy party pooper into an enthusiastic organizer.

Just an hour before the first guests showed up, Mike, the kids, and I set up the folding chairs and tables on the street in front of our house. I borrowed a yellow stand-up sign that warns people about children at play on the road from the family of seven who lives on our cul-de-sac. The Homeschoolers.

If I didn't know any better, I'd have allowed myself to enjoy the preparation. But with only seven days to live or die, I've had a hard time looking at Mike without feeling the urge to claw his eyes out. The dark forces he had unleashed on us, and the desperate times in our future didn't seem to affect my husband. I married a man with a heart of stone.

Since losing weight over the past week, eight pounds to be exact (I measured myself this morning), I finally fit into the cocktail dress I bought many years ago at Marshalls.

I don't usually purchase pretty dresses on a whim, but when I saw the model posing on the poster in front of the rack, I had to have it. At the time, I would have given an arm and a leg to look as good as she did in that dress. I used to have a body to be proud of, but that was before I got married and had my first child. But as Mike always reminds me, it doesn't matter what I was in the past. The only thing that matters is what's happening now.

When I bought the dress, I was out of shape, soft, cushioned. The largest size dress in that style offered by the store was an eight. Cramming my size-ten body into it was impossible. I bought it anyway, believing that the sight of that dress hanging outside on my closet door was going to be the greatest inspiration for me to get on the treadmill. Besides, it was on sale.

Eight years have gone by since, and the dress was still hanging in my closet, untouched. Today I wanted to look my best, so I pulled it out carefully. My heart was swelling with anticipation as I searched the fabric for moth holes but found none. At last, I slipped it on. It fit me like a perfect glove. Who knew that stress would be the cause of my shedding pounds?

I start chopping up a cantaloupe, my hips twisting to the beat of the music. As I move, the silk fabric of my dress brushes against my skin, creating a tingling sensation.

When I feel a hand pressing against my hip, I jump. Not just because whoever it was decided to sneak up on me, but also because I'm embarrassed over my dancing. I hiss when I realize that I sliced the inside of my left middle finger. Strangely, I find the pain more pleasant than painful, like when I enjoy the burn from hot peppers. Maybe this is my new thing: sadism.

Though I had my share of wild years, since becoming a mother I've turned into a person of habit, while Mike remained the brave one, eager to venture into new things, eat spicy foods, and live on the edge. In Germany—where we lived for two years in the early part of our marriage—he nearly killed himself with a bunch of hot peppers he ate on a dare. All of our friends got a kick out of how Mike was gasping for air. I was the only one who panicked.

It took Mike twelve years to talk me into eating spicy peppers again. And I'm happy I did. The pain on my tongue added a spike to my monotonous life. It was a sign that there was still life in me that I could feel and could be hurt. After that, eating food with a kick in it became a must. The only problem was that with time the pain became insignificant. I started yearning for more pain. Bruising a knee in the shower, bumping an elbow on a doorframe, even depilating my legs or plucking my eyebrows became pleasurable.

Sucking my bloody finger, I spin around to confront my overly affectionate husband.

"I didn't mean to startle you." The air becomes suspended in my lungs from the voice that is too easy to recognize. Those hands on my hips didn't belong to Mike. It was Bruce who touched me. I feel a single drop of perspiration roll down my spine. Not from the heat. Not even from the spicy food.

I pause to take a measure of his appearance. The business suit is gone, replaced by loose-fitting blue jeans, flip-flops, and a soft-looking black T-shirt bearing the sign: 'Livin' for the moment.' His hair is flowing. Wavy. Sexy.

"You shaved," I say, feeling like an imbecile from staring with my mouth agape.

He offers me an alluring smile, touching his face. "I do shave, you know. Every Thursday." He tilts his head to the side and buries his fingers into his dark, thick hair and starts rubbing his scalp.

My heart somersaults. Bruce is flirting with me. Despite my uneventful life, my decade-long absence from the dating scene, I still recognize a man's teasing.

There was a time, back when I started dating Mike, that the number of men who flirted with me increased as if they sensed that I was no longer available, and they were lured by the challenge as if the competition was worth more than the actual reward. I didn't reciprocate their flirtation.

After we tied the knot, Mike became overly jealous. For a couple of years, he suspected every male friend around us of having a crush on me. I can't count on my fingers and toes how many times I had to swear on my life that I was not having an affair.

Our last jealousy-induced fight happened in Manhattan Beach. Five months pregnant with Mason, I wore a tight black mini dress at the bar where we were to meet his friends. Mike wanted to show his long-time-no-see high school buddies how settled his life was—great job, pregnant wife.

I was waiting at the bar sipping on my virgin strawberry margarita and waiting for Mike and his friends to return from the men's room when a guy dropped himself into the seat next to me. Due to the dim lighting, my small bulging belly was almost invisible. The guy wasn't cute or charismatic in any way, but I didn't want to be rude and send him away. I was expecting my first child. It was supposed to be the happiest time of my life. Mike didn't see my gesture as a common courtesy. No apology in this universe was enough to tame his fury. He couldn't understand that our marriage was worth more to me than a cheap flirt at a bar. He asked me to prove it. I did. And I've been doing it ever since. I bottled up, locking away the sexy, available side of me in the room of unnecessary things in my head. For over a decade, I consigned the part of me that was still free and desirable to a dark corner with nothing more than a small candle in her hand. The flame was weak, only flickering vaguely on the verge of being extinguished.

Now, with Bruce standing in my kitchen, inches away from me, my nose full with his aftershave, I feel the tiny flame flicker back to life. My little candle is intensifying and turning into a bonfire. Willingly, I feed that fire. I yearn for the heat to burn me. I want that pain.

Bruce takes my hand in his. "You're bleeding."

The cut is deep enough to allow blood to trail down on my skin and drip onto the floor.

"I can imagine what you must think of me. A clumsy housewife who can't even cut up a pear without slicing her finger."

"To be honest, it makes me think twice about eating the salad Mary brought. Old lady's fingers." He pretends to shudder, wriggling his fingers.

I laugh because the face he makes is so sincere and cute. "As I told you earlier, this is an older neighborhood. I bet your girlfriend isn't so thrilled about your buying a house here."

He emits a muffled chuckle while shaking his head. "Where do you keep your first aid kit?" he asks. "We better put a Band-Aid on the cut before you bleed all over the macaroni salad, too."

I feel the heat filling up the pores on my neck and face from how masterfully he dodged my carefully phrased question, which was designed to find out if he had a girlfriend, a fiancée perhaps.

"It's upstairs. I'll go get it," I jabber, wrapping a piece of paper towel over the cut. I raise my eyes to probe Bruce's face and see if there is any sign of disgust in his expression. But there is only one expression I recognize: lust. What could have turned him on? The sight of blood?

The way he holds my gaze makes my stomach quiver. Why is he even here today? He should be on a yacht somewhere in the Pacific Ocean with a bunch of hot babes in tiny bikinis seeking ways to pleasure him.

Approaching footsteps from the living room break up our staring contest. I spin toward the sink, turn the cold water on, and put my finger in the stream.

"Honey, are you there?" I hear Mike calling for me.

"I'm here," I say. Shaking the feeling of guilt is hard. I've been feeling guilty for too long.

I hear the clatter of plates and metal against porcelain. Bruce is getting food for himself. I want to ask him—I need to ask him—to sneak out through the patio door, but I think better of it. Mike is the one with a secret lover. I've done nothing wrong. Not yet.

"Thanks for the food, Mrs. Johnson," Bruce says with affection, speaking loud and holding up a bowl of mixed fruit.

"Oh . . . no problem." I clear my throat to get more power into my voice. "Thanks for coming."

Mike appears in the doorway, blocking Bruce's way out. I envision the bottle of Bacardi in the cabinet above the boys' heads and a pack of smokes. I could use them both to calm my nerves.

After stealing a glance at me, Mike holds out a hand. "It's Bruce, right?"

"And . . . you're Mike?" They shake hands. It's hard to miss their fingers gripping hard; purple fingertips. My throat is itching for a Mojito I could make with that Bacardi. I picture the cluster of mint leaves around an old tree stump at the side of our house. My mouth starts watering.

While I wipe up the blood from the floor and countertop, Mike and Bruce talk about cars. My heart's pounding so fast that I can hardly make out more than a word or two, not as if I'd understand what they're talking about when it comes to cars.

"Thanks for the salad, Mrs. Johnson."

A hand on my hip, I lean against the cabinet. "Call me Sarah." I smile. Idiot. Dumb chick.

He bows his head. "Sarah," then faces Mike. "Great party, pal. Thanks for having me. Maybe you could come over sometime. We could grab a beer and talk more about cars."

I can't tell how Mike feels about Bruce's offer. I just hope he won't tell me because today there would be hell to pay if I have to listen to his complaining and paranoia.

With Bruce gone, my heartbeat returns to normal. Mike picks out a slice of peach from the bowl of fruit salad with his fingers. "Cool dude," he comments without making eye contact.

"Since when are you into cars and gambling," I say, hiding my injury from Mike. I don't need his babying. I don't need him to perform first aid on me. I don't need him to be anywhere near me, period.

He offers me his signature you-are-an-idiot face. Then he fishes out a cube of watermelon from the salad and drops it into his mouth. "What did he want?"

"What everybody else wants today. More fruit salad."

"Are you pissed or something?"

"No. Why?"

He shrugs, and then his mouth curves up in one corner. *Sick bastard.* He likes it when I'm spicy. I don't want him to like me.

"I'm gonna run down to Bevmo for some more beer. Need anything?"

I pretend to be busy, so I don't have to look at him. "No, thanks."

"Hey, Sarah."

"What?"

"You wanna go up to the room for a quickie?" His hands are pulling up the dress to my thighs. I press my eyes together hard. *Think of a happy place. Think of a happy place.*

With a forced smile, I tilt my head to the side. "Come on, Mike. Don't be ridiculous. We have guests."

He kisses my neck, but instead of pleasant warmth, I feel cold. I should never have put on this dress, or I should have at least eaten a bunch of that garlic bread that the old dude with arm tattoos from the house up the street brought to the party. Garlic breath would be a distinct advantage now. Like a silver bullet for a werewolf, garlic would dampen my husband's urges.

I envision the bottle of MiraLax in the cabinet. A plate of deviled eggs is within arm's reach. Just a few drops of laxative on an egg would get Mike away from me for the rest of the day. But I'm pinned to the sink, his burgeoning penis pressing against my butt. The knife I used to cut up the fruit lies in the sink in front of me. I reach for it when someone clears his throat behind us. "Do you have some cayenne pepper?"

My middle-aged paralegal neighbor Claire's longtime boyfriend is standing in the kitchen, a plate of potato salad in his right hand and a knowing smirk on his face.

To my relief, Mike releases me. And though this is what I want it's not what I need at the moment. This party has only one purpose: to show everybody how happily married we are. I must take advantage of the situation. Quickly I kiss Mike's cheek and turn to our guest with my face stretched out from a feigned smile.

"Yes, I do have some. Here." I take the container out of the cabinet and hand it to the diminutive grey-haired man. Before closing the door, I notice the bright purple label on the bottle of MiraLax in the corner. I push a jar of strawberry jam in front of it. Mike would never touch that. He never cooks. He also hates strawberries.

. . . . .

Claire: Look, my boyfriend saw Mike terrorizing Sarah in the kitchen. He said he had to intervene because Mike was pinning her to the sink, and he was very rough with her. I didn't find the story significant enough at the time to ask Sarah what happened. Probably I wouldn't ask anyway. You just don't walk up to your neighbor you barely know and ask her about something like that. You should talk to Carol. She seems to know all about what was going on in that house. Maybe Sarah and Bruce had something going on, and Mike walked in on them. I don't know. On second thought, can you please delete this last part? I won't testify to that in court anyway. Without evidence, it's all just a speculation, hearsay.

Trish: I thought the party was a success. The food was great. My husband and I enjoyed our time there. If they had any problems, it didn't show. I wasn't really paying attention though. I usually mind my own business. Although, I do remember Carol, the divorced woman who lives in the house on their right, talking to Bruce, the new neighbor. She kept offering him drinks and seemed like she was flirting with him. And it was just ridiculous because Bruce is half her age. Then she got agitated when Bruce spent a lot of his time inside Sarah's house. I have no idea what was going on inside the house, but Carol was running her mouth, as usual, bashing Sarah and upsetting all of us. I mean I don't hold a grudge against Carol, but I try to stay clear of her because once she corners you, then you can't escape her gossip train. I work all day. I'm busy. I'm also not interested in other people's lives. But the party was an excellent idea. It was good getting to know all those lovely people. I'll miss the Johnsons. They were quiet people. The best neighbors you could ever wish for.

Chrissie: Look, I have five kids at home to worry about, so whatever the Johnsons were involved in, I'm just happy it's over. We moved to Temecula because it's a very safe city. We don't need people in our neighborhood that may be part of some drug cartel or a gang or whatever the Johnsons were part of. I'm freaked out from just thinking about how my kids played with their kids. I had to take all my children to a doctor and get them checked out to see if they ever used drugs . . . Nobody told me anything about any drugs; I'm just assuming. I mean, what else could have happened?

Benny: I don't know anything about a party. I wasn't invited.

Bruce: I went inside to get a bowl of

fruit salad. Then Mike got me talking
about my car. It's a refurbished old
Mustang… Oh, yeah, is that what Carol
said? Well, she seems to know everything
about everybody… I don't want to comment
on that.

. . . . .

My hands press against the cold tile as I lean against the countertop in the master bath, my bleeding finger still wrapped in a strip of paper towel. I didn't come up here to cry, but I can't stop the tears pouring from my eyes. Maybe the sight of blood or Bruce's flirting caused it—I don't know, but as I climbed the stairs, the weight of my situation hit me hard again. I gave my life to this family, to Mike, yet he's the one who always complains about how hard married life is. He never considers for a moment that I had bigger dreams for myself than just washing everybody's dirty laundry and disinfecting bathroom floors that with two males with a bad aim in the house always reeks of urine.

I love cheering for my children at their soccer games and sitting in at their award ceremonies or school plays, but there was a time when I wanted to make my mark on the world, just always missed my chance. And now when my life may end soon, all I'm going to be remembered for will be my delicious ceviche, and that only by my children.

If the hitman takes my life next week, I won't be leaving a legacy behind. From the insurance money, Mike can easily hire a cleaner and a nanny to do what I've been doing every day. Soon after my death, all the people who knew me will forget about me, even Mason and Tammy. Maybe their new mommy will be great in the kitchen and with kids. Perhaps the world will be a better place without me. I catch my reflection in the mirror. I feel ashamed of my feeble attempt at looking sexy, like a real woman. I look ridiculous. Probably the neighbors are all talking about me right now. Who am I kidding?

"Look at her desperate attempt to seduce our new neighbor," I imagine the woman in the rental across the street to say.

"A respectable wife and mother wouldn't put on a dress like that. I always knew she had no class," would say the bitter old hag four houses up on the right. Then her husband would comment, as he always does, like an echo, an afterthought, "Oh, she has class all right, but it's all low." And they all laugh until I emerge from the house with a new plate of deviled eggs that they all love and would gobble down until they are all gone. Then they would call out their pleasantries to me, smiling and complimenting me on my excellent culinary skill.

Why am I having this party when I don't even like my neighbors? Oh, yeah. To show them how wonderful my marriage is. Unfortunately, Mike is playing his part almost too convincingly.

I rip the drawer open and take out a box of Rite Aid band-aids. The bedroom floor creaks. The same spot it always does from the loose screws. The footsteps are soft, not what I'm used to hearing. I roll my eyes because I'm not in the mood for Mike's games. As long as we are alone, I don't have to pretend that everything is all right between us.

While I wait for Mike to appear, demanding his due as a husband, I search for a weapon. Not having a better option, I grasp the electric toothbrush and rip the head off to expose the metal tip. But it's Bruce who steps into the bathroom as casually as if he belongs; as if it weren't the first time. My fingers loosen, and the toothbrush drops out of my hand. My shame at being caught crying is stronger than my surprise. I remove a towel from the towel rack and wipe the tears from my face.

"Need some help?" he asks. Why couldn't Mike be a little bit more caring and sensitive?

I gawk at him, though I don't want to. My sexy, feminine side, which had retreated into the corner a while ago, was again holding the candle with the tiny flame.

"I knocked. I swear." He smiles, placing a hand on the wall and leaning his head against it. His tan skin against the light gray wall is striking.

"I'm okay. It's just a small cut. It happens more often than you'd think." I manage to say at last searching for a box of tissues. Then I remember that the package of three is still in the shopping bag in the laundry room. I was supposed to distribute them around the house last week, but I forgot.

I step into the tiny toilet area that marks the end of the elongated bathroom like a nail on a finger and rip off a piece of toilet paper and blow my nose. I bet this classy man has never seen a girl do that.

When I move back in front of the sink, Bruce is only inches away from me. He grabs hold of my waist and sits me up on the hard tile. I don't resist.

His hands are on my thighs. He gently separates my legs and pushes himself closer. I tremble, and my breathing becomes irregular. I act like a virgin schoolgirl on her first date. I must look ridiculous to him. I'm a mature woman for Christ's sake.

He takes the box from beside me and pulls out a bandage. I lift my hand up, exposing the raw cut.

"Where do you keep your cotton balls?" he asks, and I point at the second drawer on the stand-alone cabinet by the toilet. We bought that affordable piece of furniture at an IKEA in Italy and had it shipped here, but never really found the right spot for it. Now it's pushed against the wall next to the toilet where it stands out like a sore thumb. I bet in his house everything matches like walking into a Living Spaces showroom. Not a speck of dust. Not a piece of furniture out of place. Only harmony.

He slides the drawer open. I know exactly what he'll find. Tampons, pads, an empty bottle of vaginal wash, a box of Monistat cream in case I get a yeast infection from having sex with Mike. I still can't stomach the fact that I had those nasty infections so often because Mike was cheating on me right and left. My stomach churns.

There is also a box of Q-tips and a bag of cotton balls tucked in there somewhere. He takes what he needs without a comment.

He moistens one cotton ball and wipes the dry blood off my finger. He rubs a dash of Neosporin onto the cut with the tip of his finger. The scent of his hair enchants me. I watch him ripping the paper off the bandage and placing it on my skin. When he moves away to throw the trash into the bin, I want him back close to me so badly that I have to hold myself down not to tell him how I feel.

Mike walks around me naked all the time. Forces my hand on his erection. But those moments hold no allure for me anymore. The way Bruce brushed my skin with the cotton ball made me wet.

He throws me a sideways glance. I'm still sitting on the counter. I tell myself that I'm ready to go back to the kitchen and finish the fruit salad before Mike gets back from the store. But I don't move. I'm waiting. I don't know for what because this day is about to ensure that the police would never suspect that I had anything to do with Mike's death. Today I have to prove to the world that we had no marital problems. We are the perfect image of an ideal family.

I need to go downstairs, hug my children, and kiss their cheeks. I need to sit on my husband's lap and laugh at his jokes. I need to push him gently on the shoulder when he makes an inappropriate comment about our bedtime routines. I need to come up with a few all by myself—the kind that suggests that we're still into each other and still very active in bed. We aren't one of those married couples who roll onto each other once a week to release some pressure.

But I can't get myself going. I'm clenching the edge of the counter with both hands, my legs wide open, my heart doing backflips. It feels like old times. In my head, I'm back in my childhood kitchen teasing my brother's friends. The fire of the candle is blazing again. One touch from Bruce was enough for my mind to burst into flames.

As if reading my thoughts, he launches himself at me and presses his mouth onto mine. His hands force themselves up on my thighs, pulling my dress with them. His tongue slips into my mouth. My spine flexes, and I find myself unzipping his pants. With Mike gone to the store, we only have minutes to ourselves.

One of his hands cups my right breast, freeing it from the confines of the silk bra. I'm so crazy with passion that I become lightheaded. I haven't felt this mad for ages. I don't know why but I think of Mike breathing on top of me, thrusting into me over and over again, leisurely, uninterestingly. His face says, "Here, I fucked you so shut up for a week."

I shake my head to get rid of Mike's face. I won't let him ruin this moment for me.

I cry. I shake. I'm out of my element.

I hear the clinking of a belt. Bruce dropped his jeans to his ankles. He isn't gentle as he enters me, but I wouldn't wish this to happen in any other way. His wet breath on my neck and his hands pressing into the flesh on my ass, he pushes against me over and over again. I bite my finger to keep my voice down.

For a moment, I lean back and take in the entire picture. Bruce's glazed eyes instead of Mike's. What just happened? Before yesterday, all we said to each other was a neighborly hello, and now he's invading my most private parts, doing to me the most intimate things two human beings can do to each other.

For a moment I think of tomorrow, but I stop myself. Tomorrow I might be dead, but this is today. This moment is right now.

I envision Mike's face when the coroner tells him, "She's had consensual intercourse in the past forty-eight hours. A little rough perhaps but it was consensual."

Then all the images in my head melt into white space. I have feelings between my legs I only had vague memories of from my early marriage years.

When I reach a climax, I bite my finger so hard I taste blood. Soon after that, Bruce collapses against my chest. I bury my face into his hair. We remain plastered onto each other, waiting for our breathing to calm.

"I'm sorry. I don't know what came over me," Bruce whispers, peppering my neck with tiny kisses.

I know I messed up. Now if the police question Bruce, he can say that I cheated on my husband with him.

"I'm happily married. I don't do things like this," I say, but I'm too scared to move. I wanted him. I still want him.

He straightens up in front of me and takes my face in his hand. His lips are warm on mine.

"You didn't do anything wrong. I gave you no choice."

"We always have a choice," I whisper, but I know how stupid it sounds. Instead of running away or calling the police after learning about Mike's plan to have me killed, I've been plotting to turn the tables and kill him.

He takes the roll of toilet paper from the holder, rips a strip and wipes himself. "I think it'll be better if you change your dress before you start mingling again," he says with the cutest smile that makes me want him more. He's so cool about this whole thing. He makes me feel as if we'd been friends our entire lives.

I pull my dress down. My upper thighs are sticky. I rearrange my bra. I feel like a common hooker. This was the first time I ever cheated on Mike. I'm not even sure this counts. A quickie. A type of intercourse drunk teenagers would do in the back of a van.

"Just go downstairs. I'll wash up," I say, holding back a smile. I feel alive. I don't want to die anymore. I need more of these feelings in my life. I need more Bruce.

His T-shirt is back on. *Livin' for the moment.* I wonder if he chose to wear this shirt on purpose. I dismiss that thought at once. A guy like Bruce would never fantasize over an uninteresting housewife like me.

"I think I overstepped my boundaries here. I feel like I owe you an apology." He brushes his thumb over his lips and lets out a hissing sound. "I couldn't help myself. I'm sorry. Not really . . ." he smiles again, and I love the sight of it.

I can't hold my smile back; it escapes. "You don't owe me anything other than your silence."

"No, seriously. I'd like to take you out for dinner. You and your husband. On Saturday night."

I picture all three of us around a table eating spaghetti. A strange puff-like sound breaks out my mouth.

"I don't think it's a good idea. Besides, Mike's working a forty-eight-hour shift over the weekend."

"Then just you and me. Like friends. Neighbors. Please say yes."

I look away, massaging my neck. I still feel Bruce inside me. I'm raw. Sensitive. Happy. "I don't know."

"Come on. Live a little. We can call Mary to join us if that would make you feel better." He reaches for my hand and kisses my knuckles. I want him so badly. I want him to rip my clothes off and make me his again.

"It's a bad idea."

"I promise I won't try anything." He crosses his heart. "Just an innocent dinner. Nothing more. Maybe some dessert? Have you tried the Tres Leche cake in the casino? It's to die for." He pinches two of his fingers and kisses the tips.

I give in. "I suppose it's okay. I've never been to Pechanga before."

"You won't regret it," he says. I recognize the sign of triumph that smoothes out his face. I already do regret it. "And to avoid any confusion, I won't come to your house. How about I pick you up at eight at Lowes, by the flower stands."

"Are you afraid of our mutual neighbor with big eyes and even bigger mouth?"

He shrugs, arching his eyebrows. "I thought you were." He's hypnotizing me with his eyes. I want him to take me to bed right now. But when he steps in to kiss me, I push him away.

"Now go. Mike could be back any second now." I laugh.

Despite my efforts, he plants a kiss on my lips before walking away.

On his way out his weight makes the floorboard sing again. I remain on the countertop, tracing the outlines of my lips.

When I come back to my senses, I slip out of the dress, trying to suppress my smile that refuses to stay down. I touch my breast where Bruce's tongue caressed me. My entire body starts trembling.

I avoid the mirror while I'm undressing. I can't look at myself in the shower either because all I see is Bruce's hands on me. I soap up between my legs, still overly sensitive. Maybe Mike has been seeking the same excitement when sleeping with his *adult friends* and Italian bimbo. After what just happened to me, I can't really blame him.

. . . . .

Trish: Who told you that? Carol? I don't
believe she was having an affair. I saw

186

Bruce and Sarah acting casual at the
party. Most of the time they weren't
even talking. Bruce arrived late. Then
he was the first one to leave. I don't
think it was suspicious. He's a single
young man I'm sure he's got better
things to do than spend his free time
with a bunch of old farts. Besides, I
believe he works at Pechanga or Pala
casino or some other casino. I don't
gamble. Anyway, he may have left the
party early because he had to go to
work, and not because he got into it
with the Johnsons. If you want my
advice, don't put too much stock in
Carol's tales.

Mary: It's so sad. (Sobbing sounds.) I
can't believe this has happened. She was
like a daughter to me. I loved her
children as if they were my
grandchildren. (Blowing her nose.) I
don't know what to say. She was a
fantastic mother. She loved those kids
so much. I'm sorry, but I need to sit
down. Can I get a glass of water?

. . . . .

Near bedtime, I'm in the kid's bathroom washing Tammy's hair.
She can do it herself, but I need to keep myself busy because of
Mike's being overly friendly with me tonight. I've already brushed
off one of his attempts to have sex, saying that I needed to clean
the kitchen after the party. Then I searched for more excuses. I
vacuumed the entire house. I cleaned up Mason's messy room.
That turned out to be a great idea because it took a long time to
complete.

When the entire house was in order, I hid in the bathroom with
Tammy. I needed to find a way to escape Mike's clutches without
resorting to the laxative again. He just recovered from a severe

bout of diarrhea this morning. I'm not worried about his health; I'm only concerned that he might suspect that I am the culprit here. I don't even know why I care if he finds out. He's the one who put a price on my head.

Mike shows up at the kid's bathroom door, smiling. I know that smile. He didn't give up on getting laid tonight. If there is no horse, the donkey will do. I'm nobody's backup plan. Besides, no way I'll allow him to violate my memory of Bruce.

"I shouldn't have drunk that second shot of Tequila," I tell him, pressing down on my temple.

"What makes you say that?"

"I think I got a migraine. I can't wait to get to bed." I let out an elaborate sigh.

I'm already wearing sweats. The last time Mike was aroused by my tight top, I learned my lesson about choosing appropriate attire when he's alone with me.

"I know something that'll make you feel better," he says, creating that stupid sound with his mouth he always does when he wants to get some. It used to turn me on; now I want to punch his face off.

I jerk my head toward Tammy. "Come on, Mike. Stop it." I know if I keep this up long enough he'll lose interest. I might even tell him that I started my period. Hopefully, he won't remember that I just had it two weeks ago.

The heater is blowing warm air onto me as I enter the bedroom. At this time of the night, Mike usually watches a soccer game or plays on the Xbox, with me snuggled up beside him and pretending that I enjoy whatever he's doing. But on the one night I don't want him here, he's in bed, his naked upper body glimmering in the moonlight. *Hell no!*

"I think I'll take the kids to your mom's tomorrow. What do you think?" I say, my stomach in knots.

He puts his hands under his head. "I'm sure she'd love to see them."

I slowly change out of my clothes and search for my pajamas. I pull out the black sports bra Mike hates on me from the drawer and put it on. I also jump into a pair of the biggest granny panties I can find in my drawer. My choice of sleepwear tonight will be oversized sweatpants and a T-shirt with old bleach spots on it.

"It's a long weekend. The kids need to get out of the house, and I need to do a big spring cleaning." *Make it sound more disgusting.* "You know, clean out the poop from the chicken coop, wash windows, and scrub the toilets."

"I can hire someone to do that for you. You work too much," Mike says, and the meaning of his words sets in immediately. Since when does he care about how much I work?

"I don't want you to spend money. I can do it. No problem." I reach for my temples. "Oh, gosh, my head wants to split open."

"Come here. I'll give you a massage." *What? He hasn't given me a massage since we left Guam ten years ago.*

"No thanks. I feel irritable. I think I'm gonna have my period tonight." That should do the trick.

"Let's not let this last night go to waste then. Come here." He opens the blanket for me. I wish I had a poisonous snake or spider so I could throw it at him. I still have my poisonous words.

"I'm not feeling up to it, Mike. Okay?" I'm angry now. Frustrated. Why is nothing working?

He gives me the eye. "You never do," he says and turns to the other side.

From the joy of victory, I become ecstatic. I crawl under the covers and turn to my side, my back toward Mike. But I can't fall asleep for the longest time because I keep reliving the wild intercourse with Bruce over and over in my head.

6 DAYS TO DIE

After a night of wet dreams, I get out of bed while it's still dark and quiet in the house. I have no intention of staying in bed with Mike any longer than is absolutely necessary. Especially when, after chasing sleep for days, I finally had a solid night's sleep last night.

I never remember my dreams in the morning. Either I don't dream at all, or whatever has run through my head while sleeping isn't significant enough to be remembered, but ever since the hitman called me, I'm haunted by the same series of images as if a ghastly B category horror movie had been stuck in a loop in my head. It's like when you hear an annoying song on the radio you hate yet you can't get out of your head.

The dream starts the same. I'm slowly making my way upstairs, my hand gripping the railing, my ears sharpened for sounds. I'm frightened. I don't feel safe in my home. A door squeaks, making my blood run cold. Next, the creaking of a floorboard breaks the silence.

The hair stands up on my skin all over my body and the blood pulses in my temples, but I keep going. My kids are in the house, and I need to protect them. I need to confront the intruder.

I see a shadow crossing the hallway upstairs. I pause, holding my breath. I press my back against the wall and wait for a sound or another shadow to appear. The master bedroom door is in my sight. Someone flings it open with so much power that the doorknob hits against the wall and leaves a dent. Emanuela leaps in front of me; her bulging belly peeks over the waist of a short black skirt. One glance at her contemptible face helps me regain my confidence.

"You bitch!" I yell and charge at her with only one thing on my mind: to get that bloodsucking leech out of my house and out my life. But before I can reach her, Mike confronts me at the top of the stairs. He's holding a shovel with both hands in front of him. "Look at you, Sarah. You're so pathetic," he sneers. "I'm doing the world a favor," he says and hits me on the head.

The impact of the cold metal against my skull is numbing. I fall backward while my hands grope desperately for something to hold onto to prevent me from falling. The railing is not within my reach. I roll down the hard wooden stairs. Each impact leaves a memory on my body in the form of a bruise or cracked bone.

After a sudden cease of motion, I find myself at the bottom of the staircase in a most comical position. My right shoulder feels as if it has been ripped from the socket. My neck is broken. But I know I'm alive because I'm looking at my swollen ankle next to my head, my toes facing me. My entire body is twisted and bent as if I were nothing more but a rubber doll.

I feel scared. No one is coming to help me. Mike and Emanuela are laughing at me from the top of the stairs.

I awake from the dream with a jolt, feeling angry, and realizing that there is sweat rolling down my face and back. It always seems to take a long time for my breathing to stabilize. To reassure myself that I'm okay, I run my hand over my body and discover all is well. It was only a bad dream, inspired by that stupid 90's flick *Death Becomes Her,* which I watched recently on Netflix. Then the following nights I relive the same nightmare.

I'm sick of feeling betrayed and helpless. But what I'm really sick of is that most exciting memories of the last decade come from movies and not my actual life. I used to create my own memories. Perhaps they were dangerous and reckless, but at least I lived, not merely existed. So long have I had fictional characters in movies and books as friends that I lost all sense of how to behave in adult company.

The Mike in my dreams is right. I am pathetic. I've been pathetic. But not today! Today is different. I am different. On this exciting February morning, it doesn't matter that I'm not a morning person or that I have only days left to live because for the first time in a long time I'm full of emotions and my body is gripped by readiness. I can't stay a minute longer on my back staring at the ceiling and listening to Mike's soft snoring. If I want to win this game, I need to let go of the ties that bind me to the *old* me.

As a stay-at-home mom, every day of my life has been the same, a dull repetition of events that made my head spin. At times, I tried to change the pattern, fill my hours with window-shopping or a dog walk, but those fillers only made me feel more useless and dreadful. Other times I went through fitness phases when I swore to myself to get back in shape. I developed a daily yoga routine for a while until a strained muscle forced me to drop exercise altogether. I never resumed my routine, not even after I was healed. Mind over matter, Mike always tells me. He thinks I'm lazy. He might be right.

Today I finally have a purpose. As outrageous as plotting to kill my husband may seem, it's still a purpose. Recently I've had more things to take care of and more interaction with people this year than in previous years. I feel elated, yearning to become more of the woman I want to be. Bruce might be the best thing that's ever happened to me. He burst into my life like a hurricane and swept me away. I'm still spinning, but it's a good thing. Today nothing seems impossible.

I tiptoe to my desk and pick up a black case that holds an old Sony Vaio laptop. I still haven't organized those two book promotions scheduled for next week. With everything that's been going on in my life, I completely forgot about them. Now I'm running out of time. It's imperative for me to start on the designs and get the word out. That, or cancel them both with a made-up excuse. Only I want to develop my blog. It's something I've finally come to love doing, something I also may be good at doing.

I creep down the hallway and gently pull shut the kids' bedroom doors. This morning is mine, and I refuse to share it. Besides, today is the second day of the four-day weekend, so I'll let the kids sleep in as long as they want.

Since last week, I only used the computer to spy on Mike and not for work. It's time for me to lose myself in my creative world. I need to turn off the reality switch before I go completely crazy.

In the kitchen, I plug in the laptop. I give it a second to charge while I check my phone. Benny's been trying to contact me since we parted at Starbucks, but I've been ditching his calls. Telling him how I thought my life was in danger was a colossal mistake. Making up excuses for doing so would be even bigger.

When his first call came in, I let it go to voicemail. He didn't leave a message. There was no need for it. I exactly knew what he wanted to tell me. I was going to wait a day or two to allow enough time for both our heads to cool off then call him back. Most criminals in movies have an accomplice. I pushed that idea from my head; there is no way I will drag Benny or Bruce into my sick, twisted world.

Bruce! I picture him standing by a poker table, dressed in black from head to toe.

Saturday is tomorrow. Our date night! I must keep a lid on my problems. I can't allow a word to slip out about my predicament. Telling Benny about my problems was one thing; he's my childhood friend. Bruce is an entirely different story. Though he works in a casino and most likely knows a bunch of thugs who might even own guns, I can't allow him to dig any deeper into my dark, guilt-ridden soul. What would he think of me if he found out about the things I've been doing and planning to do to my husband, the father of my children?

I send a text to Benny despite its being way too early to be bothering anybody. I'm hoping he won't get my message until later in the day so I don't have to ruin my morning talking about my untrustworthy husband. In the text message, I let him know that I'm driving north to Palmdale today to drop the kids off at my mother-in-law's house for the weekend. He responds almost immediately. He doesn't even ask what time I'll be leaving because he wants to come with me no matter what. I tell him to be ready by ten. He says he's at the gym so ten o'clock would be perfect. I stare at his words on the screen in awe. I always assumed that computer geeks stay up all night and sleep all day. Five thirty-two in the morning and Benny is already up and working out in the gym. I guess sometime after college he realized that when his mom told him he could achieve anything he dreamed of what she meant was he could achieve anything he dreamed of with the hard work and dedication.

I send him a thumbs-up and a heart emoticon. He throws a blushing face back.

I lift up the screen of the laptop and turn it on. I enjoy the gentle rattling sound in the dark as the operating system comes to life. Since childhood, I've been scared of the dark, but for some strange reason, I enjoy it at this moment. It makes me feel peaceful and calm.

The computer rattles on longer than my patience can endure. I slip off the barstool to get something to drink from the refrigerator. The beef stew tuned up with Selenium is still in there. Now that the party is over, I have to feed it to Mike.

The first thing I do every morning is to make coffee. I can't operate without caffeine. Since I didn't remember to grind coffee last night and we don't have ground coffee or instant at home—and it's too early for liquor—I settle for a glass of orange juice. I feel every drop run down my throat and disperse into my stomach. Surprisingly, I find the feeling revitalizing. I refill my glass, then snatch the soft throw off the couch and wrap it around myself. Though the days are unusually warm for February, the air still cools off into the low forties at night.

Designing both book promotions with this old laptop takes even longer than it would have on my ancient Apple computer, but I manage to stay on track. I only allow my thoughts to sidetrack a few times, and only to Bruce.

When I finished designing the banners and Facebook promo images, I lean back and admire my work for a while. They are the best promo images I've done so far.

I send out emails to over a hundred book bloggers, asking them to sign up for my tours. In the next ten minutes, already sixteen bloggers respond to express their interest in posting the promotion. Not bad for an early morning's work. Had I been working this enthusiastically on my blog last year, instead of checking out other blogs with gnawing envy, I'd have a successful business by now.

After the third glass of juice, I slip into the downstairs bathroom. As I flip on the switch, I do the same thing I always do: I check myself out in the mirror. But this time what I see curdles my blood.

And not because my hair is a tangled mess or my eyes are red. It's because three words written across the glass in black marker confront me:

SIX DAYS BITCH

My heart starts a stampede inside my chest, and I find myself gasping for air. That lowlife asshole came into the house while we were sleeping and managed to roam around without waking us. Since giving birth to my first child, I sleep with one eye open. My children's lives depend on my alertness. I should never have let Bruce push the mother in me into a corner. I was so busy dreaming about my make-believe life with Bruce that I let my guard down.

I'm also angry with Mike. He's a firefighter, dammit. Are his ears only attuned to the blare of the alarm but not for strange noises in his own home?

As panic inside my chest rising, I search downstairs. I rattle each door and check all the locks, but I can't find the point of entry. Then a cold breeze bristles the hair on my neck. One of the dining room windows is open. The screen is intact, but it wouldn't be difficult for someone to remove it and put back in place. The mere thought of a killer entering my home, the place my children should feel the safest, fills me with uncontrollable fear and anger.

I run up the stairs unmindful of the thudding sounds my heavy footsteps leave on the steps. I check on Mason first. I put my hand on his back, which is rising and falling in rhythm with his soft breathing. Then I step into Tammy's room to see if she's okay. I don't touch her. She's a light sleeper like me. I listen to her breathing for a while before I go back downstairs.

I get back to the kitchen, grab a bottle of Windex, spray the mirror and scrub off the writing. What the hell was that idiot thinking? What if Mike had seen the threat first?

I find myself sitting in front of the computer glaring at the screen.

I'd chewed my left thumbnail into a bloody chunk. I've been taking this whole execution game too lightly, as though in denial that anyone would actually kill me or bring harm to my family. I keep telling myself these things only happen on crime TV shows. I wonder if Mike has been worrying why the job hasn't been done yet. What excuses could the hitman be feeding him for taking so long?

I take my cell phone into my shaking hands, debating whether to call Benny or Bruce to ask for help. It takes all my self-restraint not to make a call.

I go out to the backyard for some fresh air. The dog is sleeping, oblivious to my presence. An odd feeling overwhelms me. It takes only a moment to realize why. The chickens are as silent as a cemetery. Every morning like clockwork, they get me out of bed at the crack of dawn, but I can't hear them now.

I slip into my outdoor shoes. I rub my dog's head. He looks at me with sleep-deprived eyes.

I shuffle to the corner of our property to let the chickens out of the henhouse while my eyes are searching for the intruder. The closer I get the harder it is to shake the feeling that something is wrong.

Once past the struggling orange tree, I can smell copper in the morning air. Then I see bloody feathers scattered on the ground inside the chicken coop. All three chickens lie on the ground, their heads torn from their bodies. I want to scream, but my voice catches in my throat. I want to run, but my body is gripped with terror.

From day one, these chickens proved to be a pain in the neck, but I loved them. They stuck their noses into everybody's business, stole food from the dog's bowl, and ran off shrieking when he chased them for it. They scraped up the dirt while I gardened. Gathered around my feet when I sat on the patio chair trying to read a book.

It was Mason's job to lock the chickens up at night, but I was the one who forgot to remind him last night. Though we live in the city, bandit rodents frequently jump our fence looking for free food.

As I approach the coop, I tell myself that a raccoon must have gotten into the henhouse and killed my babies. To even think that the hitman, who had just been snooping around inside my house, the murderer who cornered me in the garage while the kids were playing on the street, was responsible for this massacre is far more frightening than anything I can handle right now.

I don't go inside the fenced area. I remain standing in front of the chicken-wire fence, holding the dog by the leash. He looks unstable on his feet and shows no interest in his dead friends. I let go of his collar. He teeters to his doghouse as if he only has sleep on his mind.

"The kids!" I let out a panicky breath and rush back to the house. I storm upstairs and burst into Mason's room. I start shaking him awake.

"Mason, honey, you need to get up. We're going to Grandma's."

He groans and complains, then rolls to his other side and pulls the blanket over his back. I yank a duffle bag out of his closet and start packing his stuff. I shove random pieces of clothing into the bag with little regard of what I grab.

"Mason, we need to go. I need you to get up," I say, an unshakable panic riding on my voice.

I take a few calming breaths before I push Tammy's door open. I know I should sit down on her bed and caress her face while whispering to her. I should pull her blanket off and tickle her awake. I should do these things because that's what she's used to expect from me. But I don't have time for games now. I have to get to Mike and get him to clean up the mess in the chicken coop before the kids see what happened.

"Fuck!" That's all Mike has to add to my story. "Can't it wait?"

He yawns, rubbing his eyes.

On an average morning, I'd pull his hand away and warn him for the thousandth time not to rub his eyes. According to my eye doctor, the pressure might damage his vision in the long term. But right now, my smallest problem is more significant than worrying about Mike's health. Besides, he lost the privilege of being cared for or tended to by me.

"No, it cannot wait, Mike." I pull the sheet off him. He frowns. "There's blood everywhere. That damn raccoon didn't even eat them; just tore their heads off. What a waste!"

I start the shower and slip out of my clothes. "I'm taking the kids to your mom's."

He hoists himself up and leans against the headboard. "When? Now?" He peeks at his watch. "It's only seven."

I droop my shoulders in frustration. I want to tell Mike to shut the hell up, get his lazy ass out of bed, and clean up the dead chickens before I rip his head off, and throw it in with the other carcasses. He was the one who brought those innocent animals home, but he never cared a damn about them. He was the one who unleashed a murderer on us. He's the one responsible for this menace.

I duck my head under the pelting hot water. A new spider is sitting on the edge of the tile. It's smaller than the other one but just as black. I tighten my jaws and smash it with my fist in one swift movement.

*   *   *   *   *

Half an hour later the kids are sitting in the car, and I'm about to pull out of the garage when Mike decides to hold us up. He plants his hands on the window frame and asks questions: "When are you coming back? You want me to come with you?"

"I gotta go," I tell him. "Enjoy your morning."

He pokes his head in to kiss me, but I pull away. He will never, ever, put those compromised lips on mine as long as I'm alive. Which might not be long, but still.

My hands are shaking as I turn onto the street. Wasting time fending off Mike's unsolicited flirting is a luxury I can't afford right now. I need to get my children away from this twisted house.

From the car I call Benny, letting him know that we are on our way. When I get to his house, he's already waiting out front. I tell the kids that he's an old friend from high school—which is not a lie—and we are giving him a ride to his grandmother in Lancaster. The kids couldn't care less since they are still mad at me for bringing them to Grandma's and are busy taking out their anger on violent games on the DS and my iPad.

The drive is maddeningly peaceful. Benny sits next to me, unmoving, as if he weren't even there. From the corner of my eye, I can see him checking me out from time to time. He must think I'm mad. He could be spot on.

Since the block party, it's better if I'm not left alone. When alone I'm like an obsessed teenager, my head is full of Bruce, and I can't shake off thoughts of him no matter how hard I try. I need to focus on the future and get Emanuela's brother off my back, but I fail each time. My mind keeps retracing the events of yesterday. I feel Bruce's hand on my thighs, his tongue in my mouth, and his scent in my nostrils.

The drive is not giving me peace either. Random flashbacks of the bloody scene in our backyard flare up in my head, but they are not welcomed, and I blocked them out each time. I use my memory of Bruce to do so.

Benny continues to sit silently next to me. The topics we'd like to discuss can't be brought up in front of the kids. He has nothing else to talk about apparently. Like back in high school, if I didn't do the talking, we'd sit in silence for hours.

I steal a glance at him. His eyes gaze at the road ahead. I wonder what crazy thoughts going through that smart head of his. I bet he assumes I'm haunted by dreadful thoughts and anxieties. Would he care so much about my welfare if he knew that all I can think about is Bruce?

When I realize how irrational my mind is, I feel sick. I need to take frequent small sips of water to keep the anxiety under control. I brush my hand over my face from time to time. If only it were that easy to blot out the memory of that forbidden bathroom sex.

While I say goodbye to the kids, I become overly emotional. I hold them to my chest for the longest time—long enough for them to push me away and complain.

"Whatever happens in life, guys, I want you to remember that I love you more than anything," I tell my kids with a shaking voice. They seem to respond to my tears as if they sense that something is wrong with me.

"Why are you crying. mommy?" Tammy asks in her angelic voice, brushing her finger under my eye.

"It's hard for me to part from you guys." I wipe my face with both hands.

"Then can we come back home with you?" Mason whines. I ruined his plans for the weekend, and now I bid him goodbye when he's mad at me.

"I need you to stay with grandma for a while, all right. I'll see you soon," I lie. My voice cracks.

I need to compose myself in front of Grace, but it's harder than anything I've ever done. I may never get another chance to hug my children.

Grace loses her patience with me, and she ushers the kids inside her home. She's wearing a tight top over her braless saggy breasts and a pair of jeans shorts. She never seemed to possess the ability to allow herself to age gracefully. Thank God, Benny remained in the car because if he's still as openly judgmental as he was in school, he wouldn't be able to contain his laughter.

I take the kids' duffle bags into her poorly furnished minimalist home. Grace tries so hard to be stylish, but she is just not. The walls are bare, and only a few framed pictures of her dogs line the mantel. Not one photo of her late husband or her kids. A painting of a Yorkshire terrier with a pink bow rests tilted on the kitchen cabinet, a remnant of her latest failed hobby, just like the overgrown flower garden in the front, or the half-finished pond in the back. She's not too keen on spending time with me—the one-word responses, the grimacing face, and the TV remote in hand are my clues— so I hurriedly pull my kids into a final embrace that I hold for a long time with my heart aching.

"Thank you, Grace, for having them." I lean against her bony figure in an awkward hug.

"Yeah, yeah," that's all she says.

I know exactly how the next two days will play out. The kids will only be allowed to sit quietly and watch her TV shows. She will feed them frozen hamburgers and PB&J sandwiches, yet whenever I call, she will tell me how my kids have wiped her out and how they have raided the refrigerator like a bunch of locusts. She will make them take their shoes off by the door while her seven dogs run around the house like they own the place. She will tell me how much the kids exhaust her even though she won't let them get off the couch.

By the time I reach my car I've wound up myself to the point that I almost turn around to grab the kids and take them back with me. Only, our home is not safe for them anymore. It's all Mike's fault. I'll make him pay.

Leaving the 55+ senior community, I drive along Avenue M on my way back to Temecula.

"The woman is a piece of work," Benny remarks. They are the first words he's said to me since leaving Temecula.

"You have no idea," I manage to say.

I feel lightheaded. I can't concentrate on the road. I'm sick with the destructive thoughts that reign in my head. At my first opportunity, I pull over onto the side of the road before connecting to Hwy 138. All I can think of is Grace scolding my kids all day long. She treats her seven miniature-sized pocket dogs like humans while her own grandchildren have no rights in her house. If something happens to me no way will I let that woman raise my children.

"Who's gonna take care of Mason and Tammy if I'm dead?"

I look at Benny. His long hair and bearded face against the desert background paint a depressing image. The bleak city, 'beautiful' Palmdale, sucks the joy out of everything; sucks the life out of me. Desert. Heat. Fast food restaurants. Welfare communities. I could never live there.

Benny's fingers tighten against his thighs. "You can't think like that."

"But I do," I snap. "My parents are out of the picture. My brother's dead. Grace is an evil bitch who raised a murderer. Who then? Mike's foster brothers? Mike?"

I put the car back in motion. If I want to think clearly, I need to get away from this godforsaken place.

I catch Benny looking out of the window at the soul-sucking landscape of dust and lonely Joshua trees. I follow his gaze, probably wondering the same thing. No surprise Mike turned out to be a selfish bastard with no soul. Growing up here, where even God never comes to visit, must sap all the humanity out of you.

I heard his stories about living in a neighborhood where

shootings happened daily, where his mom was scared to get gas once the sun went down. At the time, I felt sorry for him. My maternal side took over, and I wanted to save him, love him till he drowned in it. I got turned on seeing his tattooed arms and rock-hard body. He had the look of an alpha male while deep inside he was a broken little boy who needed nurturing. He was the one I was destined to redeem, a broken soul I was going to save to *save* my soul.

But I was fooled. All along, Mike was no better than a narcissistic bastard. From all the guys I dated I had to marry this wolf in a sheep's clothing.

A shudder runs down my spine, and I have to focus to keep the car on the road. Pearblossom Highway is not the place where you want to lose control unless you want to wind up in a ditch kissing the airbag.

By the time Benny responds to my comments about fears that I have regarding custody of my kids, I'm miles away in my head. "What?" I ask distractedly.

"I said if push comes to shove, I'd do anything to take care of . . . you know, your children."

I let out a desperate sigh. "No offense, Benny, but I don't think you have any idea what you'd be signing up for."

He squirms in his seat, turning his upper body toward me. "Why? I know you. I mean we haven't kept in touch for a long time, but back in the old times, I was your spiritual trash can, remember? You always poured all your problems out on me. I was the first who heard about your kiss with David Gonzales in the boys' locker room . . . after his team won the championship—remember? I even went with you to buy your first box of tampons."

His words make me blush. I guess we were closer friends than I tend to remember.

"So? What's your point?"

"I know you. I know how you would expect me to raise your kids."

"Only I don't think that's the right way to bring up a child. Look at me. My mother would be ashamed."

"I don't think so. I liked your mom," Benny laughs. "She was funny. Remember how she always came up with those clichés for every question we asked?"

Reminiscing with Benny allows me a moment of laughter. "You can never step into the same river twice. You reap what you sow. You'll never know till you try."

"Actions speak louder than words," Benny snorts, slapping his thigh.

"Yep. That's my mother. Instead of setting rules in the house, or holding me accountable for things I've done, she simply attempted to resolve every problem with some proverb."

Having been mad at my mother for so long, I find it difficult to allow such fond memories to surface. "I remember when I told her that I slept with Ryan O'Donnell. Remember? Jessica's brother? I told her that we didn't use protection. Instead of taking me to the doctor, she told me, "You made your bed now you can sleep in it.""

Benny sighs. I sense his mood change. "It could be worse, you know," he says. "She could have told you how bad people are, how evil the world is, and that it's better if you stay at home and don't risk getting hurt."

I offer Benny a look of sympathy. I don't remember ever meeting his mother, but I heard stories about how disconnected she was from her son. Benny never liked to talk about her.

A few minutes of silence follow when I merge onto I-15. For a Friday morning, which is also the middle of a holiday weekend, the freeway is annoyingly busy. I switch lanes a few times until I settle into the fast lane, chasing the tail of a silver Mercedes at 79 miles per hour. Why not live a little crazy, right?

Benny breaks the silence first. "I still think you should go to the police."

"We've already gone through this. The police can't help me. Nobody can."

I hear him suck in a huge breath. He's nervous. I don't want him to be nervous in my presence.

"I can," he blurts out. "I saved up some money, you know. I could take you and the kids away from here."

I stare at the license plate of the Mercedes, trying to picture how life would be with Benny. I like him as a person, but I could never love him as a man. I've destroyed enough lives. He doesn't deserve to be used as a bridge between my first marriage and the second one. There's a woman out there somewhere waiting for him. I should cut the cord and let him loose. The more time he wastes with me and my problems, the less time he'll have to find happiness.

"Look, Benny, I appreciate the offer, but you know I'm a sick bitch whose getting what she deserves. Don't waste your time on me."

"Don't say that," he barks at me and touches my hand. His reaction comes as a surprise, and I yank on the wheel a bit. I manage to straighten the car out and calm the hell down. I'm a jumpy, nervous wreck. The feelings that coil inside me make me hate Mike to the point that if he were in front of me right now, I'd choke him with my bare hands.

"Sorry. I didn't mean to startle you."

"It's not you, Benny. You're my only friend." I try to smile at him. I believe the attempt came off as a weak grimace.

"I know that you've gone through a lot, but you must stop blaming yourself for the past."

"I can't," I sigh, passing the Mercedes. I can't follow that car any longer. The sun reflecting off the shiny silver exterior irritates me.

"You're Catholic, right?"

"I was." I don't know where he is going with the question, but I don't like it.

My mother cared about one thing, and it was for Kyle and me to attend Catechism classes at church. I could bring home a C in math or a B in English, but as long as I didn't miss Mass on Sunday morning, I was okay.

"Then you must believe in the forgiveness of sins."

"What are you getting at?" I exactly knew what he was talking about because I'd been rolling the idea around in my head for a while on my own.

"Go to confession. Here." He pulls out his Smartphone and starts typing. "Which church do you go to?"

"Saint Catherine's in Temecula, but I'd never go there for confession. What if the priest recognizes me in the grocery store the next day?"

"S'okay." I don't look at him, but I know he's wrinkling his brows. "How about Saint Martha. Confessions are every Saturday morning from eight thirty."

I'm not so keen on laying out my dirty laundry that I've been hiding for a decade, to a stranger; but, I tell Benny I'll go. Maybe I should go. What do I have to lose?

We just passed Lake Elsinore on the I-15 when Mike calls.

"Who is with you in the car?" he asks without a greeting, near to yelling at me.

"What are you talking about?"

"My mother just called and said that there was a dude in your car when you dropped the kids off."

"Oh, it's Benny, from high school. I told you about him." Why do I bother to explain myself to him? I should say mind your own fucking business.

"The fat fuck." There is a hint of relief in his voice.

"Don't call him that." I steal a glance at Benny, my heart hammering against my ribs, even though I doubt he could hear Mike on the other end. I press my phone closer to my ear just in case.

"Why is he with you?"

"He needed a ride to his grandmother's home, and I appreciated the company."

"I asked you if you wanted me to go with you."

"Well, you asked, but he offered."

"What? It doesn't make any sense."

"It doesn't matter. I'm home in half an hour. By the way, did you clean up the coop?"

"You know it." His tone has changed. I picture his smile while talking to me. "Hey, I'll be here, waiting for you, okay?" His voice is a purr now, teasing. *Why now? Doesn't your fiancée want you anymore?*

"You don't need to wait for me. I have a few errands to run. Go watch a movie or something."

"If I didn't know you any better I'd say you want to get me out of the house." I'd managed to piss him off. Good. "Are you bringing your boyfriend here?"

"Don't be ridiculous."

"Fine. I'll run over to the rental then. I gotta check the sprinkler system anyway." *I bet it's clogged.*

Bathing in victory, I press down on the accelerator. I can't wait to get home and have the house to myself.

. . . . .

Grace: Yes, I'm sure. A man was sitting
in her car when she dropped off the
children. *Hush up Puffy.* No, I didn't get

a good look at him. I got the kids running around and my babies getting all excited. *Hush up Puffy, I said*. He had long hair though. I think. Who? Sarah? No, she looked nervous. Something was going on. I called Mike and told him. Maybe I shouldn't have. *Hush up Puffy*. He wants dinner.

Benny: Yes, it was me in the car. We were organizing a high school reunion. She was always busy, so I rode with her so we could talk. *I can't now, Ma. The police are here. No, I haven't done anything wrong. They are here about Sarah. Don't call her that*. She doesn't mean it. She's kind of crazy. Says stupid things all the time. No, I didn't do it, but I should have. Sarah deserved more than this. I already told you. No more questions. I told you everything I know.

5 DAYS TO DIE

The soft padding on the pews cushions my knees as I'm kneeling to begin my confession. I never thought I would say this, but I miss the hard, rough Italian church pews where my kneecaps burned with white blinding pain. I've sinned. I deserve to be punished.

In Italy, visiting local cathedrals became a habit of mine. Not that I understood a word of the Italian mass, but the chanting in Latin and the overpowering aroma of temple incense had always gripped my soul. Every sound my heels made on the ancient stones echoed across the massive halls and resonated through me.

As I walked under the vaulted ceilings, paintings and frescoes of Jesus dying for our sins and other ghastly images of the brutality in human history forced me to feel humble. The sounds of weeping senior women, kneeling throughout the church, all the while being illuminated by gentle rays of light, filled my soul with compassion. Both Napoleon and Hitler plundered Italy senselessly, yet priceless relics in their awe-inspiring magnificence were salvaged and remain on display in Catholic churches.

As the Royal Family is one of the biggest attractions in England, the strong presence of the Catholic Church is the main reason Italy is on the map. Tens of thousands of people visit the Vatican daily, marveling at masterpieces in art and architecture of this mysterious city and seeking forgiveness.

I was too.

What could be a better place to confess my sins than Saint Peter's Basilica? I was prepared, dressed conservatively in long black slacks and white blouse despite the heat. Sadly, my enthusiasm was extinguished after four hours of waiting in line, between an American tourist couple who didn't even know the name of the basilica, and a Russian family with three whiny children, an angry husband, and a sad-puppy-faced woman.

My disappointment elevated during the Vatican tour as other slack-mouthed tourists and I were herded through the corridors like livestock. "Avanti! Avanti!" uniformed Italian guards yelled at us at every corner.

Finally, Mike and I reach the Sistine Chapel; such a holy place that you can't help but feel the need to drop to your knees on the cold hard stones and beseech God for forgiveness. That was how I thought until a group of Japanese tourists started laughing next to us, and members of a European retiree tourist group decided to take my mind away from my sins in favor of their health problems and financial troubles. Then as a final kick, a guard yelled, "Silenzio!" into the microphone, and my inner peace crumbled down completely.

Feeling cheated out of my experience, I surrendered any attempt to confess the sins of my youth to God and joined the hundreds of people who elbowed their way out of the chapel through midget doors and down the stairs, wondering why I didn't watch a YouTube movie about Rome instead.

Now, on my knees in Saint Martha's confessional booth (which is really a room, not a booth), where the air smells strongly of disinfectant, I think back about my one and only confession attempt in the cathedral of Milan. The memory makes me wish for the gloomy and isolated box with a priest who barely understood my English—a faceless man who offered no reaction to what I told him.

I want that same feeling of anonymity now. I want the pain to torture my knees. But I'm not granted my wishes in this church of our modern bedroom community. People only go to the house of God if it's big and bright, with air conditioning and friendly face-to-face encounters with the priest, where they can feel good about themselves.

I don't want to feel good about myself. I want someone to finally tell me that what I did was wrong. I wish my parents, instead of cutting me out of their lives, had confronted me and said to me that I'd been a bad girl and that I needed to change.

They should have told me that Kyle's death was a tragic accident and that it should never have happened, but it did.

Most importantly, they should have told me that it was normal to be angry about it, but not okay to hurt other people because I've been hurt.

I wish my mother would have stopped telling my six-year-old self that the painting I did was beautiful when I only spent two minutes and minimal effort on it. She should have held me responsible for all my wrongdoings.

I have to get out of my head. I want someone to rip my brain out. I want someone to take my memories away. . .

Father Gregory stands up and offers me his hand. I look down, ignoring his offer. I'm not here to shake hands and make friends. I have sins to confess.

Without a word, he retrieves his hand and takes his place on the other side of the confessional. I can hear him breathing. I feel exposed and vulnerable. Even though I chose to kneel behind the gridded wood panel instead of sitting face to face with him I can sense his presence. His proximity bothers me because what I need to talk about is very personal. I want to tell him that I'm responsible for my brother's death; I was the one who disobeyed our parents; I was the one who stayed at the party after curfew time; I was the one Kyle was looking out for; I was the one who forced him to take a break from his studies in the middle of the night, get into his car to find me and bring me home. I am the one to blame for his accident.

If I had gone home when I was supposed to, if obeying my parents had been more important to me than one extra hour with a boy and a drink, then Kyle would be alive today. He was only a couple of months away from being transferred from the community college to Berkley with a full scholarship. He had a bright and prosperous future ahead of him. I robbed him of all that.

I need to tell Father how I emotionally tortured drinkers and party boys for years. I need to confess how meanly I treated my parents. How I distanced myself from them and did not allow them to help me.

I need to cleanse my soul from the sins I've been living with for so long.

He needs to know that I was the Devil's advocate. I promised love only to take it away when it hurt the most, over and over again.

I need to make him understand why I couldn't leave Jack's apartment for three days after he hung himself because of our break up. Not reporting his death for days and lying on his bed in the insect-infested room should earn me more Our Fathers and Hail Marys. Father needs to know. And before he lets me off so quickly by saying a few prayers, he has to consider that after Jack's death, I spent a year in a loony bin to get my head straight.

He also needs to know that I entered my marriage with all these secrets buried in my heart.

I need to say that I've sinned against all Ten Commandments. I was the servant of the devil. I asked him to help me to survive the pain. I took the Lord's name in vain. I cursed God for taking my brother away from me. I turned away from the church for over a decade. I dishonored my parents and turned my back on them, too. I killed, not with my hands, but with my actions. I cheated. I stole men's hearts. I lied to save myself. I coveted successful women's lives. And now I've been plotting to kill my husband.

Instead of confessing all my sins I say, "Forgive me, father, for I have sinned. It has been a long time since my last confession. I had inappropriate thoughts of another man. I gave in to the sins of lust, gluttony, sloth, anger, and envy. I've been angry and impatient with my children."

He expresses that my honesty is the first step to forgiveness.

There is an imaginary giant cotton ball stuck in my throat that makes me want to gag.

The priest blesses me, but I don't feel any solace. *There is still time. Tell him what you did.* But I can't. This room. This environment is too open and personal. I could never look him in the eye once I told him what I had done.

I thank him for his time and make the sign of the cross. The touch of my fingertip is like a hot needle against my forehead. My heart hammers against my hand. My chest wants to explode. *Tell him. Tell him the truth.*

I push myself to my feet thinking of the five Our Fathers and ten Hail Marys I'm expected to say for my penance.

From the door, I look back at the priest. His smile tells me that he is satisfied with my confession. As I wrap my fingers around the doorknob, my knees rattle like a toy in a baby's hand. There is still time to collapse onto my knees and tell him the truth.

I open the door instead, leaving the confessional knowing that I failed to ask for total forgiveness, that I withheld my actual sins.

I don't bother with doing my penance. I can't even look at the stone carving of the crucified Jesus who died for our sins. I loathe myself. The dark arms of depression are reaching up for me to drag me down into the abyss. I envision my heart turning into a piece of dry, black charcoal. I had the opportunity to cleanse myself, but I damned myself instead. No point worrying about my soul once I kill my husband. I'll be going to hell anyway.

I take the freeway home. I know I'm losing it because I can't focus on the road. When I pull into our garage, I have no recollection of how I got there. I let the engine run and lean my head back on the seat. Would it be painful to die from CO_2 poisoning?

A series of angry raps on my side window startles me. I reach for the pepper spray I've been carrying with me ever since the hitman pinned me to the wall in the garage.

Bruce towers over my car displaying his wholly charming and confident self. I roll the window down instead of getting out. His eyes are bright and his face lights with a huge smile. Poor Bruce, he has no idea what he got himself into when he seduced me away from Mike.

"Are we still on for tonight?" he asks, placing his folded arms against the window frame and peering inside the car.

His pleasure-inducing aftershave pours into the interior and wraps around me like a soft blanket. His presence is so comforting and much needed.

"I don't know . . . It might not be a good idea," I say, taking a lungful of Bruce's fragrance with closed eyes. If he thought me weird before, I sure haven't disappointed him now.

He brushes his fingers along my cheek. "I don't accept no as an answer. I need you tonight."

Our eyes meet. I feel as if a colony of ants is marching inside my stomach.

"I need you more," I say, even though I don't want to egg him on.

He devours my mouth, latching his sensuous lips onto mine. Anyone on the street, or looking out a window, can see us. My hand gropes for the remote on the visor. I press the button. The clanking sounds of the well-oiled wheels fill the spacious garage as the door rolls back into place.

Bruce opens my door and scoops me up out of the car. He lifts me to his waist, and I wrap my legs around him as I used to do it when I was young and hungry.

I find myself on the hood of my car. It's still warm from the drive. I'm thoughtless. Shameless. Careless. While his mouth discovers every inch of my mouth and neck, his hands undo my pants. Mike would flip me onto my stomach and force my legs wide, but Bruce wants to look at my face. When he enters me, his eyes lock on mine. How can I make him feel this way? I didn't know I still had it in me.

I let my mind go blank. I block out all the self-loathing, the blame, the clutter. There is no right or wrong thing to do here. I'm here for the moment, for Bruce. He can do whatever he wants to me because I need him to liberate my soul. He doesn't try to hurt me or humiliate me. He doesn't take advantage of my willingness. He is here to enjoy this moment with me. He responds to my soft moans and the look in my eyes. The first time in a long time I feel desirable.

He picks me up and takes me to the back seat of the car. I'm grateful that he didn't try to carry me inside the house. I don't care about desecrating my marriage sanctuary, but I can't let my kids down again.

He sits me up on his lap and soon our breathing fogs up the

inside of the windows.

Back in college, I lured boys into having sex in the car. They loved it. Messing with their heads was essential to my plan. I needed them to like me so I could destroy them. I wish my thoughts would stop wandering now. I shut my eyes tight to distract myself.

The pain and pleasure come together. The mixture of two powerful feelings hits me. A desperate sob is trying to break out of me, but I can't allow myself to shed any more tears. Not in front of Bruce.

We lay on the seat with our bodies tangled. The soft sounds of Bruce's breathing are a sweet melody to my ears. With him next to me my life doesn't seem like such a dreadful place.

"I can't get you out of my head," he whispers. I feel his lips pressed against the top of my head.

"Is that a good thing or a bad thing?"

"The best." He squeezes me. I look back and stretch my arm toward the side window. I press my palm against the misted glass and leave a handprint. Bruce plants his print next to mine.

My phone buzzes in the back pocket of my pants. I don't move, but Bruce pulls it out and hands it to me. Nobody sends me texts, only Mike, and as of late, Benny. I'm in no mood to hear from either of them, so I lower the phone in my hand without checking it. Then I remember that I dropped my kids off at my crazy mother-in-law's home yesterday and the message may be from her—it could be important.

But I'm wrong.

5 days bitch

I delete the message at once.

"You okay?" Bruce asks, gathering my hair to one side.

"Yeah. Yeah. I'm fine." My voice catches in my throat.

He moves, pushing me up gently. I read his signs. He wants to get up.

"I need to get to work. I was on my way when I saw you come home."

"Oh? Did I make you late?"

He lets out a short, amused laugh. "Nobody will even notice."

"Good. Good. Go. I . . . I've some things to do too."

Out of the car, he cups my head into his hands and leans into me until he pushes me against the door. "I know you think what's happening between us is moving too fast, but what you don't understand is that I've been readying myself for this moment for some time."

I cock my head to the side. "What's that supposed to mean?" The first thought forming in my mind is that Bruce was hired by Mike to test me. Or he could be an accomplice of Emanuela's brother. Did I just step into a trap like a fool, an amateur?

My body tenses up as Bruce drops one of his hands and presses the other against the car.

"I know we didn't talk a lot since I moved in but I know you, Mrs. Sarah Johnson. I've been watching you mowing the lawn, picking weeds, and pruning your roses." His voice is gentle, yet nervous. He's not here to hurt me. "I saw you ride Mason's bicycle once when you were looking for him. You looked so cute trying to ride the small bike barefooted around the neighborhood looking for your son."

I swallow hard. I always considered myself a gray little mouse living invisibly amongst more interesting people, like that childless newlywed woman with excessive plastic surgeries who always washes her car out front while wearing a tiny bikini. Or the guy who rides a Harley and dresses like a gangster. Or the inventor who builds unique vehicles, such as that homemade go-kart last month and has his son ride them around the cul-de-sac.

"I'm not a stalker. I don't keep a journal of your comings and goings," Bruce laughs, shaking his head. "I've been just fantasizing about you for a while."

"About me?" I'm not sure how I am supposed to feel: flattered or frightened.

"Yep. You," Bruce breathes the words. His eyes are smoldering. "I have two older sisters. They both have families and kids. I know it's hard to look at yourself the way I look at you, but it's time to give yourself more credit."

I'm searching for words but come up empty. "I don't know what to say."

"You don't have to say anything." He pulls me closer but instead of kissing me he plants his lips on my forehead. "I can't wait till tonight." He brushes by me as he heads toward the door that leads to our side yard. I hear the lock on the gate click as it closes. I picture him walking in front of our house toward his car. Soon I hear the roaring sound of his Mustang as he drives away.

I stay in the garage, leaning against my car for I don't know how long. I keep running my fingers over my lips as I reflect on the events of the past week. I do not consider the future, though. There's no point. I'll let life sweep me up and carry me away to the next day.

I waste a few hours lying on my bed and staring at the ceiling. With Mike at work, Benny wants to take me out for dinner. He didn't give up on coaxing me into going to the police. I don't even consider that as an option anymore. Since I have plans for tonight, I put a rain check on our dinner.

I set the alarm for six thirty in the afternoon and close my eyes.

When my watch beeps, I find myself lying on my side in the dark room. I quickly flip the nightstand lamp on, knocking over two books I started but had no time to finish. The library already sent me an email to remind me that they are due back on Monday.

Since I'm alone and nobody has demands of me, I soak myself in a tub of hot water with sea salt. I submerge my face aware of each drop as the water pours into my ears and nose. I picture myself as a pale corpse under the glassy, smooth surface. I wonder if I am strong enough to drown myself. I've seen enough crime movies to know that drowning is a horrible way to go.

Tiny air bubbles escape my nostrils and pop on the surface. Only a strange vibration disturbs the silent underwater world. I'd imagine space to be the same. I'm floating. I've been floating for years.

I scrub my body hard with a washcloth until my skin is red and feels raw. I wash my hair and shave. Standing in front of my closet, I spend more time selecting an outfit than I did when I was getting ready for my kids' baptisms.

I have no clue what people wear in a casino. I was in Vegas once where Mike, his foster mother, and I watched the David Copperfield Show, and that was years ago. In those days the ratio between cocktail dresses and tracksuits was even.

I decide on a pair of black silk capris, a light pink blouse, and a colorful glass bead necklace. I slip into a pair of nude high-heel sandals that show off my toes. The French pedicure looks too ordinary in the nude sandals, so I redo my toenails. The dark purple nail polish gives me the look of someone wild and brave. This entire outfit is from my mid-twenties. Who knew that stress would be the best diet I ever tried?

According to a recent radio commercial, Pechanga is the number one casino in the US. I'm excited to cross its long corridors with an inside man, like I'm somebody, as if I belonged.

Bruce waits for me in his car by the gardening section at Lowe's as he promised. I'm early, but he's already there. I pop into the seat next to him. The moment I'm settled, he puts a hand on my thigh. I feel like an unattached girl on a date.

The car is as spotless, inside as well as the outside, and the interior is customized. The black leather seat is soft, welcoming. I'm starting to understand why Mike is so envious of this car.

The windows are tinted, yet every time we stop at a traffic light I lean toward Bruce because I don't want a neighbor or a teacher from school to recognize me.

After driving for twenty minutes, we arrive at the casino. I recall having heard on *CSI* that the jingling of the slot machines is calibrated to a melody that's so pleasing to the ear that it invites people to stay and play more. I'm not a gambler, but the perfect harmony of these sounds makes me feel glamorous and excited.

Bruce takes me on a tour of the main building. On our way to the elevator, he points out the restaurants, the theater, and the VIP rooms. His office is on the fifth floor. I ask why we're going up there. He says he has a surprise for me.

In the middle of the room, a table is set for two with a white tablecloth, porcelain plates, and crystal wine goblets. A bouquet of flowers in a glass vase towers over the elegantly decorated table.

Offering my compliments, I make my way to the window to admire the city view. Working in a place like this would give me back my will to live and not only to exist. Choosing to stay at home with my kids made me miss out on so much.

There is a knock at the door. White-jacketed waiters bring trays of food: roasted duck, steak, and lobster, everything fancy. I have had little appetite with all the recent stress in my life, so my stomach has shrunk. I only eat some sushi and one lobster tail with steamed vegetables. Then the famous Tres Leches cake is served. That, I can't turn down. Bruce feeds me with his spoon. He was right. It's heavenly.

More Mojitos arrive for me, and a gin and tonic for Bruce. When the table is cleared, I go back to the window with my glass in hand.

Bruce molds himself against me and drapes an arm around my chest as if he wants to make sure I don't jump. I think about it. It would be an easy way to get rid of my problems.

He claps his hands and the already dim lights go out completely. I feel his breath on my neck. I can't help but welcome it. Alcohol has this effect on me. It clears my mind of responsibilities and reality.

Bruce doesn't undress me; he only caresses my right breast through the satin fabric. I should tell him not to expect too much of me because in five days I will either be dead or dressed in orange. I want to tell him that my life is in danger and I need him to protect me but I remain silent. He doesn't need my drama. Tonight, neither do I.

It's almost midnight when we are at the bar downstairs talking to a group of people who reek of money and the life of privilege. Despite my best effort to look like one of them, I'm sure they can see me for who I am. After the fifth Mojito, I start worrying less about what they think of me. Bruce doesn't seem to be embarrassed so why should I. He's been keeping me close all night. I stood between his legs, as he was perched on a barstool. I huddled under his protective arms while watching a game at the blackjack table. I sat on his lap in the upholstered armchair. We also danced.

When our little group hit the club, a Spanish song was playing. Couples were dancing in a way you learn in a ballroom.

I must have been gawking at them with envy because Bruce pulled on my hand and said, "Let's dance."

I don't dance. I used to but not anymore. Mike has no rhythm and no interest in dancing.

"No, thank you," I said with an awkward grin. The mere thought of strangers watching me swaying my hips gives me shivers.

"Come on. With moves like yours, I bet you are good at it." He pulled me forward. I pulled him back in a childish tug of war between us. *I'm an adult. A mother of two. I can't act this foolish way anymore.* Bruce won. I let him lead me. I warmed up after a while. The cocktails that kept coming must have something to do with my looseness. We danced. I laughed. I cried. I had the best time of my life. This one night made up for all the wasted time of the past ten years.

At the end of the song, Bruce went down on one knee in front of everybody and kissed my tummy. He picked me up and spun me around. My head started to spin too. I focused my eyes on his face. Out of the blue, I pictured him hanging lifelessly on the end of the rope as Jake did. I had to wash my face in the restroom to clear my head. It seemed as if I had cast a spell on Bruce as I had done on dozens of other poor boys in my past. The devil still owned me.

"You've never been on Ortega Highway?" the alcohol-dazed Bruce yells into my face around three in the morning. Many of his friends around us express their shock and disappointment.

"No," I say innocently, shrugging my shoulders. I don't get what's the big deal.

Bruce replies, "Ortega Highway is California State Route 74 that connects Riverside with Orange County."

I shake my head. I may never have heard of the Ortega Highway, but I do know that a week before school starts Rite Aid puts a 50% off tag on school supplies.

Bruce pats my thigh, then twists his body toward the table where his Asian friends are eating something called truffle fries. "Hey, Chen, are you guys heading back home tomorrow?"

"You know it."

"Usual time?"

The guy nods.

Bruce lifts his glass to me and says, "I hope you have nothing planned for tomorrow morning because I'm taking you to Ortega."

"What's so special about that road?" I ask while taking the French fries from the hand Chen extends toward me. Since we spent the whole night together, I now feel like we are friends.

I've learned today that the fried potatoes are sprinkled with oil extracted from truffle mushrooms and is very expensive. A true delicacy. The unique flavor explodes on your tongue and once you taste it all you can think of is to have another bite. What else had I missed out on while being closed up in the fictional worlds of TV shows and novels?

"You'll see." He winks at me and forces his tongue into my mouth to steal the truffle flavor.

"Are you gonna take me home now?" I stagger a bit and giggle like a silly girl. It's been a long night of drinking and fun.

He salutes. "No, ma'am. We have a room for tonight."

"I thought you said this would be only a neighborly dinner." I feign anger.

"Why? Friends can't share a room?" The look in his eyes is intense. It makes my body shake with excitement.

He sets his glass down and pushes himself up so forcefully against me that I almost slide to the ground. While I gather myself, he snatches my hand, nods goodbye at his friends and starts guiding me along the red carpet. I don't ask where we are going because I've been in a haze of drunkenness and exhaustion since eleven. I also discover that I love being over-powered. The feeling surprises me and excites me.

In the elevator, he braces me against the wall and pins my hands above my head. No man has ever wanted me so badly. Not even my own husband.

224

4 DAYS TO DIE

The rising sun paints the dawn sky with harmonious colors. I can't stop admiring it while Bruce and I are waiting in the garage for Chan and his crew. I shiver from the draft racing through the open garage. Bruce pulls me closer to his chest and starts rubbing the side of my arm. His confidence and straightforward attitude make me feel secure. And as much as I wish Mike would see me now, and not just see me but realize that I'm not as burned out and boring as he paints me to be, I'm glad he isn't here. Finally, I have a secret life on my own. I feel as if I found my way out of the labyrinth of marriage and motherhood. I'm no longer just *one thing*. I am *many things*. I'm a great mother, had always been a good wife, and can be a fierce lover.

I owe Bruce my gratitude for opening my heart. Without him, I'd be lying on the couch right now bawling over a fictional tragedy portrayed by a soap opera character.

I listen to Bruce talking with great flair about his friends and the street racing they enjoy together. His passion is contagious, and I welcome it.

"You'll love Chan's car," he says, tirelessly running his hand up and down my arm to keep me warm. "It's a Lotus Exige S. Have you heard of it?"

I shake my head. After our last night in the casino, it has never been more apparent just how big of a gap there is between our lifestyle and age differences. Can this gap close up between us? It scares me! I'm scared of tomorrow—I'm scared of not being enough for Bruce.

"You'll see it soon enough. It's a racing demon,"
Bruce raves.

I feel my stomach flip-flop. "Are we going to street race this morning?"

He lets out a roar of laughter, but it's not mocking, or belittling, but somewhat lighthearted. "Not today. We'll only drive."

"I'm not sure what's so special about driving a car on a highway. I drive every day. It's tedious," I say.

Eyes focused, Bruce draws in a big gulp of air, most likely readying himself to explain something to me, but he's suddenly robbed of the opportunity to do so.

Competing roars of car engines fill the garage. The sound is overpowering. I felt the same sensation in my chest when my father took Kyle and me to a Michael Jackson concert when we were kids. The power of the bass speakers made my chest feel like it would explode.

Bruce leans towards my ear. "Let's talk about this after we get to Capistrano." He winks.

I have the feeling that I'll be talking about this *drive* differently when I reflect upon it in the future.

The slick nose of the first sports car appears on the ramp. The body of the car is red with cool side panels and chrome accessories. Next, a lime green car pulls in, followed by a canary yellow sports car and two blue ones. They all look different, yet similar. I can't pick out the Lotus Bruce was talking about if my life depends on it.

Bruce remains beside me, as he nods at the drivers parking side by side with mathematical precision in front of us. Then, like the main attraction of a show, a white car with streamlined body and black accessories rolls onto the platform.

"Now, that's our ride," exclaims Bruce.

Chan spills out from the front door of the car that looks unique and fast. His tousled hair and small red eyes scream of a long and fun-filled night. I knew he had a long night. I was there!

Bruce's wealthy and successful friend Chan makes his way to us. With a stern nod and half-smile, he tosses the keys at Bruce. In return, Bruce slams his own keys into Chan's hand.

None of the other drivers get out of their cars to greet us, but Chan barks a short 'wazzup' at me.

"A grand says I'll beat you to Tony's," Chan teases Bruce, waving a wad of cash. "Even with this old piece of shit."

"Whoa! Whoa! Show respect for the ride, man!" Bruce barks, but by the way his lips curve, I know he's not offended. Their tight friendship goes back years. I learned that last night. I envy their brotherly bond. I cut all ties that connected me to my friends long ago.

"Are you in or not?" Chan pushes.

"Not today, my friend. Today I need to impress my girl." He presses his mouth onto my lips. I hear windows rolling down and the various teasing chants that follow. My first thought is that I'm too old for all this, but that feeling is soon replaced with another. I decide that feeling sexy, and unique is not entirely a privilege of the young.

Bruce opens the door of the Lotus for me, and I ease onto the leather seat. My stomach is as uneasy as it used to be before an oral exam in college. The moment that Bruce shut the door, the other cars start pulling out of the parking lot one by one. I notice my charming driver pushing an earpiece into his ear.

"Are we clear?" he says, looking ahead and pressing down on his earpiece as if waiting for a reply. "Alright. Hold onto your seat," he tells me and engages the clutch.

Like rolling marbles, the six street racing cars followed by Bruce's deep-green Mustang spiral down the garage ramp at high speed. I think I'm screaming, but I'm not sure because I'm too busy trying to hold onto my seat.

At the exit gate, Bruce hits the breaks. Paying for parking seems silly now, but I'm glad for this short interruption. I can use a little more time to ready myself for the *drive* since the anticipation unsettles me.

It's six thirty-two in the morning when at last we turn onto Ortega Highway, after an exhilarating drive on I-15 and the streets of Lake Elsinore. As if an invisible hand guided us, the seven cars constantly switched lanes, passed each other and roared across the otherwise dull, straight and long freeway. But now with the rolling hills surrounding us, and the blue lake below glistening in the early morning sunlight, the road offers impressive scenery.

With little to no traffic, the cars ascend the steep winding road at racing speed. The sounds we make echo through the hills

Even though Bruce told Chan that he wasn't interested in a race, he drives fast and competitively. I can't stop marveling at him, as I take in his strong arms as he shifts, his trained legs as he manipulates the pedals, the concentration on his face, and the tiny wrinkle created on his forehead as his eyes focus on the road ahead. I remind myself that I know how to drive a car with a stick shift, too— Kyle secretly taught me when I was fourteen.

A DJ remix plays on the radio. I turn the volume up to near deafening. I'm having a flashback. It's not just a fun and exciting ride anymore. It's a time travel back to the past.

Bruce gives me a look that reaches into the depths of my heart. I start breathing heavily. I want him. I want him now.

"See you boys at Tony's. And . . . don't wait up," he says into the microphone. Staring at me with the eyes of a hungry wolf, he removes the earpiece and drops it onto the backseat. He breaks hard, and like a wave, our fellow racers pass us honking feverishly. I laugh, feeling my face flush.

Bruce navigates the magnificent Lotus towards a dirt path, away from the main road, between tall and dense trees. He brings the car to a halt so suddenly that the tires stir up dust. It envelops us, creating a cloud of privacy.

Then I pull my shirt over my head, my eyes not letting go of his. Bruce pushes his seat back and lowers the backrest. I found myself sitting on him, blinded with passion. The music continues to burst from the speakers. I'm not myself. I'm possessed. There is no thought to my actions only instincts. I'm an animal. I am a wild thing.

. . . . . .

Server #1: Look, I've been working here for two years now. Bruce never brought a girl here. He had this rule about mixing business with pleasure. Yes, I was surprised to see him with a woman. All the girls were. I always pictured him with a photo model. You know, with a tall young girl with sky-high legs and big boobs. The woman he was with on Saturday night looked nothing like that. I mean she was okay looking I guess, but nothing special. It was weird how Bruce doted on her all night. Those guys from Orange County that Bruce street-races with seemed to have a blast in her company. I don't know, maybe she's like Amy Schumer, not particularly good-looking but hilarious. Who knows?

Server #2: Just so you know, Bruce tried to hit on me a few times, but I turned him down.

Server #1: Oh, shut up Stephanie. He did not.

Server #2: Don't believe me then. Whatever.

Server #3 Don't believe a word she's saying, detective. Bruce kept his hands off us. He does have a temper, though. I saw him a few times getting into the faces of guests who were rude to us girls. He always protected us without asking for special favors in return, if you know what I mean.

Server #1: Yes, Veronica's right. Bruce is a great guy. And I'm sad to hear that he's involved in some kind of crime. To be honest, it's hard to grasp. Well, if you don't know if he was involved or not why are you questioning us?

. . . . .

I run my fingers over my lips as I drive up to the house. The taste of Bruce lingers on my lips. The combination of shame and excitement forms within my chest—under my blouse. Hidden. Safe.

Images of Bruce touching me take over my mind. This pleasant feeling is taken away from me when I spot my nosy neighbor Carol walking back from her mailbox towards me. She is watching me; her eyes are penetrating as if she wanted to look inside me. If she figures out that something is going on between Bruce and me, she will plant gossip at every house on the street, like a seed, and will nourish it until it grows out of control.

There is no escape from her now. *Why is this damn garage door not opening?* I keep pressing the button to make my escape, but the door remains stationary.

I catch her reflection in the rearview mirror. She's almost at the car. I smell of sex and Bruce. I need to get out and make a run for the door before she can get a whiff of me.

I pop out of the car and shut the door behind me. I keep my distance from her as she approaches me with a flushed face and awkwardly applied makeup. As usual, she wears a tight shirt showing off her breasts. Quickly I look away towards a pot of petunias, blooming for the second time this year.

She's caught up with me. There's no escape from her now.

"What can I help you with, Carol?" I ask, concentrating hard on keeping my eyes on her face and not her revealing shirt.

"The house was dark last night? You didn't tell me you were going away for the night. I could have watched Kona for you." She's holding the morning paper with two hands as if it were too heavy for her to carry.

"I was home. I just went to bed early." I don't allow my face to change expression. Once she senses that I'm hiding something she will start grilling me, and I wouldn't take that lightly.

I must remain kind. I don't need her vengeance again. I had enough of that when she called the homeowners association on us for tree branches that hung over her property, all because I turned down her invitation for a cup of coffee and a little chat three times in a row.

In the next five minutes she tells me about the renter across the street who always forgets to take the trash bins inside after trash day; about a family who lives on another street but walks their dog in our cul-de-sac and doesn't pick up after it; about the first house on our street that was sold a few days ago for a ridiculously low amount of three hundred thousand dollars. She complains that their decision to sell quickly at such a low price will bring down the value of all of our homes.

I take a long and deliberate look at my watch. "Oh, gosh. Carol, I have to get going. I need to pick up my kids from grandma today."

As I stand in the doorway groping for my house keys she keeps talking.

"I saw you were talking to Bruce the other day," she says nonchalantly. She's like a police dog. Once she gets the scent of something, she will stop at nothing to sniff it out. The family, who lived in our house before us, got divorced and their home went into foreclosure. I heard rumors that it was Carol who fed the wife with stories.

"Yeah. I invited Bruce to the block party." Don't say too much, or too little. Either way seems suspicious. "He seems like a nice guy," I add.

"It seemed he really enjoyed himself at the party. Did you tell him that the invitation was for a street party, not a house party?"

"What do you mean?"

"I wanted to talk to him about his gardeners," she said annoyingly, using her hands dramatically "They always park between our properties rather than in front of his home. I don't like it because the other day I could barely pull out of my driveway." It occurred to me that a minivan could turn around on her driveway. Pulling out straight should be easy for her. God! The woman loves drama.

"Okay." I make a face.

She steps closer to me. "You know I never really get to talk to Bruce because he seems to spend the majority of his time inside your home . . . with you."

"I think you're exaggerating. Bruce came into the kitchen once during the party to grab some fruit salad, but I think that was it. He also may have been talking to Mike. I'm just not sure." I tell myself not to make too many excuses. That could indicate a guilty conscience.

"Interesting."

"Carol, I really must go. But it was nice talking to you." As I open the door, I glance back at her. My eyes catch the sun reflecting off Bruce's Mustang as it rolls up in the street. My expression must have gone a drastic change because Carol follows my gaze and looks behind her.

As if being chased, I burst into the house and shut the door behind me. If the police ever came to investigate our family, Carol would be the first witness to provide testimony against me.

The moment I cross the threshold I realize the house is not as I left it. Mike's blue work backpack lies on the carpet in front of the bookshelf. I smell food.

I know I need to make a move; I should run upstairs to wash Bruce off my skin, but panic grips my muscles. I only have a split second to consider doing this or run over to Bruce's home and ask him to use his bathroom, before Kona starts whining and alerts Mike that I am home. With Carol stalking in front of my house there is no way I'll be able to sneak over to Bruce unnoticed.

Kona emits a loud cry that builds up to a series of whimpering. It's too late to run.

I poke my head through the passage into the kitchen. Mike's standing at the island, with his back to me, reading the newspaper.

"Are you home already?" I ask, but my voice comes out as a near whisper.

He begins folding up his newspaper without glancing at me. The sound of the paper makes me nervous. The storm is rising. I can sense it. There will be no way out of a fight this time. We've had enough fights for a lifetime. I recognize the signs.

I should start with an offense; blurt out what I know about his plans of getting rid of me. Put him on the spot. Question him about the Italian bimbo. I need to beat him to the finish line this time. Grill him before he grills me.

"Where were you?" He asks calmly, tossing the papers in the trash.

"I went for a walk," I casually say as I open the cabinet, take out a glass and fill it up with cold water. I used to be good at this lying game. That's how I survived college. It shouldn't be that hard to bring back the ability to deceive.

The top of the trash can snaps back into place. "Alone?" He drops a dirty plate into the sink, without as much as a glance at me.

I should cook up some believable lies or think of ways to get him off my back. Use the laxative again perhaps. But I can't think of anything useful. All violent thoughts evade me now. Bruce messed my head up.

"Whom else would I go with? I don't have friends." I take a sip of water. A whiff of Bruce's cologne hits me. My neck flexes as I take a step back. I sense the blood leaving my face.

Mike looks up and studies me for a few uncomfortable seconds. I don't move. Maybe I want him to notice how good a time I had. I want him to be jealous.

"Why didn't you take Kona?" He licks the spoon and tosses it into the sink from enough of a distance to appear violent.

I shudder from the crashing sound. "He pulls. I wasn't in the mood to be dragged around." I put the glass on the counter wondering if Bruce's cologne is noticeable. Then I ask Mike, "How come you are home a day early?"

"I traded with a buddy of mine. I hated the thought that you were home alone. I thought I'd surprise you." From everything he says all I can hear is that he traded days. How many times had he traded days to spend time with his lover and 'adult friends'? He's been playing me for a fool all this time.

"I'm sorry if your plans fell through. I didn't know I was here for your convenience." I walk away, towards the stairs.

"What's your problem?" I hear him behind me. "Why are you acting so weird lately?"

I stop, my hand grasping the railing. "I have only a few more days left, and I won't waste it on fighting." The words slip out. I use the awkward silence that follows my statement to disappear.

In the bathroom, I turn the water on and remove my clothes. I'm so angry and frustrated that I want to break something. The framed picture of Mike and me diving in Guam will do. I open the balcony door and send it flying across the yard. My throat is aching for a Mojito. It's doable. The bottle of Bacardi is still in the cabinet above the refrigerator. We have plenty of mint and lime.

When I'm about to step into the shower, I hear the floor creak. Last time it was Bruce who entered the bedroom after me. This time it's Mike. At once I'm gripped by an intensifying feeling of annoyance.

I watch the shadow he cast on the shower curtain. I picture him holding his hand up ready to pull the curtain. And he does. Even when the kids are gone, there is no privacy in this damn house.

"Why did you say that you have only days left. Are you sick or something?"

I look at him. His eyes are moist. His eyelids are sagging.

"Don't you have something to do?" I grunt. My body is not his temple anymore. He has no right to invade my privacy after what he had done to our marriage.

"So you're not gonna tell me?"

"Tell you what?"

"Tell me why are you acting like you have a problem with me?" My eyes catch the sight of a bottle of Dove men's shampoo. It contains menthol. I imagine holding Mike's head down and squirting it into his eyes. Then watch him react with pain. The violent thoughts are back at last.

"Finally the kids are gone, and I'm alone. Can I take a fucking shower without someone pulling the curtain and asking me questions?" I yank the curtain back. "Arghhh."

I search for the spider I see every morning sitting on the edge of the tile. It's still there. I splash it with water. As a cold feeling of emptiness comes over me, I watch it spinning toward the drain, desperately trying to hold onto something to save its life. With my toes, I lead him toward the hole. Then I look at the spot where he had been sitting this past week, sharing the shower with me, watching me, unmoving. A sharp pang stabs my chest. I feel horrible. I fall to my knees. The intensity of the water feels like lashes from a whip against my skin.

The curtain flies open; this time entirely one side allowing the water to spray out of the shower and trail down onto the tile floor. I look up mortified into the hard face of a madman. Mike is holding the panties I wore this morning when I was with Bruce.

"Who is he?" he shouts with a voice that sounds like a raging bear.

I can't respond.

He has no patience to wait for me to come up with an answer. He drags me out of the shower. The edge of the tile scrapes the entire length of my leg. His fingers grip my flesh harder, and he starts shaking me by the arms.

The water is dripping from my hair onto my naked shoulders. Most of the boys displayed this same behavior when they found out that I lied about loving them. They shook me. They spat into my face. But this time I do the spitting.

My uncharacteristically aggressive reaction throws Mike off balance. He lets go off my arm and slaps me across the face. I fall onto the bed. Holding my aching cheek, I watch him wiping my spit away from his face. He has an excessive amount of tattoos on his upper body and uses a ton of hair gel to look macho. Yeah, you are a real man, Mike.

He sets his hateful eyes on me. His lips are quivering. I don't give him the satisfaction to fight back. If he wants to beat up a defenseless, naked woman, so be it. I'll take pictures later. His rampage against me will be evidence in court. In public court and not criminal, because I'm not going to kill this man. I will divorce him instead. I'll make it painful, and watch him suffer in a courtroom when I take everything away from him he ever loved: his money, his children.

Mike takes menacing steps toward the sink where he rips off a towel from the hook. He tosses it at me, then marches out of the room and down the stairs. I hear the laundry room door slam. I'm not scared. I don't shudder. I'm not the victim anymore. I am once again the predator I used to be. I guess there is nothing in-between. If you're mean, people will hate you. If you're nice, people will take advantage of you. Now it's my turn again to take what I want.

While I dry off, I make up my mind about going over to see Bruce. I dress consciously; picking out clothes that will cover my fresh bruises and red spots.

I change three times before I go back to the bathroom to apply some mascara and lip-gloss. I blow dry my hair and straighten it out with a hairbrush. I don't cry. I'm not scared.

Standing in front of the mirror, I stare at the reflection of my face for a long time. I feel the muscles on my face drooping. Whom am I kidding?

All the craziness that has surrounded me in a past few days overtakes my emotions. Was I genuinely considering killing someone?

I sigh, feeling overwhelmed and stupid. With tears in my eyes, I lower the toilet seat cover and sit down. My face buried in my hands, I start crying. All those stupid TV shows and physiological thrillers made me believe that I could pull this off. That I could just poison my husband and move on with my life. All the values I've been teaching to my children would mean nothing to them anymore if they found out what I had been planning.

I have to talk to Bruce. Ask for his help. Here I am again, planning to ask a man's help to solve my problems. He will probably advise me to go to the police, just like Benny did. I will do it this time. I'm in a position to expose the hitman. I will meet him wearing a wire. I'll have proof of everything. I don't care anymore what the neighbors will think or that the kids and I will have to move. We will find a smaller, cheaper place. Start over. It's going to be tough on the kids, tough on all of us, but at least I would be doing the right thing. I would teach them that more violence is not the answer to violence.

I wash the makeup off my face and drink some water. Then I make my way downstairs. The house is quiet. Mike hasn't come back yet. I know he won't. He's probably with Emanuela, lying on her pregnant belly and telling her how horrible his marriage is. How thankful he is for her saving him from the evil claws of his wife. I don't care anymore. I'm done with Mike. I feel nothing. No anger. No disappointment. Not even jealousy.

I make my way into Bruce's backyard through the side gate like a creepy stalker. I hear music and gurgling sounds. He's sitting in the Jacuzzi with headphones on and eyes closed. I touch his shoulder. He jumps so much that water splashes all over me. Once he sees my face, he relaxes. With a hand on his heart, he says, "Jeez, Sarah. Don't do that. I almost punched you out."

"I'm sorry for scaring you."

"You didn't scare me."

He leans towards me and reaches for my hand. "Take your clothes off. Come in."

I remain unmoving. Bruce's hand moves to my upper arm. I wince from the pain.

He is startled. "What's going on?"

"He knows."

"Who knows what?"

"My husband. He knows that I was with someone last night." I fold my arms around my damp clothes. I'm shaking.

"Let me see your arm," Bruce asks of me.

"Why?" I step back.

"Pull your sleeve up. Please."

"I don't want to. Bruce, we need to talk about something." I take the towel from the back of the patio chair and hold it out for him.

He motions to take the towel but snatches my arm instead, and with one swift move pulls up my sleeve. The four long marks Mike's fingernails left on my arm are red and raw.

I drop his towel and pull my sleeve down to cover myself up.

"It's nothing," I repeat.

"It's nothing?" he snaps. I see the anger brewing in his eyes. "Your husband brings his whores to the casino, but he has the nerve to hit you for being with another man?"

I thought Mike couldn't embarrass me more than he already did but Bruce's statement makes me stagger. So many times, I wanted to go to Pechanga, but Mike always told me that he hated casinos.

"Where is Mike? Is he home?"

"No. He left."

He pushes the sliding door open. "Go home, Sarah. I'll come and see you later."

I pull him back by his arm. "Don't do anything stupid, Bruce. Please." I plead, but my words don't seem to reach him. He's mad. Coming up with a plan. I have to stop him.

I step in front of him. "What are you doing?"

"I'll go out to find him. I want to have a little chat with him."

I rub my face with both hands. "Please stay here with me. I can handle Mike."

He spins around on the top of the stairs and faces me. "Don't you see, Sarah? You don't have to do this alone anymore. I won't let that bastard hurt you ever again."

"It's not his fault. I fell. It was an accident."

"Stop it. Okay?" He pinches the bridge of his nose. "Don't you think I heard the yelling and arguing?"

Blood drains from my head, and I become lightheaded. "You heard?"

"It doesn't matter. I'm here now. And I will put an end to this."

"You won't even find him. He's probably in our rental home with his pregnant lover."

Bruce's eyes enlarge. "Pregnant? Where?"

I don't give him the address. I only say that it's in French Valley. His phone rings. It's the casino. He needs to go in. I feel relieved.

"Just go to work and let me handle this, OK. Promise me."

He looks away with clenched jaws. "I'll be back in an hour, and then we can talk, alright."

"Yes. Just go. Do your thing. I need to drive up to Palmdale today and get my kids anyway."

"I'll go with you."

"No. I want to go alone. But I'll call you. I promise."

I go home. I'm alone in the house, which I usually enjoy, but now the silence is driving me crazy. I sit down in the entry and call Benny. I need someone to talk to. I tell him everything that happened since we last spoke; except the part about Bruce and me.

He wants to come over and take me to the police.

"You have proof of domestic violence now," he said. "You can use your bruises to build a case against Mike."

I know he's right, so I agree with his plan. He asks me to stay put because he's not in town and needs a few hours to come and get me. I don't want to do this alone, so I tell him I'll wait for him.

To pass the time I do what I always do when I need to keep my mind off things: I start cleaning. I pull out the vacuum cleaner and vacuum the house. Then I go to the kitchen to empty the dishwasher when I notice the empty pot of beef stew, a dirty plate, and spoon in the sink. The note I put on the cover of the pot is on the counter. Mike ate the stew for breakfast. What idiot eats hot beef stew for breakfast?

I scrub the pot with shaking hands. I call Benny a dozen times, but each time my call goes to voicemail, I feel my nerves go on edge. I fill up a bucket with hot water and start scrubbing the floors. I keep my phone with me, waiting for a call from Bruce, Benny or even Mike. The anticipation is slowly tearing me apart. But nobody calls me. And I keep scrubbing, dusting, and cleaning until I can't feel my fingers anymore. Then I sit down by the piano and wait. I wait for fate to determine my future.

*   *   *   *   *

A slight tremor in my back pocket startles me as my cell phone vibrates from an incoming call. I yank it out of my pocket, but it slips from my hand and lands on the carpet. The shaking sensation in my stomach just won't quit, and the feeling is slowly spreading over my entire body.

I reach for the phone distractedly, my mind miles away. I've been worrying about Bruce and about what he might do to my husband. I worry about Benny because I know him too well. Revenge is his expertise. I should never have let them get involved with my life. The old Sarah, who used men for her benefit, should have stayed buried. But I unleashed the monster and now who knows what the consequences would be.

I check the caller ID on the screen while Kona's barking bounces off the tall window next to me. He isn't hostile enough to make me suspect a stranger at the door. He's just doing his job as a guard dog, warning me about the mailman or the FedEx delivery guy near our house, yet the combined forces of my nerves and uncertainty make me uneasy.

The area code is local, but the rest of the number doesn't look familiar. I think about the empty pot of beef stew in the sink, considering the possibility of Mike's already becoming sick from the Selenium overdose. But I can't know for sure that this call is about my husband until I answer it. The hitman has been calling me from random numbers; most likely, he's been using disposable phones to cover his tracks. I know I must answer. *Answer it dammit!*

"Hello," I say, not more than a ring before the call would have gone to voicemail.

"Hi, my name is Shelly Maxwell. I'm calling from Loma Linda Hospital. Is this Sarah Johnson?"

"Yes," I say, but my word comes out feebly. Deep down in my subconscious mind I was expecting a call from the police. If Mike is at the hospital sick from the stew, then I'm screwed. No way had the selenium left his system this fast.

When I read the articles online, I felt confident about the dosage I added to his food. He shouldn't be sick from one dose. I now realize there may have been some gaps in my research regarding selenium. I feel doubt taking over my thoughts.

"I'm calling about your husband, Michael Johnson. He was brought here in critical condition. I need you to come in as soon as possible."

"Critical condition? What happened?" An intense trembling in my knees makes it impossible for me to pay attention to her words. I want my legs to stop shaking so that I can concentrate, but they are out of control.

"Once you come in, the doctor will explain everything. How much time do you need to get here, Mrs. Johnson?"

Loma Linda is off Interstate 215, located in a modern white building with vast reflective windows in the color of sapphires. Before we moved to Italy, I tried to procure some business there with little-to-no success.

"Fifteen to twenty minutes," I say as an auto-response.

"Sounds great. Please check in at the front desk first. Your husband is in ICU. And Mrs. Johnson, drive safely."

The phone goes dead. I lean against the wall to steady myself. My chest feels constricted. I feel the strength leaving my legs, but I can't allow myself to be weak now. I need to keep my wits about me and to get rid of any evidence from the attempted poisoning of Mike before the police come to sniff around the house. If Mike is at the hospital suffering from a heart attack and his blood test shows a high level of Selenium, they surely will come to investigate me.

Gaining support from the kitchen countertop, I make it to the dishwasher. Above it is the cabinet where I keep the bottles of Selenium. I take all three containers into my hands along with the bottle of MiraLax. The back of my neck is hot, and I feel my scalp burning as I stagger to the toilet where I flush all the pills and the entire contents of the MiraLax.

I peek at my watch. I've already wasted three minutes of my time, but I can't go to the hospital just yet. First, I need to get rid of the empty bottles. I make my way to the backyard fence, unstable and off-balance. My movements are not my own. A puppet master is controlling my limbs.

I toss all four bottles into the thick shrubs behind the backyard fence. Nobody will look for them there. And even if they do, there is no way they'll find them in the overgrown, rodent-infested shrubbery.

The containers are still soaring high in the air when I realize that I didn't wipe my fingerprints off the bottles. I bang my fist against my head. All those hours spent watching TV crime shows, yet in the moment of panic, I forgot that the most apparent trace criminals leave behind are fingerprints.

I grunt angrily and kick a flowerpot into the air. It goes flying several feet. Suffering from a sharp, throbbing pain in my toes, I limp to the garage. I'm sure the ceramic pot lifted at least one of my toenails, and now my toe is bleeding into the sock.

After taking care of my injury, I go to my car and place my purse next to me on the seat. I then pull out of the driveway and start driving down the street at an excessive rate of speed to make up for the lost time.

By the time I reach the freeway exit for the hospital, my hands are so damp that when I try to make a sharp left turn, they slip off the steering wheel. I wipe them both on my thighs, but it only solves my problem temporarily.

As usual, a sea of cars fills the designated parking area, but I somehow manage to find a spot relatively close to the emergency entrance.

By rushing to the main door, my legs become tangled, and I nearly trip a few times. All I can think about is that if the nurse wasn't allowed to share details about Mike's condition with me, then it could only mean one thing: I'm a suspect.

When it comes to murder and suicide, poison is the number one choice for women. I just turned myself into a statistic. I'm fucked. Freaking TV shows!

Determined to avoid eye contact, I check in at the front desk, and a hospital volunteer escorts me to a waiting room where people are pacing around or sitting with their heads buried in their hands. These are people who might have lost loved ones or fear for their children's lives.

What have I done?

"Do you know why my husband's here?" I ask my escort who stops at a chair and motions me to sit down. I shake my head no at her offer. I'm too nervous to sit.

"Someone will be with you shortly and explain everything," she says with a sympathetic smile and presses a hand against my back.

I picture her saying the same thing and offering the same gesture to every confused and devastated visitor. I don't know why but I think of my nosy neighbor Carol. Perhaps if she volunteered in a hospital, she wouldn't be so bored and desperate, and wouldn't need to live vicariously through other people's lives.

The minutes crawl by, and though I'm determined to stand, I feel lightheaded, so I take my place on an upholstered chair. I braid my fingers over my lap and affix my eyes on the door closest to me and wait.

Three chairs to my right a short blonde woman in her forties sobs quietly. A man who looks like as if he had just driven here from a golf course has his arm drooped over her shoulders. His worn yet somewhat handsome face is devoid of expression as if suddenly his life just lost all meaning to him. My heart twitches.

What have I done?

A group of people comes through the double door. The wailing of the woman around whom they all huddle hurts my eardrums like a Q-tip pressed in too deeply. I'm grateful when they leave the room because I'm not sure how much longer I was going to be able to endure the tormenting sounds she made.

What have I done?

The minutes roll on, and I feel drained and emotionally exhausted from the crazy thoughts that have been flashing through my mind.

I picture Mike with defibrillator paddles on his chest as the paramedics are trying to revive him. I picture IV tubes dangling from his arms and an oxygen mask on his face.

Next, I see his hostile expression as he pushes me against the wall and spits in my face.

Then I recall his loving face as he tells me that I'm the love of his life.

I should have never let things get out of hand. I should have asked for help long ago. Perhaps a marriage counselor. Domestic violence advocate. Sex therapist. Anger management. Anything.

When a nurse finally appears in the hallway, I jolt up from my chair and grab her arm. I tell her my name and ask her about Mike. She says that my husband is still in surgery and I'll have to wait for the doctor to hear more.

"Surgery? What kind of surgery?" I ask.

"The doctor's are trying to remove a bullet from his chest."

"My husband was shot?" I manage to ask through the veil of shock.

My reaction seems to come as a surprise to her. She watches me with small beady eyes. "Yes, he was. He was brought in with two gunshot wounds in his chest. But you have to wait for the doctor to tell you more."

I should cry or display some degree of panic, like someone who just learned about her beloved husband's accident, but I can't see past the shock. I stare off into the distance, my face utterly devoid of emotion, while considering all types of scenarios.

"Are you all right?" the nurse's voice penetrates the cloud in my head.

"No, I'm not okay," I tell her and collapse onto the chair.

*   *   *   *   *

Darkness began to descend on the streets a while ago, and I can barely see a thing, but I don't stand up to turn the light on in the living room. Ever since I discovered Mike's dirty secrets, I've been preparing myself mentally to kill him, yet now the pain pins me to the couch. The hospital staff thinks I'm mentally challenged. The police think I'm guilty. After all those preparations, I completely blew the whole thing.

"Mrs. Johnson, I want you to know that we did everything possible to remove the bullets from your husband's chest, but unfortunately, we couldn't stop the internal bleeding. I'm sorry that I have to be the one to tell you this, but your husband lost a lot of blood, and he didn't make it," said the doctor.

"Thank you, doctor," I responded, shaking his hand. "I appreciate your hard work. When can I talk to him?"

"Mrs. Johnson. I don't think you understand. You won't be able to talk to your husband. He's passed away."

"No. You don't understand. I just saw my husband a few hours ago. He was fine. I mean, we had an argument, but he was perfectly healthy when he left the house. I need to see him. Can I see him now?" It was only a misunderstanding that needed to be sorted out.

"I need you to sit down first, ok?" The surgeon folded his fingers around my arm. I shook them off violently.

"Stop patronizing me. You don't understand. I need to talk to my husband. I have to see him. I have to apologize for the things I did and said."

The doctor waved his arm at someone behind me. When I turned a saw a nurse in fashionable black shrubs rushing toward us.

"Mrs. Johnson, you need to sit down and take a moment to compose yourself. I need you to understand that your husband was shot multiple times and his injuries were fatal. He died in surgery from internal bleeding. Two detectives are here. They will want to talk to you."

"Shot with what?"

"A handgun most likely, but I'll be able to tell you more after the autopsy."

"Autopsy?"

A woman and a man, both dressed in suits like the cast members of the *Men in Black*, walked up to us. The doctor introduced them as Detective Sergeant Tom Long and Detective Sergeant Silvia Morales. If not for the business cards they pushed into my hand, I'd never remember their names.

They invited me to a row of chairs in the corner of the waiting room, where we sat down in a circle as if we were at an AA meeting. They both looked at me as if they expected me to say something like, "Hi! I'm Sarah. I'm an alcoholic."

In alternating order that seemed rehearsed, the detectives asked me questions that I thought were too personal. They were teaming up against me. I felt entrapped. I kept asking for a chance to talk to

Mike. I can't tell how many attempts at explaining to me that my husband was dead it took for me to accept it finally.

For days, I've been thinking of this moment. I tried to imagine how my meeting with the doctor and the police would go. Yet, given a chance to perform, I completely shut down.

I told the detectives that I didn't know anybody who would want to hurt Mike. We weren't involved with criminals. I had never done drugs in my life—which was the truth—and neither had Mike. I wasn't sure about Mike though. After all the filth I uncovered about my husband, nothing seemed impossible. But even if Mike took drugs at parties, he wasn't tangled up in some drug war or anything.

I admitted that we had a fight earlier in the day, but I lied when I said that we fought about money.

After an hour of the detectives' grilling me about my marriage, I asked them to continue this interrogation some other time because I had completely lost my voice. They offered me water in a plastic cup. The liquid went down my throat burning like a shot of moonshine. I tried to swallow, but my throat closed up again as it had happened many times lately. For months, I've been suffering from a sore throat that refuses to heal. I should have seen a doctor about my symptoms, but Mike thought I was being a hypochondriac.

My throat still feels dry and raw when I'm back home staring in front of me at the living room carpet—a light-gray shaggy rug I picked out at Lowes with Mike's approval. Soft. Stylish. Also mainstream and boring.

Kona is whimpering at the back door, asking me to let him inside. I don't move. I sit with my back against the couch. My knees hugged to my chest. Who shot Mike? The Hitman? If he did, what on earth could be his reason? Mike needed to stay alive and take care of his sister and baby once I was gone.

Could it be Bruce? He was stark raving mad when he saw my

bruises, but for Christ's sake, we barely know each other. He would never kill a man for someone he banged a few times. He would never kill anyone period.

Then who? Benny? Yeah, he likes to put his nose into other people's business, dig up dirt on everybody, expose them, humiliate them, but murder? That's way over Benny's head. Come to think of it he had always felt responsible for me.

When my brother Kyle died, he offered to inject chlorine into the tire of the drunk driver who killed my brother. He said the chlorine would wear the rubber out and the tire would pop. And if we were lucky enough, the murderer would be on the freeway driving ninety miles an hour when it happened.

At the time, I found solace in his plan even though I knew he was joking. Now? Well, now that Mike had been killed, I'm not so sure he was joking back then.

My cell phone chimes. A new email has come in. The sound makes me remember that the kids are with Grace. I know I should call her and let her know what happened to her son but I can't bring myself to move. I'm not ready to tell the kids either. Especially on the phone. I'll wait a couple of days until I work out a deal with the hitman. Then I'll drive up to Palmdale to get my kids and bring them home. It's not safe here now. Not until the police find out who shot their father.

Kona's barking suddenly shifts from high-pitched begging into mad barking. This warning sound is different from the one he directs at the mailman.

My heartbeats accelerate. The TV remote is within reach. I press the 'on' button to provide some light. White noise emits from the screen. I'm groping for the light switch on the wall when a series of powerful knocking echoes through the living room. Kona's furious behavior could mean only one thing: there's a stranger at the door.

The police would contact me before they showed up at the house, especially at this late hour. Detective Long promised to call if they needed to talk to me again.

I creep to the kitchen and pull out a knife from the drawer. I have several bottles of pepper spray placed all over the house, but they are all upstairs.

The knocking stops. I make it to the front door and press my face against the glass. With the dark inside and the streetlights illuminating the outside, I'm able to sneak a peek without being seen from the street.

The entire cul-de-sac looks deserted. I keep scanning the street when I hear the gate that opens to the side yard slam shut. Did I lock the garage door? I only remember that I unlocked it when I took the trash out in the afternoon. Did I lock it again? I can't remember.

The laundry room door squeaks. I hear someone knocking over the container of fabric softener I use to hold the doors open to get a breeze into the house. I must have left it on the floor.

Holding the knife in my grasp, I squat down and move closer to the wall. The pressure in my chest is squeezing my heart. I start hyperventilating. I clamp a hand over my mouth to muffle my heavy breathing.

"Sarah?" A man's calling my name.

Where did I leave my cell phone? I have this image in my head of it lying next to the coffee grinder, but I'm not sure.

"Sarah? Are you home?" The voice is softer now. I know to whom it belongs, but I can't find the courage to come out of hiding.

"I need to talk to you. Are you upstairs?"

Ascending footsteps bounce off the staircase. I look up at the wall behind me and see the row of light switches. I jolt upright and flick them all up at once. Brightness pours over the room and illuminates the family photos on the piano. I swallow hard to contain my emotions, but my throat is closed up again and aching.

"Bruce," I call out with my croaky voice. "I'm down here."

He comes rushing down the stairs. I wait for him with my arms dropped to my side, still holding the knife.

His face is panic-stricken as he takes hold of my arms and starts examining my face. "What's going on? Are you all right?"

I let out the breath that has been stuck in my lungs. I feel my eyes welling up.

"Mike's dead," I say, but I'm not confident enough to determine how the words came out. Did I sound sad or scared?

He stares at me but says nothing.

I lick my lips. Why does my throat feel so dry? I feel sick, not just emotionally but physically too. I'm weak. I can barely stand.

"Bruce, you had nothing to do with this right?" I blurt out even though I promised myself not to confront him about Mike.

He jerks his head back in surprise. "What do you mean?"

"Somebody shot Mike in his car at a traffic light. Please tell me it wasn't you."

He lets go off my arms and staggers backward until his back crashes against the piano. "How can you think that? No. I don't even own a gun."

I drop the knife and bury my face into my hands. "I'm sorry, Bruce. I'm so confused." I cry for the first time since I learned about Mike's death.

His arms slip around me like a soft blanket. I lean against his chest and soak his T-shirt with my tears.

"I came here because I was so worried about you. After what Mike had done to you. . . I was so angry. I wanted to confront him, so I drove to French Valley to look for him. But I couldn't even find his car. Then I drove around for a while to cool off. I went to the casino and lost two grand in a poker game. Then I came home and saw that it was dark inside your house. I was worried about you."

His lengthy explanation makes me feel suspicious again. I peek at the knife on the floor next to us.

He bends down and picks it up before I could get to it. "Who are you so scared of?"

I shake my head to brush off his question. "How did you know the side door was open?" I sob, wiping my nose with the back of my hand.

"I didn't. I was lucky I guess."

I lower myself onto the piano bench. Bruce crouches in front of me and places his hands on my knees. I know he isn't the killer. He's tough on the outside but quite gentle on the inside.

"Can you tell me what happened?"

I tell him about the phone call from the hospital. About what the doctor said, about how the police were questioning me. Then we sit next to each other on the narrow bench, our legs touching, my face resting between his chest and arm.

I should be happy that someone killed Mike for me and solved all my problems with the hitman, but I feel just the opposite. I've never been so desperately sad in my life, not even when Kyle died.

3 DAYS TO DIE

A call from Detective Long wakes me in the morning. I'm tucked in bed wearing last night's clothes. Bruce is sleeping next to me in his jeans and T-shirt.

"Who was it?" he asks, looking at me through sleepy eyes.

"The police," I tell him with a voice that should belong to the devil. I clear my throat a few times to clear the mucus away, so I'm able to finish my sentence. "The preliminary toxicology report came back on Mike. Now the detective wants to talk to me at the station."

"This fast? Wow!" Bruce rubs the back of his head, looking at me. "Do you want me to go with you?"

There's an annoying humming in my ears making Bruce's voice sound as if it had been coming through a filter.

"I don't think it's a good idea," I whisper.

I'm too weak to make it to the bathroom let alone shower, dress and drive to the police station but I have no choice. Detective Long said it was important and it was imperative for me to come in as quickly as possible.

Bruce offers to drive me, but I can't take the risk of being seen together, although it would be logical for me to go in his car instead of driving my own because most likely I won't leave the police station today. I'm afraid the coroner's findings will be reason enough to arrest me. Then there will be no one to take my car home.

By the time I get out of the shower and come downstairs Bruce has made coffee. He hands me a cup. I inhale the aroma deep and long. It's crazy to think about the fact that I needed such a devastating event in my life to appreciate simple things like the aroma of coffee. Bruce is about to pour creamer into my cup when I stop him. Everything happened so fast between us and he didn't have the time to learn about my habits. Even Mike knows—I mean *knew*—how I like my coffee.

Bruce promises to feed Kona while I'm gone. He plants a kiss on my forehead and wishes me good luck. He says after he takes Kona for a walk he'll be at home in case I need him.

I want to bid him farewell. I have this feeling that I'll be arrested today for attempting to kill my husband. But the words escape me. So I leave him standing in front of my house, waving me away as if I were going to work or on a short trip.

Once I reach the police station, I remain in my car. Since my visit to the hospital yesterday, I can't stop reflecting on my life. I started a mental list of things I must take care of in order to provide a safe and peaceful life for my children. The most challenging task on that list is to reach back to my past. But it's something I must do.

I look up my mother's telephone number and quickly dial before I can talk myself out of it. It's been sixteen years since I last spoke to her. Now listening to the ringing tones makes my entire body shiver.

"Hello," a voice so fragile and strange to me answers.

"Mom," I say, even though I know that she won't recognize my voice either. Since we last saw each other, it became deep and cracked like a whiskey-drinking smoker.

Silence. Then faint sobbing sounds.

"Mom? Are you there?"

"Oh, Sarah," she whispers. She sounds like an old lady. Tears start to press against my eyes.

"Mom, I'm sorry. I'm so *so* sorry for everything." I cry. My chest quivers. I press my fingers against my temples.

"Oh, no Sarah. Sweetheart." Her voice breaks. "I'm so happy you called. Let me get your father."

"Mom, no. Please don't," I blurt out.

"Are you all right?"

"Mom, I know we haven't seen each other for a very long time, and I know that you and dad hate me…"

"Oh, no, Sarah. We don't hate you. How could we?" She interrupts. "I'm so happy you called. Jonathan, come quickly."

"Mom, no, please, don't tell dad it's me."

"What's going on?"

"Mike—my husband is dead." I take a moment to gather some strength. "I'm calling to ask you a huge favor."

"Oh my goodness! Sarah, Sweetheart, how can we help?"

"Mom, I have two children." My voice buckles. "They're very good kids. You'll love them. My son …" I need a second to continue. "My son Mason is so much like Kyle."

She's crying on the other end of the line and the voice pulls me deeper into emotional waters. I blow my nose and wipe my face, but the tears just keep coming.

"If something happens to me I need you to look after them, Mom. Can you do that for me?"

"Sarah, Darling, what's going on? Can I come and see you?"

"Mom, I don't have much time. I need to go to the police station. But first, I need you to promise me that you will watch after my children if something happens to me. There's no one else I can ask."

"Of course I will. But you must tell me, are you in danger?"

"No, I'm not. And I promise I'll call you back soon, but I need your word now. Please, Mom."

"I promise, Sweetheart."

The pain is real in my chest. Sixteen years had passed, yet I'm a kid again depending on my parents.

"Can you please come to my house as soon as possible? I live in Temecula. I'll text you the address."

"Of course. I'll start packing right now."

"Thank you." I take a few shaky breaths before I say, "Mom! I'm so sorry for not being the daughter you wanted me to be."

"Oh, Honey, we never stopped loving you. But don't worry about that now, okay? Just be safe. We're coming."

"I love you, Mom."

"I love you too, Sweetheart."

After hanging up, it takes a few minutes to compose myself. I'm sitting in my car, bawling like a dumb heartbroken teenager. But this emotional journey is not over yet. I have to call Benny because he's the only one who knows what's going on. I don't want to cry again, but I must dial him up soon. I'm running out of time. If I don't wish to Detective Long to call me back, I must surrender myself at the police station at once.

While the phone rings, I try to envision Benny pulling up next to Mike in the intersection and pointing a gun at him. I fail. The only scene I can put Benny in is when he hunches over his computer and types away.

That doesn't mean he didn't shoot my husband. It's common

knowledge that intense violent video games make people immune to violence and blood. And Benny had grown up on them.

I wait for him to answer the phone with a knot in my stomach.

"Finally," he barks at me. "I was wondering when you'd call me." I sense a hint of hostility in his tone.

"I've been busy."

"Oh, I know. Busy fucking your new boyfriend."

His hostile tone is not what I expected. That's not typically how Benny talks to me.

"I'm . . . not . . ."

"Save it, Sarah. I saw you last night with him. I thought you learned your lesson with Mike, but I guess you like them though, don't you?"

"What are you talking about?"

"I'm talking about you and your choice of men. I just showed you what kind of guy your husband is, and now, you hook up with a casino floor manager! I mean, are you kidding me? Did you miss the day at school when brains were handed out?"

"Don't talk to me like that."

"Why not? Isn't that what you enjoy?"

I take a deep breath and say, "Mike is dead. Someone put two bullets in his chest. I was just calling to tell you that the police want to talk to me so if there is anything you want to tell me, now is a perfect time."

Only silence comes through the line.

"I didn't do it if that's what you are implying," he says at last, sounding offended.

"Well, neither did I, but considering that you've been seen with me a few times lately, I wanted to warn you to watch your back."

"Was it the guy Mike hired to kill you?"

"I don't think so. It wouldn't make any sense."

"Hey, Sarah. Are you all right?" He's all milk and honey now.

"Don't worry about me, Benny. I gotta go."

"Hey, I'm sorry, okay. I . . ."

"No need for an apology. You're right. I'm toxic."

I hang up, and before Benny had a chance to call me back, I turn off my phone.

The interrogation room looks nothing like those on TV shows. The bare and off-white walls of the small room make me claustrophobic. There aren't any pictures or posters to look at or a big window disguised as a mirror. I'm seated on a small wooden chair with a curved back. Detective Long is close enough to me to allow me to get a whiff of his aftershave.

Detective Morales leans against the wall next to the door, guarding the only exit. Her folded arms perch on her chest, and her right hip is high enough to offer a peek at the hilted gun under her blazer.

After a short exchange of pleasantries, Detective Long picks up a stack of papers from the table. I've been told that this conversation will be recorded and I wish he hadn't mentioned it to me because this information only makes me nervous. Probably that's the plan.

Detective Long looks up from his papers and locks eyes with me. "Did your husband have a health condition? Problems with his thyroid or arteries?" he asks casually as if we were at the doctor's office filling out my medical history report. I know where he's getting at with these questions. He won't trick me that easily.

"Not that I know of," I say. There is a glass of water next to me on the table, but I decide not to drink from it. That would show that I'm nervous.

He flips the page and examines the preliminary lab report. "This report states that there was an unusually high amount of selenium in your husband's system. Did you know he was taking selenium?"

"Selenium?" I manage to come off as someone who heard something out of the ordinary. "I didn't know people take selenium. What for?"

"They usually don't, unless someone is trying to poison them." He slams the papers onto the table and looks me in the eye. I'm not intimidated. I played this game enough in college. Although then I was the aggressor.

"You told me my husband was shot." I stick to the say-as-little-as-possible rule.

"Yes, he was shot, but it has been determined that he was also poisoned."

I don't respond to that. I pretend that I'm deep in thought.

"Mrs. Johnson, I had the opportunity to talk to a couple of your friends and neighbors yesterday, and I'm not sure what to make out of their statements, so if you could help me figure this out, it would be very helpful."

At the mention of friends, I feel my core temperature drop, which is odd because whenever I'm in a tight spot, usually my body heats up.

"I don't know to whom you have been talking. I don't have many friends."

He takes out a notepad from the inside pocket of his jacket and opens it at the bookmark.

"Your neighbor, Carol Bowman, said that she heard you arguing with your husband quite often. She also said that you might be having an affair with your neighbor, let's see, yes, here it is, Bruce Adelardi."

I want to scoff, but I'm able to contain my outburst and remain poker-faced. "Carol isn't my friend, but if she said I'm having an affair, then it must be true, naturally."

"Do you deny that you engaged in heated arguments with your husband at times?"

"No."

"That's it?"

"What do you want me to say? We've been married for fourteen years. Yes, we argued sometimes. Who doesn't?"

"What do you have to add to the part that you were cheating on your husband with Mr. Adelardi?"

"Why don't you ask Mr. Adelardi if you don't believe me?" I do feel uncomfortable when I say this. Would Bruce lie to the police to protect me? I should have asked him when I had a chance in the morning upon waking up next to him.

Detective Long glances at Morales behind me. Then he consults his notes again. I need to come off more emotional because I look like a cold-hearted bitch. My husband has been shot, and I'm accused of poisoning him. I should act as would be expected from a loving, caring wife in a dire situation like this.

I brush my finger under my eyes as if wiping away tears. I also sniff three times.

"Can I get you a tissue?" the detective asks, and I nod, pressing my fist against my lips as if I had trouble keeping a sob down. I can't mess this up. My children need me.

Detective Morales hands me a box of tissues. I pull out two and dab my eyes.

"Alright, let's continue. So, you are saying that Ms. Bowman's statement is not accurate."

"I'm saying that she is a nosy neighbor who likes to look important. I'll let you draw your own conclusion. I've done nothing wrong. I don't feel the need to defend myself." I sip at the water now. My throat is killing me. The raspy feeling is the worst it's ever been.

He drops the notepad on the top of the toxicology report. He pulls his chair closer to me and leans forward. His eyes are more focused now. He's changing his demeanor. He drops the Colombo style. I'm curious to see what he will come up with next.

"We still have to wait for the full autopsy to get a better picture of your husband's health, so until then let's just talk about what we know. How about the million-dollar insurance policy your husband took out on himself? That's high coverage for an Air Force firefighter to carry, don't you think?"

"Mike was serving his country in the Afghan war. I'm a stay-at-home mom. He wanted to make sure we were taken care of if something happened to him."

"But if my information is correct your husband had returned from Afghanistan years ago." He consults with his notes again. "Ten, to be exact. Right?"

"Sounds about right."

He's irritated by my response. I can tell by the way that he clenches his jaws every time I answer.

"I can only imagine how high the monthly payments are on a policy that big. Why didn't your husband change it once he was home safe?"

"Some people spend their money at Disneyland; we spend ours on security. What's the problem here?"

"Well, it's just convenient that with him out of the picture you will get all this money."

I need a melodramatic response here now. I jump off the chair. It falls back and slams against the floor.

"Do you ask every widow the same question the day after their husband died?" I know my face is red because I feel the burn. I grab my purse from the table and knock over the cup of water, which then spills onto the floor. "I think we are done here."

Detective Long jolts up and snaps his finger at his female partner. They sandwich me between them, but I don't panic.

"You need to sit down, Mrs. Johnson. We're not done yet."

I squint behind me. The door hangs open. Detective Morales is consulting with someone I can't see.

"Fine, but let me ask you this, detective. Are you divorced?"

My question doesn't seem to sit well with him. He tucks his shirt back into his waist and directs me to my chair, all the while looking at me with a distorted face. He puckers his lips and creases his brows as if about to say something mean. The guy has anger issues when it comes to women.

"This interview is not about me."

"Well, let me guess. Your wife left you for someone else and took your kid with her. Even if she is living with someone else, you still have to pay alimony because they are not officially together. Your kid likes his new daddy better than you, and it makes you angry. Now you're a self-proclaimed protector of mistreated husbands. You swore an oath to put away all ungrateful wives. Am I close?"

His doesn't respond only looks at me with piercing eyes. He's struggling to keep his cool, to remain professional, but it's too late. I know men. I used to take pleasure in torturing them emotionally. Kyle might not have been proud of me but the skills I developed sure come in handy now. And I'll do whatever it takes to keep out of prison.

I win the staring contest. Detective Long pushes himself out of his chair and leaves the room. At the same, time Detective Morales reappears and drops a bunch of paper towels on the puddle of water on the floor.

She pulls the chair even closer to me and sits down. She looks like an FBI agent with her white blouse and a black pantsuit.

"Look, Sarah," she begins in a soft voice, smiling, trying to be friendly. "I grew up in an abusive family. My father was a drunk. He used to threaten my mother all the time. Sometimes a few plates would fly. A slap here. A push there. They were fighting about money, too."

I don't say anything. Don't even blink an eye.

"It's tough to make a living here in California. You have two kids, a big house, and cars. I can imagine that the cost to support that lifestyle was high. Your husband is an Airman. I mean he can't make that much money, can he? Was he angry with you for not working?"

"Yes, he was, but it doesn't mean I killed him."

"Look, we already checked his phone records. We know about the house in French Valley and the other woman. And I'm sure you know about her, too. We women always sense when something is just not right." She rests an elbow on the table and shakes her head. "My husband and I also have our share of problems. I know how it is."

"What are you talking about? What do our renters have to do with Mike?"

"Renters? You mean the pregnant woman your husband calls every day? We also found a box of See's and a beautiful bouquet of flowers in your husband's car. I can't show them to you because they were both covered in blood. They are evidence now. But you probably wouldn't care about seeing your husband's presents to his lover anyway, would you?"

My jaws clench. I feel my face droop. How could they find out so much in one day? Damn, these officers are good!

"No, we have a family living in the house. They are renters. You must be confused."

"Are you sure it's not you who's confused?" She takes on a

cynical attitude. I like her less for it.

"You know you really have to change your tone because I don't like it," I say.

"Yeah, I get that a lot. Fortunately, you're not here to like me. We're here to find out what happened to your husband."

"Then maybe you should go out and investigate his shooting and stop wasting your time with me."

I lick my lips, craving the water to cool off the burn in my throat. "Are you charging me with something? Because if not, I'd like to go my mother-in-law's and bring my children back home. I didn't have the chance to tell them what happened to their father."

I stand up again, this time sans the dramatic flair. As I turn, I feel lightheaded. My head starts to spin. The face of Detective Morales blurs in my eyes. I hold my arm out for support but grasp only air. Then my knees give way, and I fall, hit my head on the edge of the table and black out.

2 DAYS TO DIE

My head is pounding against my skull when I open my eyes. The furniture and the smell of disinfectant suggest I'm lying in a hospital room. I have difficulty swallowing My eyes are swollen and aching. I attempt to hoist myself up on my pillow, but a tube that connects the needle in my vein to a hanging bag next to my bed stops me.

Analyzing my last memory, of me being in the interrogation room with Detective Morales, I grope for a button to call for a nurse. Handcuffs don't tie me to the bed frame. My hands are not cuffed to the frame of the bed. It seems the detectives didn't arrest me. Yet.

Underneath the medical wrap, there is a sizeable area above my right temple that is sensitive to the touch.

A nurse enters my room and orders me not to press on the bump. When I ask what happened, she tells me that I fainted and hit my head. Although it was an unfortunate accident, I'm lucky it happened because when the ambulance brought me to the hospital, and upon examination, the doctor discovered that I suffer from progressive Laryngeal Cancer.

When I tell her I don't know what it means, she explains that the doctor found an abnormal mass of tissues on my vocal cords; lab results are still pending to determine the extent of the cancerous tumor. She tells me that the doctor will see me soon and explain my options for chemotherapy. Then she mentions again that to know for sure how widely the cancer has spread we need to wait for the lab results.

She knows that I just lost my husband yesterday, so she sits next to my bed and holds my hand while looking at me with pity. I'm not the one for pity. If I have throat cancer, I will fight it. And I will win. I'm the only parent my kids have left. Dying isn't an option.

I could start wallowing in regret, blaming myself for not seeing a doctor when the first symptoms appeared. I could blame Mike for telling me that I was a hypochondriac when I complained about the changes in my voice and the pain in my throat. I could blame the universe and the stars for my predicament, but I won't do any of that. I request a meeting with the doctor because if there is anything we can do to stop this sickness from spreading, then I want to do it.

I only allow myself to cry into my pillow when I'm alone. Nobody knows I'm here so I won't have visitors. When the nurse returns and asks me who should be notified to come and get me, I tell her there's no one.

After the doctor explains what to expect from this disease, and the medical regimen is to move forward, I'm released from the hospital.

I take a taxi from the hospital to my home. I already puked my guts out this morning, but it could happen again, so I don't mind taking a cab. However, to be fair, I'm worried about the backseat upholstery. It would be embarrassing if I ruined it with my half-digested hospital breakfast. So I keep a bag close at hand—just in case.

Upon arriving home, I get out of the taxi, feeling like a broken china figure that's just been glued back together.

As I drag myself to the front door, Carol rushes out of her garage to meet me, but I ignore her. She's her usual aggressive self, as I comb through the various items in my bag looking for the keys. I drop them a few times before I'm able to open the door. She doesn't stop blabbering about the police, and I want to shut her up, but I don't have the energy to do so. I slam the door in her face instead.

The house is quiet, almost abandoned. I notice the dust and lint hovering in the air, highlighted by the sunlight that pierces the family room through the windows. Mason's soccer cleats are under the dining table. The duffle bag Mike carries to work is on the chair. Kona's slobbering face is framed in the patio door. I don't love this house anymore.

I take a breather in the entry, then start toward the junk drawer in the kitchen where I keep the phone chargers. Kona whimpers outside but I won't let him in now. I'm too weak to withstand his jumping and frolicking.

I sit down at the breakfast nook and wait for my phone to charge enough to be turned on. I need to make a few calls.

The night in the hospital took a great deal out of me, and my mind can't form a coherent thought. My head feels heavy. I rest it upon my folded arms on the countertop and then close my eyes. There is so much I must figure out and take care of, but I doubt I will do anything useful today. If the police came to question me again, I'd give them everything they wanted. After all, I have planned and done, cancer will be my end. How ironic!

I turn on my phone and text my mother first. I don't mention my hospital trip; I only ask her to come as quickly as possible.

There are worried messages from Bruce and Benny, but before I could respond to them, first I need to write a power of attorney naming my parents as legal guardians of my children just in case I can't beat this cancer. They did a good job raising Kyle. They will do right by my children, too.

Once I finish filling out an online Power of Attorney I print it out. I then pack a suitcase for necessities for my hospital stay. Carrying my bag downstairs puts as much a strain on me as if I dragged a bag of stones.

I open the garage door and pop the trunk to put the suitcase inside. The recent events drained all my energy and I stubble and crawl back to the house to call Grace. I tell her about Mike and, finally, I allow myself to cry with her as long as I need to. I ask her not to mention any of this to the kids. I also tell her that my parents will come and get the kids tonight or tomorrow morning at the latest.

She sounds shocked at the mention of my parents. We never talked about them before. When she asks for the reason why I don't drive up to get them, I tell her that I need to spend a few days in a hospital. I fail to mention my cancer though. We were never close. We'll never be. She shouldn't be the first one to hear about my illness.

I call both Benny and Bruce, but neither of them answers the phone. I don't leave messages because now I know that the police are checking phone records. They will need a warrant to request mine from Verizon, but the high level of selenium in my husband's bloodstream might be enough for the judge to rule in favor of one.

As much as I'm devastated by the news that I have cancer, it might come in handy. No jury would sentence a sick mother of two to prison. Especially when the police have only circumstantial evidence. Besides, Mike died of gunshot wounds, not from poisoning. They will never tie that to me since I don't even know who did it. Based on all the dirty secrets Mike was harboring it could be anyone, an old war buddy, a pissed off 'adult friend,' an underpaid pimp, Emanuela's angry father.

I have a few hours before I have to return to the hospital and check in. I'm all packed and ready to go, but I still need to see a notary about my power of attorney. Quickly I refill Kona's water bowl and give him some food. Bruce promised me he'd feed him yesterday, but I don't want to take chances. Too many times men have disappointed me. Not because they are trying to be mean. Only most of them can't think past their personal needs. They are wired like that.

Reading my mom's text saying that they will be here in less than two hours, I step through the laundry room to go into the garage. The moment my foot touches the concrete floor I feel something hard and cold pressed against my temple.

"Your time is up, bitch!"

I hear a cracking sound. It sounds as if a small sonic bomb has exploded near me or someone has cracked a bullwhip inside my garage.

In the same time, I feel my strength leaving me.

The phone drops from my hand. My knees let go. I'm falling weightlessly into the abyss.

Bright and blurry images of my children running towards me fill my mind. Laughing and pushing, they're racing on the sand as they always do. The vast blue ocean washes against the shoreline behind them. I see green clusters of tall and thin grass swaying in the wind. I feel happy.

Then the image turns brighter until it's nothing more than a blinding white light.

I don't feel when my head hits the ground. Pain isn't racing through my bones. There is only one thing I feel now, and it is regret.

I should have run away; grabbed my kids and started a new life without Mike.

Will they ever be able to forgive me?

EPILOGUE

"You damn fool!" Emanuela screams, banging her fists against her brother's chest. "I hate you!" She doesn't attempt to keep her voice down; has no concerns for the neighbors.

Even if people heard her yelling, they wouldn't understand a word. In the past few months, she had been taking daily walks in the neighborhood, admiring manicured yards with beautiful flowers, and chatting with fellow residents. And since most people's first question to her was always the same, "Where are you from?" she figured out long ago that nobody in her proximity spoke Italian.

To fend off the outburst, Sasha seizes his sister's fists in a way that a woman could not escape and pushes her onto the couch. "Stop it! You've messed it up not me."

Emanuela's body drops to the side like a sack of potatoes, and she buries her face in her hands. Her seven-month pregnant belly protrudes from her fragile frame.

"What am I going to do now?" she cries.

Seeing her so emotional eases the wrinkles that anger created on Sasha's forehead.

"I had no choice, Ella," Sasha says, calling his sister by her nickname that she so loved. "He wasn't going to leave his wife for you," he continues while taking out a gun from the back pocket of his jeans and setting it on the mantel.

One glance at the gun that took her future husband's life is enough for the emotionally imbalanced woman to freak out again. Without consideration for her unborn child, she starts banging her fists against her bulging belly, screaming hysterically.

Sasha leaps to her side and restrains her arms again. "Are you out of your mind? If I see you hurt this baby again, I don't know what I'm going to do to you."

"Why do you care? You ruined my life!" she screams into his face.

Sasha grits his teeth and leans closer to his frenzied sister. "He asked me to help him to figure this situation out. He literally cried in the car next to me telling me how much he loves his family; how he thought he could leave them but he cannot. He told me that he just wasn't capable of hurting them anymore."

"I don't believe you," she cries, fighting to free her hands.

"Calm down, Ella. I'm not lying. He chose his wife and family over you."

Ella stops struggling and looks deeply into her brother's dark eyes.

"Why did you kill him?" she asks on the verge of crying.

"What was I supposed to do? That stupid bitch wife of his believed that her husband hired me to kill her. What do you think Mike would do if he found out that we framed him? And if he planned to tell his wife everything, then I do not doubt that he would have found out."

"You should have given me a chance to talk to him. I could have changed his mind."

Sasha straightens up and kicks the side of the couch. "The spell you cast on him was gone. Don't you understand?" He grunts.

Ella senses that he's losing his patience with her.

"I told you not to get pregnant," he says, pointing his finger at her. "The day you did was the day you lost him. He was seeking an escape from the mother of his children. You were that escape. Now, look at yourself. You turned yourself into a mother of his child, too."

Ella takes a shuddering breath, trembling with cold. In a matter of few hours, her whole world crumbled around her. It was a lot to digest. She was so sure that this time she found the right man to give her the life she deserved. All the other American airmen loved her, sponsored her, but Mike was the first one who promised her a life together. She followed him blindly to America. She spent her days dreaming about being the new Mrs. Johnson, pushing a fancy stroller, shopping at Macy's, taking her kids to Disneyland. Now with Mike gone, she's left alone. And what's worse. She's left alone and pregnant. Nobody will want her with that baggage.

"Are you sure that old hag didn't tell Mike about you?" She asked through clenched teeth.

Sasha takes a glass from the cupboards and pours a glass of whiskey, without ice. After taking a sip of the whiskey, he emits a revolted grunt and hurls the glass into the sink.

"Don't you try to put this on me," he roars. "I did my part. All you had to do was to keep that fool under your spell."

At the sound of beer bottles clanging in the refrigerator door, Ella licks her lips and pushes herself off of the couch. She takes a Heineken for herself, but Sasha yanks the bottle out of her hand, and gives her a look of disappointment and disgust, reminding her that she is pregnant.

"What are we going to do now?" Ella asks, running her hand up and down on Sasha's arm to win him back.

He doesn't move, just stares ahead with unblinking eyes.

"Sasha?"

He turns his head toward his sister slowly, the look of deep rage still embedded on his face.

"Pack your stuff. We're going home."

Ella kicks the refrigerator door shut. "No!" she screams. "I've come too far to go back now. Get the money from that bitch and let's move somewhere else. I'm sure I can entrap another fool with money here in America."

Sasha gobbles down the rest of his beer, throws the empty bottle in the trash and opens the refrigerator for a new bottle.

Ella lunges at her brother's chest with both hands. "Talk to me!"

"I popped the bitch, too," Sasha whispers, rubbing his face with a sigh.

"What the fuck did you just say?" Ella blurts leaning to the side swiftly enough to make her lightheaded. She staggers reaching for the countertop for support. Her blood sugar has been a problem ever since the beginning of her pregnancy. Mike kept telling her to eat more for the sake of the baby, but she was determined to keep her figure as long as it was possible. Her eating habits were the only reason that she and Mike argued. But those arguments were never volatile enough for Mike to leave her.

"I went to the house to collect the money from that dumb bitch when I saw her suitcase in the trunk of her car. She thought she could skip town without paying me." Sasha lets out a wry chuckle. "She thought she could fool me."

Ella's knees start to buckle, while she slowly slides against the cabinet, and finds herself sitting on the floor. "What the hell is wrong with you?" she hisses.

Her hothead brother had erased everything they planned in a matter of moments—a comfortable life more than a year in the making. The smiles. The kindness. The passion. The willingness. Everything she offered Mike was in exchange for a better life. But now, all that effort was for nothing.

"Good job, Sasha. You just fucked us big time. We don't even have money to buy tickets to get home."

"I got some money. Mike was always bragging about his gold and silver collection. I turned the place upside down to find it."

A weak thread of hope fastens Emanuela's heartbeats. "Did you?"

Sasha walks to the dining table and snatches a Rite Aid plastic bag from a dining chair. He pours the contents onto the table. A few dozen silver and gold coins roll out of the bag and a small wad of cash drops onto the cheap IKEA table.

Emanuela jumps to her feet and rushes to the table. She scoops up a bunch of coins and starts to examine them. Then she takes the cash into her hand. "How much is it?"

"Not much. Five grand. Your boyfriend's doom's day stash."

"What do you think these coins are worth?"

"No idea. We can get them evaluated once we are home."

With the new hope at coming out on top, Ella feels slightly better. Even as far back as her earliest memories, money was the only measure they used to count the family's happiness. If they had money, it was a happy day. If his father couldn't scrape together enough, it was a sad day for her and her brother.

"Fine. But I'm not going back to Pisa. We need to relocate to another city with Americans. All my friends believe I'm living the American dream with Mike. If we go back without Mike, I'll die of humiliation."

"I don't give a shit. You can pick the place. Vicenza? Sicily? Aviano? Makes no difference to me."

Vicenza sounded tempting. The city is near Venice and Milan. That means there are a bunch of tourists to rip off. There is also a huge Army base in Vicenza; thousands of soldiers seeking pleasure for their dollars.

There is still one problem though. "What are we going to do with this baby?"

"I don't know. I'll look into how much we can sell it for. I'm sure there are websites where rich American families look for babies to adopt."

Ella puts her hand on her belly where the baby just kicked. "I don't know, Sasha. This baby is Mike's. I think I want to keep it."

"Mike brought flowers and chocolate for his wife. He wanted to tell her everything and ask for her forgiveness. You really want to keep his baby?"

Suddenly Ella's images of pushing the stroller with a cute little bundle of joy in a park with Mike by her side begin to fade and new bitter images of Mike crying for his wife's forgiveness replace them. The failure tastes bitter on her tongue. Men don't say no to her. Men don't choose their boring wives over her. Maybe Mike wasn't the man she thought him to be. What kind of man leaves his pregnant girlfriend anyway?

"You're right." She wraps her arms around her brother's neck and kisses him on the cheek. He hugs her back, pulling her tight.

"Don't worry. We'll find someone else. You're still young and beautiful."

"I don't know what would I do without you," Ella weeps, but not from sadness, but rather from deep gratitude. Her brother was always her anchor, the strongest point in her life. When their father was arrested for extorting money from local farmers, it was Sasha who stepped up and provided for her. When their mother ran off with their father's business partner, it was Sasha who stayed and took care of her. She owed him. And she would do anything he asked of her to pay back his support and loyalty.

"Thanks, Sasha. For looking out for me."

He brushes his fingers along the side of her face. "I told you I'd always take care of you." He offers her a warm smile, and she reciprocates. "Now go and start packing. We have to disappear before the police come looking for us."

Ella starts towards the bedroom to gather her meager belongings, while Sasha fills up a spray bottle with a mixture of bleach and water. Then he grabs a rag and starts wiping everything they might have touched, getting rid of every bit of evidence that either of them lived in this house. Without DNA and fingerprints, only the neighbors' descriptions will help the police to identify them. But with over seven billion people on earth, there is no way they will ever find them based on sketches. After a few days, the papers will stop writing about the double murder. After a few months, the police will give up on the investigation. The collected evidence will be placed on a shelf in a cold and creepy warehouse to gather dust until the end of times. The Johnsons story will become a cold case, just one of many thousands. The planet will continue to rotate. Life will move on. And those who survived will have a second chance at doing it better next time. No harm's done. It's evolution. It's life.

ACKNOWLEDGMENTS

Writing is a very lonely and lengthy process. As a result of spending hours—that turn into weeks and months—in front of the computer typing and reading, my children have a hard time understanding why it takes so long. But after four years of writing novels, my family has learned to be patient with me and to give me space when I'm in a writing frenzy. Thank you Danny and Allison for understanding that writing is something mommy loves to do.

Enormous thanks to my husband for enduring the mood swings I experienced while working on each chapter.

My mom is definitely one of the most enthusiastic supporters of my dreams. She truly believes that the day will come when we will be watching the movie adaptation of one of my books together. Mom, I hope your wish comes true.

I would like to thank everyone who helped me to make this novel what it is today.

Much thanks to my longtime friend and proofreader Dennis

McCarthy, who has been supporting me through good and bad times, and to Kathy Wood, who when obstacles almost caused me to abandon the whole project, stepped up and gave me hope, and to Amy Robb, who is just as passionate about a good thriller as I am. Without their hard work and dedication, this novel would have remained unfinished.

I owe considerable gratitude to my book critique group members: Lisa Hessler, Christine LaLonde and Carrie Lewis. Your insights helped to shape this story in positive ways.

My deep appreciation goes to Mary Rees at the Grace Mellman Community Library for giving me an opportunity to introduce my manuscript to the members of the Mystery Book Club.

Finally, thank you to the stay-at-home and soccer moms I came to know, who shared bits and pieces of their lives. Although none of the characters are based on any of them, their life experiences allowed me to develop new ideas for my story.

ABOUT THE AUTHOR

A.B. Whelan resides in sunny Southern California with her family, among soccer fields, manicured lawns, and beautiful homes, where everybody's lives 'seem' perfect. Here is where she cooks up unique psychological thrillers that delve into suburbia life. Also, as a medical professional, she meets interesting people and draws inspiration from them for her characters.

She is a James Patterson Masterclass graduate and credits her writing style to her favorite suspense writers: Gillian Flynn, Liane Moriarty, and Paula Hawkins.

Her first psychological thriller, *14 Days to Die*, is about a good marriage gone terribly wrong. The book earned praise from reviewers and readers alike, describing it as, "…is like peeking in the window of your neighbor's house … you just can't turn your eyes away."

Her second psychological thriller, *As Sick as Our Secrets*, is about family secrets, a hidden journal, a girl gone missing, and an unorthodox serial killer. It's been reviewed as, "a fast-paced tale that delves into a dark subject matter that should not be read by the faint-hearted."

Whelan also writes YA romantic fantasies, inspired by her fascination with the ancient Egyptian culture, 19th century London, and our vast universe. In her *Fields of Elysium* series, *Kirkus Reviews* describes the first book, "the novel's take on otherworldly travel is a compelling one, and the romantic plot will likely appeal to Twilight fans."

If you'd like to connect with A.B. Whelan, learn more about her books and giveaways, and read advanced material before anyone else, you can find her on Facebook, Instagram, Goodreads, and Twitter. Or on her blog at abwhelan.blogspot.com.